BEHOLDEN

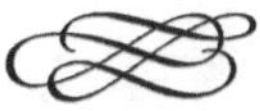

FRANCESCA CRISPO

IBSN: 979-8-9885719-6-4

Cover illustration by Melissa Hudson - www.mhudson-illustration.com

Editing and proofreading by Three Fates Editing - www.threefatesediting.com

Formatting by Nezhda Seyfulova - www.nezhformatting.org

CONTENTS

CONTENT WARNING

This book contains explicit descriptions of sexual activities; mentions of loss of a family member; as well as depictions of human and mythical creature ("monsters") death. Other potentially triggering topics include spiders, swearing, weapons/injuries/death threats, and dental... stuff.

To golden retriever himbos and those who love them.

The Invisible Cliffs
KINGDOM OF BARRIEN
Grimmaker Woods
Beast's Breath Tavern
Dalcester Street Market
DALCESTER

THE WILD OPEN
KINGDOM OF EMYNOR
End of the Road Inn
Max's House
Isle of Wyrms

FORTUNE TELLERS

MAX

There aren't too many career opportunities where I'm from, but a fortune teller in Dalcester once told me that I was destined to be a matchmaker. I remember the faraway look in her smoky eyes as she stroked my palm and muttered her musings about my "innate ability to seek out what people are searching for." I guess that panned out; I do find people that others are searching for, but instead of matching them with a love interest, I turn them in for a bounty or, if the price is right, I kill them myself. It's a dirty job, but the price is right often enough for me to have become hardened to it. When your options are as limited as mine and you have the responsibilities I do, you take what you can get, even if that means gutting people in the street so that you can afford to eat for the night. I guess that's why they call me Max the Menace. Max is short for Maxine. I'm a mercenary.

Ugh, I can't believe I wasted three crystals on that fortune teller. Looking back, it's possible that the "faraway look" was just her thinking about how she was going to spend my hard-earned money. If I had known then what I know now – that I'd have to capture the most obnoxious rogue viscount in order to earn those three crystals back – I wouldn't have bothered using them on as frivolous a notion as fortune-telling! That was back when I had less riding on my shoulders and more money in my pockets. I'm more practical now.

Eventually I got sick of working for a few crystals at a time. I found myself face-to-face with work that could be life changing for me. No more slaying dragons for a pittance or stalking royal men to catch them cheating on their wives. While some other hired hands found the drama interesting, I just couldn't get into it. No, this would be different. This would change the course of my future and set me up for a long time to come. I could feel it. I wouldn't have to count my crystals just to buy the necessities or go days without food to get by, and I would finally be able to take care of my little brother, Danny, without worry. Hell, maybe I could even buy some new boots; it really gives the phrase "being one with the earth" new meaning when you can feel the ground through the non-existent soles of your shoes. So, when I reached the kingdom of Barrien in the hot night air of midsummer, I had a spring in my step. I had to stifle that spring, of course, because you can't sneak into a castle while jumping for joy. It looks suspicious and is bound to get you either kicked out or caught.

"Stay here," I instructed my partner, a black Percheron named Wraith. The beast whinnied as if to say she understood, but nipped the back of my pants when I walked away. For a creature who couldn't speak, she never missed an opportunity to make her feelings known. She was massive, and although she was relatively quiet given her size and opinionated demeanor, I often had to leave her out of sight so as not to draw extra attention to ourselves. And also so that people didn't see me struggle to climb onto her towering frame; it really takes away from the "stealthy assassin" image when you practically need a stepstool to mount your steed.

Recently, though, I had been experimenting with different ways to get onto my horse. I tried climbing onto a tree and dropping down onto her – that one earned me a swift buck off of her back accompanied by an onslaught of loud neighs that sounded a lot like a lecture about respect. I also attempted to get a running start and swing onto her back after taking a leap. That method needed some fine-tuning but showed promise. I thought so at least. Wraith would probably roll her eyes at my confidence if she could.

I'd actually won Wraith as a filly several years prior, and she had been colossal even then. I was generally hesitant to take anything but straight crystals as payment, but the moment her previous owner showed her to me, I decided that she would be a fine payment for taking down the griffin that repeatedly kept eating this farmer's livestock and subsequently, his livelihood. Though she was just a weanling – and too small to ride – when we became partners, we instantly clicked, and her presence made the long weeks and months on the road bearable. Her intimidating energy, with her raven hair and her pitch-black eyes, also seemed to ensure the other mercenaries took me more seriously. Sometimes, though, I braided her mane and tucked moonflowers into it just to make sure she felt pretty.

The castle and grounds of the kingdom of Barrien were much like all of the others I had visited in my time spent traveling. The land was vast, with wide open, immaculately pruned walking gardens, stables, and a space for every royal activity one could imagine. All of the kingdoms in the continent looked similar to me, and I felt equally excluded from the luxury and lifestyle of those who inhabited them; I was able to tell them apart solely by their locations on the map in my pocket. This one was only special to me because it housed my prize: the prince of Barrien, who would fetch me a hearty reward if I delivered him, alive, to the kingdom of Emynor. Barrien is a kingdom of humans, and Emynor is a kingdom of elves, but I don't pick sides. I just do the job, collect the payment, and move along.

In addition to my map, my pocket housed the rolled-up wanted notice for this man's capture and delivery, including a rough sketch of the prince, the fee that was promised for him, and what he was wanted for, though I hadn't bothered to look at the latter. It was part of my personal code not to pass my own judgment on the people I encountered based on why other people wanted them captured or killed. If I learned too much about them, took the time to form my own opinions, I felt too close to them. I didn't want to give my captives that much thought; it made the job harder to do. I had to view my captives as assignments, not people.

Guards monitored the castle grounds at every possible entrance, and several patrolled the open areas, like an intricate hedge maze, tennis court, and outdoor celebration area that was still set up from the evening's festivities. They'd been celebrating their successful acquisition of a nearby village; it was my job to keep tabs on these types of events, even if the details bored me. Even with all the guards, it was easy to remain unseen, thanks to my size, dark clothing, and general familiarity with sneaking around. The garden, which was right outside of my target's window, was filled with towering shrubs, marble sculptures, and even a water feature, all of which I fit behind easily. As I squatted behind the fountain, I studied its details: a sculpture of a mermaid, whose bare granite breasts were spraying water into the mouths of two fish balancing on their tails. The moonlight reflected off the small pool's surface. "Rich people…" I muttered to myself. I kept my cowl pulled up high around my neck and slipped from one tall cover to another until I was right beneath the bedroom window of one Prince August of Barrien. Lucky for me, it had only taken me one afternoon of observation to determine which bedroom window belonged to the prince. He kept all of the curtains pulled wide open in his chambers, which meant that my stakeout had awarded me many less-than-desirable sights as he dressed for the evening, not to mention a personal training session in his bedroom that included some sort of high-energy dance. It was all very strange to me.

I stood in silence until I was passed by two guards who were laughing hysterically at a joke, then timed the release of my anchor and rope up so that their laughter perfectly masked the sound of my wall-scaling equipment being installed. They were none the wiser. It was only when I realized I was standing next to an amaranth plant, to which I was wildly allergic, that I had to stifle a sneeze. I couldn't fight it, and just my luck, the guards' laughter ceased right as the sneeze exploded from my puckered face. My eyes watered, and I tried to stifle the onslaught of sneezes that wanted to follow. If I hadn't already given myself away, continuing on with my allergy attack certainly would. My vision blurred. I held my breath.

The two men, who had been clunking along in their bulky armor, stopped walking and turned my way. It was no wonder they had been meandering so lazily with the equipment they were required to wear. Certainly no one could expect them to be stealthy or prepared for battle, but perhaps the kingdom of Barrien didn't have enough actual enemies for their safety to be a concern. "Oy, you hear that?" one of them asked.

I held my breath and slid a hand to my hip, where I kept a small dagger. I hoped that I wouldn't have to use it on one of the guards. After a moment of silence, the other guard grunted with a shrug. "Yeah, my stomach's rumbling. Let's see what they've got in the kitchen." Truly, the guards of Barrien were top-notch protectors.

I let out a sigh of relief once they were out of sight, then began my ascent of the castle wall. The rough and weathered stone, still warm from the day's sun, was worn in a way that provided perfect handholds for climbing. Once I was at the bottom ledge of the window, I pulled up the remainder of my rope and tucked it away so that I didn't leave a clue for any wandering eyes. Then, I surveyed my target.

Prince August Theodoric III was a "caste-hole." That's what I called rich, castle-dwelling royalty that gave absolutely zero shits about anyone lower than them; the insult worked on multiple levels, I thought. In fact, as I scaled the side of the castle of Barrien, identified his bedroom window, and peered inside, I had to stifle a chuckle at my own creativity. Traveling alone was clearly starting to get to my head; I longed for adult interaction, but most people that I ran into were either my victims, prisoners, or employers, so there wasn't much room for amicable relationships there. I couldn't very well ask someone how their day had been right before slitting their throat. Well, perhaps I could… I hadn't tried yet. Wraith, while lovely and a true asset to my work and life in general, offered little in the way of conversation. In fact, sometimes it felt like she wished I would shut up. What I saw inside the room, however, cut my internal laughter off immediately. I'd expected opulence, greed, to see him sitting on a pile of money, maybe, but I hadn't expected to be peering in on the start of an orgy. Maybe if I had observed from a distance just a little longer, I would've noticed all of the female visitors prior to climbing the castle wall.

The prince of Barrien was, by all counts, a traditionally attractive royal man, much like a prince character from a children's storybook. He was tall and broad shouldered, with a chiseled abdomen. How did I know his abdomen was chiseled? Well, he was lying on his bed shirtless, all but covered in nearly naked women, as I peered in through his window. As one of them threw their head back in amused laughter, his face came into view. Seeing him in person made me question the artist who had done his

Wanted poster sketch; it was undoubtedly him, but they'd failed to capture the details of his face. His jaw was so sharply angled it looked as though it could slice anyone who touched it. The only thing that softened his razor-like jawline was the soft, dark stubble that made it look like he only shaved when his mother insisted he should. His brow, thick and perfectly manicured, cast a shadow over his deep-set eyes. From where I watched in the window, the candlelight of his bedroom reflected off of them – a honeyed hazel color. His hair was chestnut brown and fell in short curls against the pillow upon which he rested his head… and his cheeks were flushed with amusement and perhaps the effects of alcohol, in contrast to his otherwise fair skin. He looked as though he hadn't a single drop of sweat on him, despite the sweltering heat of summer.

Meanwhile, as I propped myself up and out of sight on the windowsill, I could feel sweat dripping down my lower back into the crack of my ass. Did rich people just sweat less? How was that fair? Speaking of… when was the last time I showered? I lowered my arms around my body and continued to watch the scene unfold, waiting for the perfect moment to strike. It occurred to me then that showering might actually help my stealth level; if people could smell me, it would be harder to hide. I told myself to return to my job and worry about my armpits later. Finding the prince with a room full of other people was inconvenient, but I would make it work.

I didn't know exactly why I had been hired to retrieve and deliver this man – likely to his death – but based on his appearance alone I could tell he was everything that was wrong with the world: rich, obnoxious, and beyond full of himself. As if on cue, I heard him say, "Now, now, ladies, there's enough of me to go around, I assure you." I stifled a groan. The women, meanwhile, giggled, all too pleased by his announcement.

Apparently, I had been perfectly content to continue my observation, and it wasn't until I saw one of the women crawl across the bed and begin to undo the prince's slacks that I remembered I had a time-sensitive job to do. "Shit." The last thing I wanted was to haul an unconscious prince out of a building with his dick out, so I felt around my waist momentarily until I found what I was looking for: a vial of Forty-Winks[1]. The bottle came loose with a satisfying pop. One swift chuck sent it sailing, where the vial shattered on the floor and emitted a puffy cloud of purple smoke. I'd even sprung for the lavender-scented variety, a nice touch from Beatrice the Apothecary.

"Auggie, what was that?" one of the women, a leggy blond gal who was already fully naked, asked.

Auggie? Barf.

But before any of the orgy-goers could investigate, they were swaying and collapsing across the room, as the potion's smoke filled the room. I pulled my cowl up around my nose and mouth to protect against the tendrils finding their way toward the open window, but even so, a yawn overtook me. The way some of the women fell on furniture, like one brunette woman who flopped gracelessly onto the chest at the end of the prince's bed, made me cringe. They were going to wake up with quite a few bruises, but not as many as August, who I'd have to carry out of his bedroom on my own. I wondered if I might be able to toss him onto a few soft bushes down below, but then decided against it when I remembered that his being in good condition was part of the terms outlined on the Wanted poster. When everyone was down for the count, including Prince August – thankfully with his pants still zipped – I slipped into the room. I didn't bother being too quiet; if the sound of ten people dropping to the floor wasn't enough to rouse other people in the castle, which was loud with other merry-making, then my footsteps should have been inconsequential in comparison. I did, however, slip over to the door and ensure it was locked. The fact that it hadn't already been caused me to question the prince a bit. Was he expecting additional guests or was he the type to enjoy an occasional accidental voyeur?

I almost felt bad as I tied the prince's wrists and ankles with rope, then tossed his big ass over my shoulder. Almost. He had at least half a foot on me, but when your job is hauling prisoners around, you get strong pretty quickly. Something jingled as I carried him through the room, and I realized he was wearing a silver necklace with some sort of locket or vial on the end; I made a mental note to grab it before he woke up. Maybe it would fetch me enough to buy those boots I had been looking at. I side-stepped the naked bodies in the room, realizing that one or all of them would be blamed for his disappearance when they woke and alerted the rest of the royal family. I didn't have the time to care.

Forty-Winks was effective and quick, but the downside was that it didn't last very long. The alternative called Fifty-Winks[2], however, had led me to accidentally kill a few of my prisoners in the past. Thankfully they'd been requested dead or alive, but I still hadn't let Beatrice live those down; dead bodies are a lot more of a pain to transport than live ones because they don't help at all, and they start to stink faster than you'd expect. You also can't bribe or threaten them into cooperating. She'd since agreed to name that concoction The Final Wink[3] instead and dyed it black, with no fun added scent. My suggestion of black licorice had been promptly rejected.

It took me a few minutes to rig a pulley up to the prince's windowsill and then lower his body down with a rope. He groaned a little as he was set on the ground, and I waited on the windowsill to see if he'd wake, in which case I'd probably have to jump down and tackle him. He didn't rouse, though, and I made a mental note to find someone else to tackle; clearly, I had an itch I needed to scratch. Then I turned back into his room and grabbed what I assumed was his shirt, as well as a few other articles of clothing, and threw them down on top of him. We had a long road ahead of us, and I assumed the prince of Barrien wasn't used to wearing the same clothing for days or weeks on end. Once I was back with him again, I signaled for Wraith, hoisted the prince's body onto her back, and hopped on. The reward money was so close I could practically taste it; I just had to get him back to Emynor. It was a long journey, however, and I was eager to get a move on.

"Buckle up, Wraith," I told the horse. "You're gonna have to get used to carrying a lot more weight if we're bringing 20,000 crystals home with us."

---

1. Forty-Winks: sleeping potion with a purple haze/smoke. Smells like lavender.
2. Fifty-Winks: stronger sleeping potion, sometimes dangerous. May have caused the death of a few people by accident.
3. The Final Wink: lethal, produces black smoke.

PRINCE AUGUST THEODORIC III

AUGUST

When you come from a disgustingly wealthy royal family, you can be anyone you want. The opportunities are endless! Personally, I'd chosen to be a lifelong bachelor. What can I say? I loved doing whatever I wanted, sleeping with whoever I wanted, and spending whatever I wanted. I didn't have to bother with much of the royal dealings, though my father said that I would eventually have as much responsibility in the kingdom as he did. I preferred not to think about it. He did, however, occasionally have me sit in on tedious meetings and assist with signing decrees to better serve "the people who rely on us." I'd perfected my signature to sign where Father and his advisors would tell me, and then I'd go on my merry way.

The proverbial guest list for my bedroom varied by what I was in the mood for and, that evening, I wanted nothing but tall, thin women. They were easy to find, what with the celebratory dinner that had just concluded moments before they joined me in my bed. I'd shown my face at the event by request, but couldn't be bothered to care what we were celebrating for. My parents, the king and queen, insisted that our triumph over a warring kingdom full of "ruthless savages" was "worth celebrating" because I had been the one to sign the decree that made it a reality. Personally, I wanted to get out of the stuffy clothing that came with public appearances. After the party, things had been going swimmingly until my captor arrived to ruin all of the fun.

To say that I was surprised to find myself captured by a mercenary would be an understatement, to say the least. Even more surprising was waking up on the ass end of a horse; it was the bouncing of said horse's ass that woke me, actually. Normally, I wouldn't be fully captured, but instead would be held at knifepoint until someone realized I was in danger, then negotiated with my attacker for my release. "Negotiating" typically meant that someone would offer the attacker whatever they wanted until I was safely retrieved, then they'd capture the attacker for public execution or murder them on the spot. Not so this time, apparently. I groaned and eased my eyes open to find the darkness of Barrien's main road surrounding me, unmistakable with its looming architecture and overall beige coloring.

"Really, you didn't even bother to wait until I was dressed before kidnapping me?" I grumbled at the hooded figure atop the horse. Just because this man had gotten me farther away from the castle than others had didn't mean I was impressed. "My nipples are chafing against this damn horse, for fuck's sake!"

"It's summer," my captor replied in a shockingly smooth, feminine voice. "You'll be fine. You're not going to freeze to death. Besides, if I had waited any longer, it looked like you were about to be far less clothed than you are now."

I had hardly expected the voice of a woman to come from my captor, and somehow, that made me even more irate. I had no clue how she'd gotten me out of my chambers and onto this horse by herself. Magic, probably. I had yet to meet even a man who could overpower me. In fact, my trainer always told me that I was the most muscular of his students, which was odd given that I was his only student.

"I'm not really concerned with your nipples," she continued. "Also, language. Aren't royals supposed to be well-spoken?"

The horse clip-clopped on, and my head bounced off its thick leg in rhythm with its steps. I rolled my eyes. There was no way this wasn't messing up my hair, which I'd just gotten to the perfect fresh-out-of-bed tousled look prior to my visitors arriving.

"And aren't mercenaries supposed to be big, burly men?" I groaned. "You can turn back around and head for the castle now. I'm sure the king and queen are wondering where I am, and I assure you, they are prepared to pay whatever ransom you're looking for."

My parents had always insisted that this was one of the perils of being the heir to the throne and something that all princes had to deal with on a regular basis. I only hoped that my guests would still be waiting in my chambers when I returned. Slipping them each a discreet invitation at the dinner and then guiding them to meet at my bedroom without causing alarm to the guards or my family had taken quite a bit of orchestration; I would hate to lose all of that hard work. When the hooded figure didn't reply, I repeated myself, the horse's gait causing me to inadvertently emphasize each word. "Hello? Castle - ransom - nipples - are - chafing."

"Afraid that's not part of the plan," the figure told me without turning my way. Despite the bouncing of my head as the horse walked, I could make out that she was small, definitely shorter than me. My captor's cloak camouflaged her figure, especially in the darkness of the evening, but she was thin, the fabric hanging over her shoulders in loose waves. I wanted to be curious about this woman, but I couldn't get past my irritation. Her voice was calm, almost as if she were bored with the whole ordeal, and I didn't like that one bit. People weren't bored in my presence regardless of our relationship… it just didn't happen! "We'll stop once we're farther from the kingdom, and you can get fully dressed, but for now you're just along for the ride."

I opened my mouth to speak, to tell her that wasn't how this whole system worked. I had never been taken away from the kingdom before, and I wasn't about to let it happen now. Everything and everyone I knew and loved was there; this was not the time for an impromptu adventure across the continent or wherever she was planning to take me! "But—"

"I suggest you hush and play along, or I'll have to knock you out again, and that'll really put a damper on my plans." It was almost as if she could sense my tendency to argue because she added, "Though I'd rather put a damper on my plans than listen to your whining all night, so I guess the choice is yours. Awake or not, I'm gonna need you to shut up."

"My, my, she has quite the attitude. I wo—" I don't remember anything after that because everything went black.

THE KINGDOM OF BARRIEN

AUGUST

hen I woke up sometime later, light assaulted me. I winced as I eased my eyes open. "Where the hell am I?" I asked with a groan, fairly certain I wasn't going to like the answer. If not for the fact that I was still using a horse's rear end as a pillow, I would've assumed my capture was just part of a strange dream or a prank by some of the previous night's guests. But alas, the only female visitor in sight sat across from my dangling head, resting against a tree, picking at her nails with a dagger. Her hood was still pulled up and covered most of her face, but the onyx tangles of her hair peeked out from beneath the fabric.

When she finally looked up, what felt like far too long after my question, she sheathed her dagger. "Good, you're up."

"I mean, it's not like I was taking a nap," I retorted, straining against the rope that still held my wrists and ankles bound. The bristly fibers were biting at my flesh, not to mention the very clear rash I was developing from the hulking beast I was strapped to. "You knocked me out!"

She ignored me. "Before I let you down to get dressed, we need to go over a few ground rules."

Despite my brain's fogginess from the blood pooling in my head, and while I was certain that being practically upside down and half naked did nothing to make me seem intimidating, I attempted to assert myself. "Great, I have questions that you'd do well to answer. Who are—"

"Max. I'm a mercenary. You are my captive per the wanted order in my pocket. I am delivering you to the kingdom of Emynor. No, I don't know what will happen to you once we get there, but I will get you there in exchange for the offered bounty." The woman looked at me intently, as if she dared me to argue with what she had just told me.

"Says who?" Despite having been kidnapped before, I wasn't really used to this direct explanation of what to expect. I also had no clue why I was being captured and, supposedly, delivered to a kingdom I'd only heard the name of once or twice. A prank, perhaps?

She sighed. "Says me, my sword, and my reputation for always completing jobs."

I scoffed.

"Listen, this is going to be a long trip. The kingdom of Emynor is on the other side of the continent, and I'm not one for small talk, nor do I feel like chasing you all over the place. It gets tiring after a while." She still looked bored. "I'd advise you to follow my rules, or it will be not only a long trip but a very uncomfortable one. Got it?"

"Did you have that speech all planned out?" I asked, trying to turn my head so that I could see her upright, but failing.

"Not until I had to knock you out for being obnoxious. I figured I should think one up then," the mercenary told me. "Now," she began again with a sigh, rising to her feet from the ground. "If I untie you and let you get dressed, are you going to run?"

"No."

Max raised an eyebrow. "Okay, because I just said—"

I waved her off as well as I could with my wrists bound. "Yeah, yeah, it gets tiring."

Needless to say, the second I was unbound and upright, I ran. Or, I attempted to. The thing about being upside down for so long is that right side up suddenly feels very disorienting. I think I made it maybe ten feet before dizziness overtook me, I wavered, and a strategically placed foot from Max sent me falling on my face. I hit the ground in what felt like slow motion, then lay there in defeat as Max stared down at me.

"I just said," she scolded me.

"To be fair," I protested, squeezing my eyes shut in an attempt to stop the woods from spinning around me, "I don't think anyone would call that running."

The mercenary didn't dignify my comment with a response. Not even a small chuckle! Instead, she walked off, then returned to drop a shirt on my face. "Get dressed, it's time to move."

When I opened my eyes after a moment of careful consideration, I agreed. "Okay."

"Okay?"

I shrugged. "Yeah, okay. I mean, I've always wanted an adventure, maybe this is the way I'm gonna get it."

The mercenary's eyes widened. "Adventure? I don't think you're still going to be calling it an adventure when I hand you over to Emynor."

I waved a hand to dismiss her fearmongering as I hoisted myself to my feet, shirt in hand. "I can deal with them. Besides, my people will probably find me before we make it there—"

Max narrowed her gaze at me. "Is that—"

"Don't worry! I'll make sure you aren't punished for kidnapping me; I'll tell them I came willingly." Before the mercenary could comment again – though she looked at a loss for words – I clapped my hands and headed back to the horse. As I walked, I yanked the shirt over my head. "Let's go!" The horse, meanwhile, nipped at me the second I approached her.

THE INVISIBLE CLIFFS

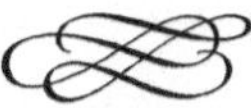

MAX

At the edge of the kingdom of Barrien, there is a steep drop-off known as the Invisible Cliffs. They're not really invisible, of course, but they're named as such for the dense thicket of fog that has permanently settled over them. It moves as if it's breathing, but I've never seen it clear away. It seems to be the only place nearby with such an accumulation, but the weather doesn't really call for it. One misstep, and you'll find yourself tumbling down the cliffside… it would be more of a bounce, though. Word is it's freckled with sharp, jutting ledges, and the drop is very, very far down. If you were to survive the fall – you wouldn't – you'd find yourself amongst piles and piles of bodies at the bottom. It would be a sight to behold: a gory, gruesome sight with mounds of bodies that had broken every bone on their way down. Perhaps some of their faces would still be distorted in their screams of agony from the trip down. Not a very pretty mental image. I don't imagine the Invisible Cliffs are on most people's list of landmarks to visit.

But people do visit them. You see, the royals of Barrien use the cliffs to execute people. I've heard they bring their criminals to the top of the cliff, then force them to walk at swordpoint until they step off the edge. Perhaps they'd been inspired by pirates. If they don't walk, they're pushed; sometimes this results in them pulling the executioner down along with them, but the kingdom of Barrien doesn't seem to mind the occasional loss of personnel. To them, it's a bit of a game or at least a social event. They publicize the executions, and there are many people in attendance, but from what I've heard, it's just the nobility. The townsfolk are invited solely as a way to show them what can happen if you disobey your leadership, so naturally they don't attend the executions of their fellow townsfolk. I've never seen an execution in Barrien, but if you travel the continent for as long as I have, you hear lots of things about each kingdom you visit, even if they're things you'd rather not know. If anything, that information taught me that I wouldn't want to be imprisoned in Barrien.

Most of the bodies at the bottom of the cliffs are people who have been executed by the kingdom or those who got tangled up in the execution, like I said. The others, however, are workers who have fallen to their deaths. What they're working on before they fall, however, is what really makes the cliffs interesting and mysterious. You see, in the face of the cliff, there is a very precious, very powerful—

"What's going on there?" August asked, interrupting my inner monologue as he looked as far over the cliffs as was possible. He was like a small child who had absolutely no concept of danger or decorum. I reached out to grab his shirt and stop him from sending himself over the edge. Because of our size difference, I had to lean the opposite direction to have any effect on him.

Wraith snorted behind me. I, too, was concerned about my ability to keep this royal moron alive long enough to get him to the people who would pay me. "This is less than a mile from your castle, and you don't know what your people are doing here? Have you ever been outside of those four walls?" I couldn't imagine spending all of my time in one place, though I had never really been given the chance to settle down. To never have experienced the sunset in a different place, to have only met the people who had been allowed into his kingdom; what a boring life that must have been.

August looked at me as if I were the dunce in our partnership. His golden eyes, overshadowed by his heavy brow and the shifting fog, stared at me in confusion. "First, it's a castle, so there are more than four walls… and yes, I've been outside to the garden and pool and the—"

"That's it?" I asked, still unimpressed. I watched his curls float in and out of view, thanks to the rapidly shifting fog; he was nothing but a giant, petulant child. I imagined him with a giant lollipop and overalls on and had to stifle a chuckle.

"If you'd let me finish…" August said, his voice thick with irritation. "I've been to other kingdoms, but we always travel by carriage, and I don't get out until we've reached our destination. Honestly, though, why would I need to go anywhere but the castle grounds? Everything I need is there." There was the kicker I had not considered: to have all of your needs met in one place, without having to travel the continent and scramble on a regular basis. Perhaps that would make being stationary worth it. Perhaps I would consider stopping for the comfort and stability of knowing that my needs would be met, of knowing I'd never have to wonder about my next meal or worry about providing for those who relied on me. It would never happen for me, though, so I dismissed the thought just as he continued to pester me. "Are you going to answer me or just continue with the criticism?"

"I can't promise I won't criticize you for the remainder of this trip." I let go of his shirt with a sigh, then folded my arms over my chest. The leather of my pauldrons squeaked a little as the plates shifted against each other. They made that sound when they were recently polished, a routine I engaged in prior to a big job. "First off, the edge of the cliff is closer than you'd think. Stop trying to look over it, or you're going to fall to your death."

"It sounds like you know what's at the bottom," August mused aloud, leaning forward as much as he could without moving his feet. It made sense to me then that someone who had never experienced real danger, had never faced actual harm, would be braver than most when it came to testing limits. If Prince August's life had been so privileged that he'd never gotten more than a papercut, he probably assumed he was impervious to injury. Boy, was he in for a rude awakening…

"Bodies," I told him simply, pausing to emphasize just how bleak the answer was. "This is where your family executes people."

"I knew that." He swallowed hard in discomfort, then carried on with his commentary as if I hadn't noticed. I didn't know enough about the executions to know if the entire royal family, prince included, were always present, but based on his reaction I concluded that he either wasn't invited or opted to skip such events. "But I meant that sound? What is it?"

What am I, his damn tour guide? He's acting like he hired me to lead him on an adventure. "They're mining the face of the cliff." The clanging of metal against stone was unmistakable to me, but perhaps not to someone who had lived such a sheltered life. The cliffs were far enough from the castle that he would not have been able to hear it from there. When he looked at me in confusion, I continued. "See that sickly green glow, there, through the fog? It's —"

"No, it's too blurry." August squinted into the fog, searching for the target I was describing. He looked unsteady, but I chalked it up to the way the fog made the whole world seem like it was spinning around us.

I grabbed his shirt again, this time with more enthusiasm and secretly hoping I would knock him off balance and let him see the cliffside with his own two eyes. "Go ahead, take a couple of steps closer."

His eyes narrowed again. "You're going to push me over."

"Are you always this paranoid?" I rolled my eyes for what felt like the millionth time since I'd met Prince August of Barrien. I was going to have to work on that for my own sake, but goodness, he was irritating. Did he possess any deductive reasoning skills at all?

The laugh that burst from his lips was incredulous and disbelieving. "Only when I'm… oh, I don't know… being kidnapped, held hostage, and dragged across the continent for a bounty!"

"I haven't dragged you anywhere in at least half of a day," I told him. "And we're not quite across the continent yet. We're just down the road from your home. Besides, we both know that pushing you off a cliff would be a stupid move on my part. I can't climb down there to retrieve your body, so I'm forced to deal with your incessant commentary from here on out."

"How comforting." August eyed me in suspicion, then glanced at the grip I had on his shirt as if to evaluate its effectiveness, and took a few steps forward. I stayed still and held on tight, digging my boots into the loose dirt of the clifftop, then waved him forward with my free hand.

"It's calcinite[1]. Most people call it the Neon Shackle, though." Before I could explain further, however, I was being yanked down toward the ground; August was falling, and in the fog, I had no idea what was happening. "What are you—"

I hit the ground next to him, my fingers still tangled in the cloth of his shirt, and the ground shifted. Despite the swirling white, I could see that he'd fallen unconscious. I didn't have time to ponder how or why... we were closer to the edge than I had expected, and the flaky gravel beneath us was crumbling. The weight of his body and now mine had added pressure to the fragile ground that it couldn't withstand. If I didn't move quickly, we would be exploring the bottom of the cliffs in short notice. The clifftop groaned as if to warn us that it was about to give way.

A chunk of the ground broke loose only a few feet from us, and the workers on the cliffside shouted below as if it were a common occurrence. "Loose rocks! Tuck in, gents!"

I wondered if they'd be able to hear us down there if we called to them. "Wraith!" I yelled, searching through the dense fog for any sign of my companion. It wouldn't be safe for her to step much closer to us, but if she could just toss her reins my way, I'd have something to grab on to. Her massive black head slid through the thick, shifting air, and her nostrils flared in panic. "Stay back!" She bucked her head repeatedly as if she had read my mind and sent the reins flying into the air. Each time she nodded, they let out a satisfying snap that cut through the fog. After several attempts to reach them, I caught the reins in my free hand. They whipped against my palm and sent a stinging sensation up my forearm. The ground crumbled more and August's limp, unconscious body started to slip from my grasp. "Got it, Wraith! Go!" I instructed her, trying not to panic but knowing very well that this could end badly for all of us.

The Percheron complied and backed up slowly, pulling us with her beefy neck until we slid across the rough ground. The gravel crunched beneath our bodies and scraped the leather of my pants, but Wraith pressed on steadily, her wide hooves planted firmly with each step. I was barely hanging on to August, who hadn't budged since he'd fallen; if this man had just died on me out of nowhere, I was going to be pissed. What a waste! The leather of the reins dug into the bare flesh of my hand. With the weight of our two bodies, my skin tore, and the hot stickiness of blood trickled down my arm. As we got farther from the edge of the cliff, the prince finally groaned, and I thanked the stars that his stupid ass was still alive at least. If he was messing around and testing my desire to keep him alive, I'd kill him myself once we were safe. "A little more, Wraith!" I yelled into the fog.

A few more steps had us horizontal on steady ground again, and I finally let go of August's shirt and the reins. I flopped down next to him with a groan. "Thanks, girl," I told my horse. "I owe you… I don't know, whatever you want." She snorted and nudged my hand with her velvety nose. "Apples, a hundred," I agreed. Then she retreated a few more steps away; she'd been scared off by the fragility of the cliff. I couldn't blame her for being cautious. If the cliff wasn't able to hold two human bodies, the weight of the giant beast would've surely sent us down to our rocky deaths. I lay there, trying to calm down to the noise of my own labored breathing and the far-off clinking of pickaxes against the rock face of the cliff. It occurred to me that the work on the cliffside would have continued even if the workers had seen us tumble down to the bottom, screaming for help. Would they have peered over to watch us fall? Would they hold a moment of silence in our honor? Or would they see us pass with a shrug and carry on, knowing that each moment wasted would likely be docked from their daily pay, or worse, they'd be sent to the bottom of the ditch with us for slacking off? No matter the horrors I encountered on a regular basis, it still shocked me the way that humans could become so desensitized to the pain and suffering around them. I wasn't quite desensitized to it, but I had gotten good at storing it away; it was only a matter of time before all of the trauma associated with my job caught up to me and I was forced to process it.

Then, August took a gasping breath. He sat up as if he'd been shocked back to life. "Did I fall? Am I dead?"

"You're not dead, idiot. But you almost killed all three of us!" I didn't bother looking at him, just stared up at the murky sky in annoyance. The fog shifted and swayed, and the sense of urgency fluttered back into my body. It was time to move again. No more tour guide antics, no more sight-seeing. We had to go. Like the miners, each moment wasted was money lost for me. I had to keep August alive, which meant I had to keep him fed and clothed and well. The faster we could get to Emynor, the faster I could stop wasting my resources and my patience on him.

"I didn't do anything!" August argued. "You were showing me the edge of the cliff!"

I scoffed. "Yes, and then you decided to take a very sudden nap near the edge of that cliff while I was holding you up by a thin scrap of fabric!" Oh hell, maybe the Forty-Winks had a stronger effect on him than I had planned for. I hoped he wouldn't be drowsy for the remainder of the trip.

The space between August's eyebrows knitted in confusion, but I didn't offer him any further explanation. "You're bleeding," he said suddenly, gesturing to my hand. When he sat up, he almost looked as if he was going to reach for me and inspect my wound, but the sight of the blood must have put him off.

I held my hand up in front of my eyes and winced as I pushed the torn flesh back over the now open wound in my palm. It made a sick sucking sound as it shifted and another trickle of blood ran down my wrist. I wiped it on my shirt. It would heal. Until then, it would be annoying. Hands were the hardest to heal because I needed them for so many things, but there wasn't time to dawdle. When we stopped next, I could dig through my bags for a healing potion from Beatrice. "We need to get going. Back on the horse so we can see what other life-threatening situations you'll get us into."

August shook his head in disbelief. "Don't you need to... I don't know, pour some whiskey on that or something? Cauterize it with some fire from a dragon? Or does the feeling of pain escape you like every other sensation?"

I looked over into his stupid, honey-colored eyes and snorted. "The latter. I mean, I do have some feelings. Annoyance, irritation... regret, for example." Sensations were a topic for another day.

---

1. Calcinite (also known as the Neon Shackle): a neon green gem mined from the Invisible Cliffs. It is harmless to most beings, but depletes the magical abilities of elves and for that reason was weaponized by the kingdom of Barrien during their war with Emynor. The gem is no longer mined, sold, or utilized.

THE CITY OF BURIED MEN

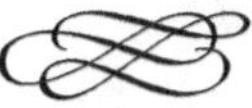

AUGUST

The actual city of Barrien is called the City of Buried Men by the people who don't live in the castle, as in the townsfolk. That's what my captor told me as we walked the streets. I'd never heard of this nickname, however, because apparently they use its rightful name in public. She also said they roll their eyes every time they have to call it that. I'll defer to her on that; Max may be an expert in expressions of irritation like eye-rolling. Also according to Max, the townspeople call it that because living in our fair city is a bleak existence, with people dying left and right. I'd heard no such thing myself. In any case, midday found us traveling through the neighborhood streets with the big, black horse walking behind us. We agreed to keep me unbound in order not to draw attention to us, but I continued to search for ways to slip away. Had I been more involved in the daily lives of my people like my father insisted, I probably would've had a chance to get noticed by one of them. It would take a lot of convincing for one of them to believe that I was the prince of their kingdom and had been kidnapped, but I hoped to find a way to get someone's attention. Maybe I could convince someone to inform my parents… Until then, I would have to stay put.

Being captured again after running had done some serious damage to my ego, and personally, I was looking to avoid a repeat if at all possible. Better to play it cool until I was rescued than to foolishly try to leave and fail once again. Rather than lament the ways I could have set myself up for a quicker rescue, I kept my mantra of "this is an adventure!" on repeat in my mind.

Up close, the city was dirty and depressing. The buildings were gray, and the streets were littered with refuse and sewage. No wonder the people of Barrien kept dying.

"Keep your head down," my captor told me, hissing through her teeth with each word. The cobblestone of the ground was unfamiliar to me, and it felt a little like I was learning to walk again as I gracelessly marched in front of her. Although she let me walk unbound, Max kept her dagger between us, pointed discreetly at my back as we moved. I'd already told her I wouldn't be going anywhere, but I supposed it would have been foolish for her to trust me.

"Why? No one here is going to recognize me." I mentally palmed my face at that admission. It probably would've been in my best interests to keep that information to myself.

Max halted in her tracks, and I stopped too, following a poke from her dagger, then turned around. Her dark eyes locked on to my own even under the cover of her hood. "Don't you think that's weird?"

I pulled away from her gaze and attempted to keep my voice low, the windows of people's homes only feet away from our now very public discussion. "Why would that be weird?" I asked, looking around the street so that I could avoid her face. "It's not like I visit the city."

She shook her head as if there were no words that could make me understand her high-level way of thinking and resumed our walk. I tried to brush it off, but being spoken to like an idiot was certainly a new experience for me. Then again, everything about this situation was new and surprising to me. So far, I knew that Max was a mercenary who had been hired to deliver me to Emynor for what must have been a hefty fee. She was surprisingly strong for someone so little. I couldn't make her laugh, which significantly decreased my chances of charming my way to freedom. Also, she and her horse only liked each other and no one else.

When she spoke again, I was intrigued by the fact that she was giving me more than one-word answers. "You're supposedly the beloved prince of an entire kingdom, and no one knows what you look like—"

I cut in to correct her. "People that visit the castle do. Like my guests."

"Well, none of your subjects do. So you're telling me you don't make any appearances… and there are no paintings of you anywhere? You're walking the streets of your city, and your subjects will treat you like any other commoner. That's not strange to you? Shouldn't they be flooding the streets to get a peek?"

I chewed the inside of my lip before shrugging her questioning off. I'd had similar questions once, but my parents had been quick to give me the answer I was about to give her. "It's for safety."

"You're literally being kidnapped and taken for a bounty, and no one knows to help you. I also don't see anyone out looking for you. Guards? No posters, no one yelling in the town square. How can that be safe? I mean, I don't mind. Makes things easier for me, but you'd think you'd want one of these people" – she gestured to the townspeople we passed by – "to recognize you and… I don't know, *do something*, because you're with a mysterious cloaked figure."

"You're not that mysterious," I assured her. While my instinct was to deflect, I couldn't help but dwell on her questions. Eventually I had to push them into the back of my mind and remind myself that my parents had my best interests in mind, so if there weren't royal guards scouring the city for me, it was for good reason.

"You're missing the point."

Before we could get further into it, someone peeked out of a window above us. "Oy! Are you Max?"

We halted, and my captor looked up to the middle-aged woman who had demanded our attention. Her dirty blond hair was piled high into a bun on top of her head, and she wiped her brow as she looked down at us, as if she were taking a break from some strenuous work to speak with us. Even from our place in the street, the bags under her eyes were obvious.

"Depends on who's asking," Max replied. She kept her hood on still, and I couldn't help but wonder how she'd been identified. Perhaps potential customers knew to look out for her horse. Wraith was hard to miss.

"I've got a job for ya," the townsperson said from her window.

Max nodded up at the woman, who then disappeared back into her home.

"Aren't you on a job right now?" I asked.

Max nodded a little. "Yeah, but unless you smuggled some crystals in your ass as I was kidnapping you, we're going to need money to get to Emynor. You know, for food, lodging, travel. I already checked your pants."

I scoffed. "Not my ass, though, right?"

Max kept her gaze on the door of the building that the woman had peeked out of, no doubt waiting for her to come speak in a more private manner than yelling into the street. I found myself curious about what the job could be. It wasn't like she had space for another captive; I was not going to let some prisoner be an awkward third wheel on our adventure. "Come on now, I'm not a monster," she said coolly. "I wouldn't do that to someone without their permission."

"But you'd kidnap them," I noted, fighting the smile that was creeping onto my face. I was glad she wasn't looking at me.

"And kill them." Her face remained unmoved.

I must've been staring at her wide-eyed when the woman finally came down because she halted at the door and looked between us, making sure she wasn't interrupting something, before speaking again. "Will you come in? Your friend, too."

Max shook her head. "We've got to keep moving, so I'll need to hear about the job before we agree to stop." She wasn't rude, but she certainly wasn't friendly either.

"We've got tooth faeries."

TOOTH FAERIES

MAX

The laugh that burst from my captive's mouth caused every hair on my body to stand on end. It was loud, and hell, it was downright embarrassing. We'd barely made it through a day together, and his behavior had me regretting my decision to keep him conscious throughout the trip. Here I was trying to make some money to keep him alive until I forked him over and he couldn't even control his giggles. "Excuse him—" I began to tell the woman, but August, in typical male fashion, cut me off.

"You're joking," he said, still laughing. His dark curls bounced as he spoke through his laughing fit, his hand on his midsection as if it were sore from his endless amusement. "That's a children's story! Tooth faeries aren't real." Yes, he would be well versed in children's stories given his level of maturity.

I elbowed him in the ribs harder than I had intended and sent him staggering to the side while in a coughing fit. "As I said, excuse my travel companion. He's... an idiot."

The woman watched August for a moment before returning her gaze to me. She wrung the front of her dirty yellow apron as she spoke. The exhaustion in her pale blue eyes made her look far older than she was. "Please help us," she pleaded, the desperation in her gaze one I was very familiar with. Life outside of the kingdoms was rough to begin with, but being plagued by tooth faeries would certainly add another layer of misery to things.

I continued my pre-employment interview. "How many are there?"

"Two, three maybe. The children can't sleep anymore, they're so terrified."

"Three?" I shook my head in frustration. Three tooth faeries was practically an infestation. Once their appetite for a particular child's or family's teeth was whet, they were particularly hard to get rid of. Her mention of children didn't pull at my heartstrings like she hoped. "How much are you paying?"

The woman avoided my gaze when she answered. "We don't have much, twenty crystals maybe…"

I turned to leave; it wasn't anything personal, but I only did jobs that made sense to me financially. They needed to look out for their family, and I had to look out for mine. It was that simple. August was still coughing, hunched over with his hands on his knees. "Kind of dramatic…" I murmured, grabbing his sleeve to pull him along. "Pull yourself together."

The woman turned frantic and dropped her apron to reach out to me. "Wait, wait, we'll feed you, too! And give you a warm place to stay for however long it takes." I didn't like the implication in the last part of her offer.

I sighed. "And the horse?" I jerked my thumb at Wraith behind me, who let out a snort.

"And the horse, yes!" The woman nodded frantically. "We've got a place for you to tie him up and feed for him—"

"Her."

"Feed for her, of course."

When I realized that I was, in fact, agreeing to the job, I nodded with a sigh. This was bound to happen. People would recognize me, and I'd be offered work as we traveled, just like I was when I wasn't transporting a captive. The only difference was that I had to drag August along to each of these jobs to ensure he didn't escape. That, and I wasn't particularly fond of dealing with tooth faeries. "We're headed for Dalcester in the morning, so it'll have to be done in one night."

Relief washed over the woman's face. "Oh, that would be a miracle, if ya think ya can—"

"I can."

UNFORTUNATELY, I couldn't.

Later that evening, Wraith was tied up and eating, having gotten a sufficient amount of petting from the villager's two young daughters. They had even braided her mane, which she tolerated when I told her that her meal and boarding depended on it. As I packed up my belongings to bring in from the stable with me, the pitter-patter of rain gave me pause and put a damper on my plan to make this job a quick one. Tooth faeries never come out in the rain, so when I made my way back to the home of the woman who had hired me, I was feeling defeated.

"Looks like it'll be more than one night," I told the mother as I slipped into their home. I pulled my hood off, which sent droplets of water cascading down my back. When she gave me a confused look, I added, "The rain. They won't be showing themselves if it's raining… I'm not sure why, but that's just how they operate."

"Ah, makes sense that they didn't start popping up until summer then… and it's been quite the dry summer at that," the mother replied. "Well, it'll be a relief to have you nearby when the rain lets up… and as I said, you're welcome to stay as long as you need to."

I offered her an appreciative nod despite being displeased with the circumstances. A job was a job, and I couldn't back down just because the weather had changed. When I entered the kitchen to find August setting the table with the two young daughters of the villager, I stood in silent shock for a moment. I didn't say anything, just took the seat I was guided to at the table. It was a small, cramped table with one wobbly leg. August and I sat shoulder to shoulder on one side, while the girls sat across from us. Their mother's place setting was at the far end of the table, and the last seat at the opposite end remained empty. It had a place setting with a bowl, spoon, and glass, though.

I was thinking it, but August wasted no time in blurting out his question. "Don't you have a husband?"

The woman, whose name we'd learned to be Ermaline, stared at him with wide eyes. She paused on her way to the stove to grab a pot of whatever we were having for dinner. "Well, yes, but—"

"Pa is working on the cliffside," the older daughter, Mabel, told us proudly. "Sometimes he doesn't come home until very late, so we leave his dinner out for him once we're done. That way, it's there when he gets home."

Ermaline nodded and smiled at her daughter, then turned to us again. "Yes, their father works very hard."

I shot August an irritated glance. He may not have noticed it, however, because he was busy looking around the tiny home. I hadn't bothered looking around myself, but given the stark difference between any villager's home and the royal castle, I said a silent prayer that he wouldn't make any more thoughtless comments. I was still surprised that he'd helped set the table and that he knew what components went where on the surface; I imagined that he had servants to do that back home.

Ermaline ladled each of us a bowl of cabbage stew and tore a hunk of bread from a large loaf. My stomach growled; it had been quite some time since I'd eaten a warm meal, let alone one sitting at a table, no matter how rickety this one was. I primed my elbow toward August in hopes that he would graciously accept the food. This time, he noticed, and scowled at me silently, but said nothing. Our host also poured us each a glass of beer and two small cups of milk for the children.

I took the beer graciously. When I noticed Mabel staring at me over her cup of milk, I cocked an eyebrow in her direction. "What is it?"

"Is it true they call you Max the Menace?" she asked.

Before I could respond, August was chuckling again.

Darkness fell late that summer evening, and sleepiness was looming over me following our food and rest, but a sense of unease bubbled inside of me. I didn't like not knowing how long we'd be in one place or how much of a delay this job would put on our overall trip. Ermaline rolled out a thin mattress in the middle of their main living area and piled it with blankets and a couple of pillows for us, then left to put her daughters to bed. They all looked exhausted, but they seemed relieved that they would get at least one night without the stress of the tooth faeries. I hoped that it would allow them to rest whenever I would get to exterminate their pests, as that would undoubtedly be a long night for everyone. I had information to gather, a plan to formulate, but I decided to let the small family rest that night.

It wasn't lost on me that August of Barrien had likely never slept in anything smaller than a king-sized bed and that he'd probably never shared a bed with someone out of necessity. Or a room. Or a bathroom. He folded his arms over his chest as he stood above the makeshift sleeping bag on the floor and looked at me. "Look," he whispered harshly, "I know that I'm a prisoner here, but this really feels like cruel and unusual punishment. Surely even you can admit that."

I gestured for him to keep his voice down even more, not wanting to offend the people who were being so hospitable with us. What happened to the August who had just helped set the table only hours before? "Which part?"

"All of it. Sleeping on the floor, on... what is this?" He shoved the mat over with the toe of his boot. "A stack of newspapers? Not to mention the fact that we have to share."

"Yeah, well, sharing is the only way I'll be able to get some sleep and make sure that you don't take off in the middle of the night," I told him as I shoved the thin mattress against the front door, the only exit to the house unless August was willing to take a fall from one of the windows. Then I yanked my boots off and sat down on the makeshift bed, not bothering to remove my weapons. The accommodations certainly weren't much, but it was a welcome break from sleeping on the ground outside, which, even in its rustic wonder, got tiring after a while. I was grateful for a warm meal, the safety of walls, and the sound of falling rain. Even though it put a damper on my plans, it forced me to slow down and breathe. The windows of the small home were cracked, and a slight breeze whisked through the open living space.

August grumbled to himself, but eventually kicked off his own boots and lay down on the mat, which was large enough that there was significant space between us.

Ermaline's husband didn't come home that night.

Two more days of rain came and went. The girls and their mother spent time inside, cleaning, playing, and drawing on scraps of parchment. I forced August to play with them because I didn't trust him to leave the house alone, and I didn't want to have to keep an eye on him whenever I stepped out. He seemed to have a softer spot for children than I did; hopefully he was enjoying this part of his adventure. On the third day, the rain finally let up.

"When did they start visiting you?" I asked, standing in the doorway of the girls' room as their mother tucked them into their beds. The room was small and dingy, with the girls' beds next to each other and Ermaline's slightly larger bed at the far end underneath the window. It was a tight fit, with only one night-stand to share between all of them, but each bed was neatly made with clean bedding and a small toy propped up on each girl's pillow. I had no doubt that, despite the limitations of their resources, the girls were well cared for and went to bed feeling at peace, aside from their recent run-ins with the tooth faeries. In fact, the room reminded me a lot of my own home growing up: small, cramped, but kept clean by someone who loved me and my brother a great deal. August stood behind me in the hall. I didn't think he'd run, but I also didn't trust him on his own. He was so unused to this way of life that I could just imagine him accidentally destroying their home or asking where the theater or sauna were, both of which no one in this town had ever seen in their lives. That would be sure to set off an alarm in the woman's mind.

Ermaline looked to Mabel, who hid her face in shame beneath the edge of her blanket. "I lost my first tooth," she said, hesitation thick in her voice. She chewed her lower lip before forcing herself to meet my gaze. When she lowered the blanket a little and spoke again, I caught a glimpse of the missing front tooth she was referring to. Cute. "All of the kids at school said that if you put your tooth under your pillow, the tooth faerie will come and leave you crystals!" Her voice was so eager as she recounted the tale that my heart ached a little.

"See?" August whispered behind me. "That's the story I was talking about."

"And we really need the crystals, ya see, so I was in such a hurry to put it under my pillow that I didn't think to ask Mama if it was the right thing to do or not." Mabel sounded truly remorseful, but who could blame her for believing her classmates?

I knew the story, everyone did. The unfortunate truth was that there was no tooth faerie like the one Mabel and August were talking about. Childhood tales would have you believe that the fabled tooth faerie was a petite, girlish pixie with glittering wings. In those tales, she flitted in through the windows of children who had lost a baby tooth, plucked the tooth from beneath their pillow, and left a few crystals in return. She would then fly away peacefully, but not before sprinkling a bit of magic faerie dust in the air for added good dreams! It was no surprise that this story was shared far and wide by children everywhere, especially those in poor cities where the idea of swapping a useless tooth for some crystals to buy candy or toys seemed too good to be true… because it was. The real creature that showed up when you left teeth under your pillow was something completely different. Real tooth faeries are more like a mutant spider than a glittering pixie, and they're less interested in making a child's day than collecting their teeth for consumption. I felt sorry that this family – and soon August – had to find out the truth the hard way.

Ermaline stroked Mabel's tangled mess of hair and kissed her forehead. The younger sister, Eleanor, stood by her mother's side as she tucked her in. When she spoke, it was the first I'd heard her little voice during our entire visit. "Is she gonna be okay?"

"It'll be alright," I told them in the dark. "Nothing is going to happen to you while I'm here." I'd said that exact phrase to my little brother, Danny, more times that I could remember, and I hadn't let him down yet. Once Ermaline and Eleanor were out in the hallway, I tucked myself into the youngest girl's bed and blew out the candle on the shared nightstand. Beneath the blanket of the younger sister's bed, I ran my hand along my weapons' usual holding spots: dagger on hip, check; knife in boot, check; darts in hip pocket, check; potion on belt, check. "Go to sleep," I told Mabel, then called out to the hall. "August, you stay there. Settle in, it could be a while."

FUCKING TOOTH FAERIES!

AUGUST

I had just dozed off on the creaky floor of the villager's hallway when I awoke to the sound of skittering, scampering claws. At first, it sounded like rats maybe, a vermin that even royals have to deal with; no matter how rich you are, they still find a way into your chambers. They eat your furniture and shit in your shoes. The only difference is that we have people to come and handle them. When I finally shook myself awake and lucid, it took me a moment to remember where I was. The scampering continued in addition to the soft snoring of the little girls asleep in their room. But then, there was another sound: a grunt, then a squelch, then a shriek.

I turned the corner into the room to find Max on her back in the bed she'd tucked herself into, one arm wrapped around a squirming, wriggling shadow while the other held her dagger up in the air. On the end of the dagger was another shadow which looked a lot like a giant spider. It seized a few times before falling limp. Before I could respond, she whipped her blade so that the creature's body flew off of it and into a nearby wall. It hit the wall with a squelch that would take months to shake from my memory. The sound reminded me of what it might be like to throw a sopping wet steak at a wall.

"August, grab that one!" Max yelled, still wrestling with the creature she had pinned under her arm. Apparently, she'd gotten a lot done while lying down.

"What? 'That one' what? 'That one' what?" I stammered, completely unprepared for whatever the hell was happening. "You didn't say I'd have to do anything!"

"That tooth faerie!" she yelled, pointing at a third shadow that was scampering toward the open door and consequently, me. It ran so quickly it was almost a blur, each of its eight legs coordinating perfectly with each other. "You don't have to do anything, just don't let it leave! That's the last one!" she added as she speared the second faerie she'd been wrestling with. It emitted a shrill screech, and when she threw it down to join its dead partner, it made a tinkling sound like a jar full of marbles.

As the escapee came closer to the dim light of the hallway, I got a better view of just what we were dealing with. It did, indeed, look like a giant spider, but it was easily the size of a cat. At the end of each scurrying leg, however, were pincers. They were undoubtedly the perfect tool to rip teeth right out of a person's head. Its eyes, huge and milky, scanned the room as it crawled.

As if the situation couldn't get hairier, our conversation and the creatures' cries woke up Mabel, who immediately started to panic. "Oh no, they're here, they're here!" she squealed, then threw her covers over her head. "Don't let them take my teeth!" She kept screaming, but I couldn't make out the rest of her words over the sound of Max's frantic directions and the eight legs making a run for the doorway I happened to be standing in. My head swam. This, alone, would've made me work harder to convince Max to bring me home in exchange for a ransom payment. Between the cabbage soup, sleeping upright in a hallway or on a thin wafer on the floor, and the tooth-eating spider monsters, this was feeling less and less like an adventure.

By the time I caught sight of my target shadow again, it had flitted past me in a shocking display of speed and disappeared down the hallway, the same tinkling and rolling sounds accompanying it. I gagged a little and involuntarily pressed my lips together over my teeth when I realized what was making the sound; they were all full of teeth, their treasures, which were jumbling around inside of their bodies as they ran. Those critters were practically living piggy banks filled with pearly nuggets.

Max flew past me in an instant, and I was left dumbstruck, staring at the lump of a little girl under her blanket. I wished I could hide under my own blanket and wait for all of this to blow over, or better yet, call for my own mommy. When Max returned, she was panting, and Ermaline and the younger daughter were close behind. The mother scooted into the room to comfort Mabel while Max spoke. "I've sealed the doors and windows, so I'm hoping it's in here somewhere. We just need to lure it out."

I highly doubted that securing the windows and doors would make this home escape proof, but I wanted her to be right because I desperately wanted to be done with tooth faeries. If we could skip the prolonged cabbage soup, too, that would be a bonus. Then, I realized what she had said, and unease passed over me. "Lure it out… how?"

Ermaline and the girls followed my gaze to Max, and we all looked at her expectantly, fearing the worst.

"We need teeth," Max stated finally, wiping her brow with the back of her hand. Her breathing slowed while the rest of our nerves seemed to escalate. She shot me a quizzical look. "Obviously."

I shook my head, then threw up my hands and began pacing in the tiny hallway. "Fuck that."

"Language." Max gestured to the young girls huddled up next to their mother.

I groaned. "Fine, screw that, if you please."

"We don't need *your* teeth, idiot," Max told me. Was that my new nickname? Kind of rude... but at the same time, perhaps it was a sign that my captor was growing to like me.

"Then whose?" I dropped my voice to a whisper and leaned closer to her, trying to keep part of our conversation private. "I don't believe for one second that you're not planning to use your prisoner as bait." I clenched my teeth and parted my lips. "But these," I told her, gesturing to my teeth, "are staying inside of my head!"

"Shut up," Max scolded me, then pushed past me to face the family. She closed her eyes for a moment as if to gather her thoughts, then looked at all of us again. "I mean, as I'm sure you have all noticed, they prefer children's teeth."

The shock must have been clear on my face because Max threw her hands up, even more frustrated than before. "I'm not going to rip out their teeth, August!" She looked back to the family in annoyance. It was then that I realized the father was still not home yet. I remembered what Max had said at the Invisible Cliffs and wondered if he had fallen. How long had it been since he'd joined his family for dinner? Did the children realize by now that he wasn't just working? I didn't have time to theorize any longer because Max spoke again. "But does anyone have any loose teeth?" she asked. "Mabel?"

"No, just the one so far... and they took it." Mabel shook her head. "And Eleanor's too little. She still hasn't gotten all of her baby teeth." Ermaline held the girls close as if she wasn't sure if Max was going to snatch them away and pluck the molars right from their mouths. I also felt uneasy about the situation, but when Max let out a low groan, I realized that she meant to meet her goal of exterminating the faeries tonight, no matter the cost to herself.

"Everyone out," Max said finally. "Except you, August. I need you to close the door once I lure it in here."

"What are you—" Ermaline attempted to ask, but Max ushered her out even quicker.

"Out, please. The later it gets, the less energy I'll have to deal with this." She wasn't rude per se, but any rational human would not have ignored her directions. "This time we really do need to leave for Dalcester in the morning."

I let the family file out nervously before turning to my captor again. "I need to know how you're planning to do that. I know you don't have a pouch of spare teeth on that belt of yours, and if you're not going to use me, then…"

"As far as I'm concerned, I don't owe you an explanation about anything given the situation here. But if knowing will get you to participate, then the answer is I'll be using my own." Max's voice was even, surprisingly calm, as she dug around in her pockets and along her belt until she found something that resembled a pair of spindly pliers. I had to stifle a gag when she put her fingers into her mouth until she found what was apparently the perfect tooth and jammed the pliers into her gums until it loosened with a sick pop the likes of which I'd be hearing in my mind for days to come. Not a single whimper escaped her, but her eyes were shut tight against the pain; no matter how tough Max the Menace was, there was no way that didn't hurt like hell. Blood coated her lower lip almost instantly, and she held the tooth up to the glow of the candle, still slick with her spit. It glimmered in the light: a perfectly pearlescent little bud with the roots intact, ripped from its home without a second thought. "Perfect. Remind me to get this back when we're done." Then she wiped her mouth with the back of her sleeve, where it left a streak of dark red.

What she was going to do with her own disconnected tooth, I had no clue, but I suddenly didn't have it in me to argue with someone who was willing to rip their own tooth out for twenty crystals. I inadvertently ran my tongue along the inside of my mouth to make sure none of my own teeth were missing.

Max yawned a little, which caused more blood to dribble onto her lower lip, then pointed to the door. "Stand by," she told me as she tucked her freshly plucked tooth under the pillow of the little girl's bed. That was going to leave a stain, I could tell. "Remember what I said: once it's in here, close the door, and stay out of the way. I'll handle the rest."

"Yeah, I don't doubt it," I told her with an impressed grunt. "Hell, how did you do that so quickly?"

"I'll tell you later," Max smirked, then crawled into the kid's bed again. "Or if you continue to get in the way, I'll give you a personal demonstration." She made a gesture with her hands like a pincer and snipped her fingers in my direction. This was the most lighthearted I'd seen her, and all on the tail of ripping her tooth out of her own damn mouth.

I cringed. "That's sick… but there's no way that was worth twenty crystals."

Max gestured to a spot by the door, cloaked in shadow, and mused aloud as I got myself into position. "No way, not even close," she agreed. Again, she surprised me with more information than I deserved considering I was her prisoner. "But if you knew anything about tooth faeries, you'd know that once they have a target in mind, they'll stop at nothing until they've pulled all of their victim's teeth out. For little ones like Mabel and Eleanor, that means all of the teeth they'll ever have, all the way up into their skull." She sighed and settled into the bed, her murmurs of contentment making it clear that she hadn't slept in a bed in a long time. Once this was over, I wondered where we would sleep next. I was already starting to miss my bedroom. "Even a big idiot like you can surmise that they wouldn't survive that."

My heart sank as I pictured those spindly-legged creatures pinning the little girls down to take their teeth. The thought itself was horrific, especially after I had heard one of their small voices plead for help earlier. Perhaps that alone was worth the loss of one adult tooth.

"Goodnight," Max murmured, then leaned over the nightstand to blow the candle out once again. It might've been because of the blood or the sudden onset of darkness, but the scuttling came much faster this time. I held my breath as I stood by the door and waited.

This time, the critter paused near the entrance of the door, and I turned my head ever so slowly to get a better look at it. It didn't notice me, but I noticed everything about it, from its spindly, hairless legs to the way it was sniffing intently at the air in the room. It could smell the metallic tang of Max's blood, but must have been too stupid or too tempted to care that its sisters' bodies were piled up in the corner of the room. I waited for it to get farther into the room and slid my hand along the door toward the doorknob. Farther, farther, until it was inches away from where Max had stashed her bloody pulp of a tooth under Mabel's pillow. Then, I closed the door as quickly and quietly as I could. The age of the building did us no favors, and it creaked loudly as it closed, the latch making a heavy *thunk* rather than a sharp click.

The creature let out a harsh screech in response and bolted for the door again, but Max was up in seconds and sent her knife sailing through the dark. It hit its target with a crunch, and I looked toward the door to see the small creature impaled into the wood of the doorframe and wriggling in pain. We really weren't going to leave the place better than we found it, that much was certain. Max said nothing as she walked over and twisted the creature's neck to kill it completely, then removed her blade and wiped the blood off on her pants before sheathing it again. She didn't bother to light the candle before gathering the tooth faerie carcasses. Instead, she just piled them up, cut a slit in each of their spider-like appendixes, and then shook them over the wooden floor of the bedroom, as if emptying a purse. A small mountain of molars came tumbling out, many with gold caps or fillings, which glistened in the moonlight streaming into the room. She sorted through them, selecting those that she would be able to sell for a profit, and swept the rest up into her hand to dispose of them. I imagined she didn't want the girls to see the results of her kill, but she didn't make any effort to clean the splattered blood out of the room.

I didn't need to remind Max to find the tooth she pulled. When it flopped out of the faerie along with the rest of them, she identified her own gleaming tooth in the pile and pocketed it. Again, I found myself wondering what she planned to do with it. I was no doctor, but as far as I knew, teeth didn't just get reattached. Then again, I hadn't known that tooth faeries existed until that day, so I would be willing to admit my own ignorance when it came to magical beings. We threw the carcasses in a bag that we'd load onto Wraith in the morning, then we made our way back into the hall so that Ermaline could finally get the girls to sleep. Max leaned against the hallway wall next to me and slid down until she was sitting on the floor.

"Thanks," she said with a sigh.

I sat next to her in silence. Before I could think of anything to say, she was asleep, and a few moments later, she'd slumped to the side with her head on my shoulder. She smelled a bit like blood. I didn't move my captor.

BEFORE WE LEFT the next morning, Ermaline packed us a few hunks of bread and a piece of cheese and pulled Max aside to pay her. I couldn't hear all of the conversation, but I heard enough as I buckled the bag of faeries onto Wraith's saddle and packed our small ration of food away as well. Wraith looked less than enthused about my being the one to prep her, but she tolerated it as well as she'd tolerated her mane being braided by the girls. Personally, I wasn't sure how I'd been talked into having responsibilities and chores on the trip to turn me over, potentially to my death, but I dutifully completed the tasks at the threat of Max's wrath. I didn't want to see what that would look like after I watched her pop one of her own teeth out like it was an ordinary occurrence for her.

"He's not coming home, is he?" Max asked bluntly. "Your husband."

"I— I don't rightly know." Ermaline sounded shattered at the way Max had forced her to face the severity of her situation. It didn't feel like the kindest parting gift, but then again, Max had done the promised job of ridding the small family of their tooth faerie problem.

"And this is all you have?" Max asked. She must have been looking at the sad handful of crystals she'd agreed to this job for. I half expected her to berate the woman, but she then said, "Keep it. The teeth are enough… I can sell those… and you fed us and Wraith. That'll do."

Ermaline began to argue, but Max shut her down immediately. "I'm not going to be responsible for solving one problem and leaving you with another. Just… keep this to yourself, I can't have people thinking I'll work for free."

We loaded up in silence and were off.

DALCESTER STREET MARKET

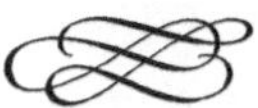

MAX

We were accompanied by the hearty clop of Wraith's hooves against the cobblestone of the Dalcester Street Market, a place I had frequented for as long as I could remember. It had served as a spot to restock supplies, gather food, and people watch; even though I didn't have the time or energy to connect with other humans in the way I wanted to, I could observe from afar and enjoy little bits of their interactions as if they were my own. The time I spent observing people and their habits only made me better at my job. I didn't have to get close to people to understand how they worked, and at this point, most behavior was far too predictable for me.

The market was bustling with exuberant vendors, haggling customers, and loose animals dodging the feet of the former two. Prior to our entry, I had told August to stay near me; although we still had no reason to believe anyone would recognize him, I didn't trust that he wouldn't run off. Whether he would run off to escape his captor or just to look at the wares at each stall remained to be seen, but the business of the open-air market made it harder for me to keep track of him than it had been in the near-empty streets of Barrien.

Our first stop involved selling the gold and silver teeth that I'd acquired the previous night. The buyer didn't ask too many questions, but also didn't spare us his judging glances either; it was clear that he was used to purchasing unusual items, but teeth in bulk were a bit too unusual for any common wares dealer. When all was said and done, we made out with a bit more than the twenty crystals I was supposed to get from Ermaline. I held on to my own tooth because it was more valuable to me than to any market buyer, and we traveled through the market to prepare for the rest of our trip. As we walked, I ran my tongue over the tender pocket in my gums and felt grateful that I hadn't picked a smaller but more obvious tooth near the front of my mouth. Even though it was a habit for me to keep my face covered, I still cared about my appearance as much as anyone else. Well, maybe not as much as Prince August of Barrien, actually. Either way, I didn't think I could sport the missing-tooth look, even if it did seem to give male mercenaries more of an edge.

"Ooh, check these out. I haven't seen one this color before," commented August as we weaved through the market stalls, Wraith dutifully walking behind both of us and causing several traffic jams along the way. I had thought we were next to each other, at least, until I realized his voice was farther away than I'd remembered. When I followed the sound, I found him at a stall with miniature dragons for sale. They were all balancing on different perches, their tiny ankles shackled and chained to the wooden rods beneath them, although they hardly looked like they had the energy to take off anyway. Occasionally, one would let out a little puff of fire, but their display of magnificence was lackluster, to say the least. These little pet-type accessories were always a thing in the realm of Barrien, but the type of popular creature often changed. Years prior, Glitterats had been all the rage until people discovered that they were literally just rats covered in glitter. That and they'd been told the creatures' feces had magical properties only to learn that they'd spent months eating plain old rat shit.

Before I could respond, the stall owner attempted to talk up his wares. He was a short, portly man with thick glasses and oven mitts on both hands. His shirt was singed in several places, and even one of his eyebrows had been burned off. Nevertheless, he delivered his pitch with the enthusiasm of a man who really needed to recoup his investment. "They're all the rage right now, ya know. Why bother with a full-size dragon? They're dangerous and expensive to maintain. I mean, who can afford to slaughter an entire flock of sheep a day to keep one satisfied? And the housing, forget about it! You gotta build a fortress or a dungeon for them. These miniature dragons are the perfect companion! They're practically pocket-sized! Plus, all they need is a single mouse per day! Perfect for keeping your chambers clear of pests! You got mice, you got roaches? Not with these little gems!"

I rolled my eyes. "They're not looking too hot on one mouse a day." I reached out to stroke one of the little creatures under its chin, and it rested its head on my fingertip in exhaustion. Its tiny throat radiated heat, though it wasn't enough to burn me. I didn't believe it had the energy to take down a mouse.

The salesman ignored me. "And they come in a variety of fashionable colors! You'll be the talk of the town when you show up to a party with the limited edition turquoise micro dragon, and for today only, you can get your own for just three crystals!" I groaned internally. Three crystals was more than I could afford to waste on an accessory, even if I was interested in purchasing a "designer micro dragon." I wondered if August even had any concept of the value of money.

"See? Fashionable colors!" August said with a grin, gesturing to a tiny blue-green dragon that looked to be on its last leg. It let out a dry cough, and a puff of gray smoke left its petite mouth. I half expected it to keel over next. "I think you need one. Wouldn't Wraith love a sister?"

I grumbled, then pulled August along by his sleeve. I was already regretting my decision to let him travel unbound. "I don't do pets, especially not wild-caught, imprisoned creatures that look like they've been abused for profit. Wraith is a companion."

The dragon vendor called after us. "I'll cut you a deal! Two dragons for four crystals! You can have a matching set for the two of ya! What better for two charming lovers?"

We passed stall after stall of things we didn't need: hats for people, hats for horses, horses to put on your hats, overpriced exotic fruits, and more. "Besides," I mused aloud as I searched the market for necessities. "Wraith would eat one of those in a heartbeat. She's easily annoyed. Like me."

Wraith snorted in agreement.

August chuckled to himself. "I bet that'd give her some mighty heartburn."

"Enough messing around," I continued, stopping our leisurely stroll to look August in the eyes. "If you keep wandering off, I'll have you bound and back on the horse. Besides, I'm still not convinced you won't be recognized." I added the last part in a whisper.

"By who?" August asked, louder than I would have liked. "We've already talked about this; the villagers living right outside of the castle didn't even recognize me. I've never been to this market before. Hell, I've hardly even been outside the castle walls. No one is going to recognize me. It's not like there are posters of me all over town. Though, I wouldn't blame the people for worshiping this." He gestured to his face and attempted a smolder, which, in my opinion, fell short.

As if on cue, we passed a group of young women who were all sporting miniature dragons on their shoulders; each one had coordinated their handbag with their fire-breathing accessory. While the sight solidified my decision not to partake, August seemed even more enamored with the little creatures. "They've got the right idea," he argued. Even as I pulled him with me, August's eyes remained glued to the group. They followed his gaze in return, and one of them blew him a kiss. "Don't worry, they don't know who I am. They just know a beefcake when they see one."

"Bound and on the horse," I told him. "Last warning, don't test me."

"The number of times you've threatened to tie me up is alarming," August mused aloud. I didn't have to look at him to visualize the smirk on his face. Was this man flirting with me? I couldn't say this was the first time someone had tried to get out of capture by attempting to woo me, but this one had me more annoyed than usual.

"It almost sounds like you'd prefer it." When he leaned closer to me to whisper in my ear, a chill coursed through my body. "Shall I continue to misbehave?"

Before I swung my arm back to punch him in the stomach, he chuckled a little in amusement.

"Worth it," he said.

We spent the rest of the afternoon wandering the market to acquire the other essentials we'd need for our journey, which, unfortunately for my pockets, included clothing for August. He just wouldn't make it through a cool night in the woods with only a thin shirt and pants. Thankfully I'd thought to snag his boots on my way out of his chambers, but it remained to be seen how long those would last; they were made of very soft leather and looked to already be damaged just from walking around the market. The contrast between attire made for real life and that made for life in the castle, where he likely didn't lift a finger unless he wanted to, was bizarre to me.

I spotted a stall with clothing and pulled August to it, determined to keep him away from the flirtatious gaze of nearly every woman that noticed him. Not only was it annoying, but it was slowing down our progress. Besides, he may have been traditionally handsome, but he wasn't that good looking. They also had no idea what his personality was like; it certainly took his physical attractiveness down a notch. "You need a jacket," I told him.

"You think so? I thought you said it was summer, and I'd be fine," he said with a laugh, gesturing to his thin white shirt, which was unlaced so much that the crux of his chest, sprinkled with dark hair, was showing. "Remember? Zero concern for my nipples."

I rolled my eyes and turned to the merchant, who was hanging up clothing around the edge of her stall. I scanned the array of jackets and pointed to one hung high up; it was simple, made of what looked like thick brown minotaur leather, and appeared to be August's size, based on my guess alone. It was significantly bigger than my size, at least. "How much?"

Before the merchant could respond, August scoffed, and I turned to find him wrinkling his nose. "But that's so… plain."

I rolled my eyes again and looked back at the jacket. "What are you talking about? It's a perfectly good jacket." It was far too big for me, but I was planning on taking it back from him when I finally turned him over; I could always use a backup.

The prince's eyes lit up as if he'd been hit with a marvelous idea. I immediately knew it would be something ridiculous. "You know what would really spice it up? A matching micro-dragon." He held the jacket up after the merchant handed it to him and gestured to the shoulder of the garment. "See, right here? That would be the perfect spot for it to hang out. Can you imagine?"

Later that evening, we made camp at the edge of Dalcester. Despite Wraith's size, I traveled light for the sake of convenience, so we didn't have a tent or even a bedroll to lie on. That was standard for me, but I expected protest from August III. I threw a blanket on the ground and bundled up one of my jackets to make myself a pillow. Because he'd been such a pain at the market, I considered forcing August to make do with what he had – which was very little – but instead, I threw him my other blanket. I gave Wraith a bunch of carrots I'd traded for at the market, then plopped onto the ground near our fire and tossed August a chunk of bread I'd torn in half for us to share. We were silent as we ate, and when I looked over at the prince, he was staring at the city lights from our quiet vantage point. To my surprise, he ate his bread without complaint, even though it was undoubtedly bland compared to what he ate at home. Somehow, he was on multiple days of eating commoner food without whining. Maybe he really was viewing the trip as an adventure…

"How are you so content?" I asked. That was my job, to know the plan and to be confident in its implementation, even if it involved some gruesome components. As my captive, his job was to panic. Resist. Fight back. Attempt to run. Apparently, it also included making casual passes at me, as if that was going to change the course of our plan. He'd done a few of those things, but not nearly to the extent that I expected, and frankly it confused me. I didn't like being confused.

August shrugged. "Why shouldn't I be? I get to explore the land outside of Barrien for a few days, then my people will find me, pay whatever you're asking for, and I'll be back home in no time… maybe so soon that those girls will still be hanging around my chambers. I can tell them all about how I helped kill three tooth faeries with an infamous mercenary."

I shook my head. He was too busy admiring the view to notice.

We ate in silence for a while before August piped up. "Why do you do this? It seems like the hardest way to make money." He chewed thoughtfully on his bread, watching the sun go down.

I smirked a little. "I think it only seems hard to you because you don't have to work for money. Have you ever?" When the question left my mouth, I found that I was actually curious to know that answer rather than just trying to make a jab at him.

"No," August responded, still chewing thoughtfully.

"Well, there are certainly easier ways, but they don't pay as well," I explained, looking off into the distance as I spoke. "This work gives me the freedom to work when and where I want to and only take on jobs that interest me. That, and the pay. Makes the gruesome parts worth it, I suppose."

"And if you could do anything else and still make the same amount of money, what would it be?"

I turned to August in wide-eyed shock, unsure if I was still speaking to the same stuck-up prince who had been flirting with women at the market only hours before. "I… um…"

"Would you peddle dragons at the market?" August smirked a little, then took another bite of his food.

"No, I don't think so." I turned back to the skyline. "I'll have to get back to you on that."

I'd never really had the time to think about hobbies or jobs that were fueled solely by interest like other people do. I knew those jobs existed, of course; I'd seen plenty of people make a living, though not a lavish one, creating art, making music, or farming.

Given my station in life, however, I'd never considered any of those an option for me.

The short of it is that I was raised by two parents who loved me and my younger brother, Danny, very much. My father was a soldier and a very good one at that, but much like Ermaline's husband, he just didn't come home one day. The kingdom he fought for didn't even bother to let us know he had been slaughtered defending their land, nor did they offer help to his widow and young children. My mother cared for us as well and as long as she could before she fell ill… and I held her hand when she took her last breath. After that, it was up to me to care for myself and my little brother. The only profitable skill I had left was the self-defense and weaponry skills that my father had left me with. I wasn't proficient with a sword, nor could I defend myself against the monsters that roamed the continent, but I started small and practiced a lot. Unfortunately, a lot of my practice came from fending off male mercenaries who didn't think I could run in their circles and wanted to "teach me a lesson." I could run a household just fine, but that wouldn't keep my brother fed, so I left those tasks to him when I moved us out to the Wild Open. I vowed to never be ruled by a kingdom again.

Perhaps one day when Danny was old enough, he'd be able to accompany me. But he was so much younger, and I was so determined to keep the last remaining member of my family safe, that I had holed him away from the rest of the world. When I spent time at home with him, I tried to teach him to the best of my ability. I hoped that this job, turning August over, would give us a windfall and allow for a change of pace. I couldn't see us ever living in a big city, but I wanted Danny to have the childhood experiences that I wasn't able to.

The next few days of travel were uneventful, so much so that August didn't even surprise me with genuine questions. I feared that there may be a change of tone once he finally realized that he wasn't going to be rescued by someone from his kingdom; even if they had everyone out looking for him – which they didn't, surprisingly – I was experienced enough to know how to keep him hidden.

GRIMMAKER WOODS

AUGUST

"What are they called again?" I asked over Max's shoulder as Wraith brought us into the looming, suddenly very dark woods. The way the sunlight went from bright and radiant to almost non-existent felt like we were entering an entirely new world. I'd never stepped foot in a forest before and had only seen paintings of such scenery. The murky darkness of the trees was offset only by the shimmering of wet moss on every surface. It felt alive. Mesmerizing, in a way. The sound of critters skittering across Wraith's path took away from some of the magic, though, and made me realize that I was glad to be up off the ground. In Barrien, I had a cat that lived in the castle. His name was Terrance, and he underwent weekly grooming by the groundskeeper, which kept him smelling pleasant. I decided then that aside from Terrance and Wraith, who I had been forced to cohabitate with, I was content to observe other animals from a distance.

As usual, Max seemed annoyed by my questioning. I just wanted to know how to refer to all of these places when I recounted my adventures to the women of Barrien; they would be impressed by how worldly I had become in my time away. I'd heard that nothing gets the ladies going like a well-traveled man. "Grimmaker Woods," she replied over her shoulder. Her tone was hushed, as if others were listening. "Haven't you ever seen a map?"

"Why would I need a map?" The way Max continued to question the life I lived was getting old. Was it jealousy or just straight judgment? Perhaps she truly thought she was going to bring me to justice by turning me over, but I still didn't know why I was even being captured for a bounty, and it seemed she didn't either. We'd had some variation of this conversation several times since my capture, and still, we couldn't see eye-to-eye when we came back to it. We would never understand each other's worlds. I felt like I was trying, at least a little, to understand hers... I couldn't say the same about her approach to my background.

"Yeah, yeah, I know, you've never left the castle." Max put a hand up to wave me off.

I kept my chin up despite her constant jabbing. "And right now, I have the perfect tour guide, so I think... Map: zero. August's plan: one."

"There's no way this was part of your plan." Max scoffed.

"You know how they say you have to laugh or you'll cry? This is what they're talking about. I'm trying to look at this in a... less negative light." Couldn't she let me have one ounce of triumph? After all, I was the captive here. It wasn't like I had any chance at actually being in charge. I shrugged. "Whatever, okay, Grimmaker Woods. Why do we have to go through here?" A shudder ran through the horse beneath us, and I found that I was the only one enchanted by the shimmering greenery of the forest. Was I supposed to be uncomfortable?

"It's the only way through," Max said plainly. "There isn't a boat that'll take Wraith until we get to the end of the road. Even so, the ones that would take humans around to Emynor aren't safe or affordable. It's almost as if by design… you know, since the elves of Emynor don't exactly love humans." She stopped talking for a moment as if she'd caught herself oversharing. "Not that you need all of that information."

I shrugged again. I'd likely never come through these woods again in my life, but I guess I didn't mind hearing about them. I wouldn't tell her that, though, because then she'd have a reason to remind me I'd be dead in a matter of days and no one would hear about my travels. That was what she thought, and she was entitled to her incorrect opinion, but I was getting sick of hearing about my untimely demise.

"There's a tavern halfway through," she added, almost as if she had just remembered. "That's where we're headed."

"In the middle of the woods?" Part of me liked the idea of visiting a tavern – another first for me – but the premise seemed suspicious. Foreboding, even, just like the woods.

"Yes," she told me with a nod. The tip of her hood bobbed along with her head like a tiny mountain peak, and I fought the urge to pinch it. "Along this path. We need to make it there before nightfall."

I chuckled a little. "Why? You don't wanna sleep under the stars? We've done it so much already, I'm kind of getting used to it… Isn't that a thing for you rugged types anyway?"

Max groaned, and I sensed that it was taking a lot of restraint for her not to reach back and knock me off the horse. I wondered if she ever smiled. Hell, I wondered if she ever got laid. Maybe that would make her smile for once.

"Sleep under the stars in Grimmaker? Not likely. If you're out in the woods past nightfall, you'll be sleeping in a monster's belly. The Beast's Breath Tavern is really the only spot to stop… and we have to stop. There's no way to get through the woods in one day, no matter how early you start or how fast your horse is." She leaned down to pat Wraith's neck in reassurance.

I couldn't help but laugh. All of Max's fearmongering had done nothing to dampen my spirits, which I'm sure was much to the dismay of her prickly self. "You're saying there's something out here more vicious than you?"

"Only barely," Max told me as the horse slowed down. "Lucky for us, we've got plenty of time to get there."

I wasn't sure what made me say it – perhaps the strange air of the woods or the mention of some unnamed beast that apparently had an appetite for people – but I asked, "Wouldn't it make more sense to just… head there now?"

"The sooner we get there, the closer we'll be to me handing you over. I don't mind, but you should. Besides, this tavern isn't some-where you want to hang out casually for too long… Lots of shady characters, you know… and I have a few things I'd like to take care of along the way." Max clicked her tongue, and the horse pulled off the path, heading off into the woods instead of straight on the clearly designated part of the ground. I didn't have a ton of experi-ence riding horses, other than lessons in the castle stables, but I found myself impressed by the way that Max and Wraith worked so intuitively together. Perhaps part of it was just routine and they were used to traveling the same roads, at the same pace, together, but when Wraith led us straight to a small pool of water beneath a trickling waterfall with what felt like no guidance from Max, I was surprised.

The sun filtering through the canopy of the forest caused the surface of the water to glitter. It was then that I realized just how thirsty I was. "Water…"

My captor hopped off of the horse with little effort, landing successfully on her feet despite the steep drop to the ground. I watched her in awe, amazed at how stealthily her small body moved, then snapped myself out of it. When you're used to every woman you encounter being a potential lay, it gets easy to view them all as such... even if they're holding you hostage. And as much as I tried to keep my chin up and allow my joking side to shine, I was still a hostage in this situation. I had to remember that. Max didn't explain the plan, which, I had recently learned, was her style; in fact, she often seemed to operate as if I wasn't there. I looked down at her. "Should I... get down as well?"

"Yes, your highness," Max told me with a sigh, holding her hand up to me as if I were a prissy princess. Oh hell, that was probably just how she viewed me. When she looked up at me, I was taken aback by the depth of her dark eyes, which sparkled with the reflection of the glimmering woods like stars in an endless night. "Shall I lend you a hand?" she asked.

I grunted. "Certainly not," I told her, sliding off the horse and landing next to her. I flexed my toes in my boots as they settled into the soft forest ground and peered around our stopping point.

"Give me your wrists," my captor told me. I snorted a little and held out my hands to her, certain that this was her attempt at a joke. She wasn't very good at joking. She'd threatened to tie me up so many times in our short few days together and never followed through aside from her initial capture of me, so when she pulled a length of rope from her pocket and began securing my wrists to each other, I was speechless. Why now, when there was nowhere for me to run to and no place for me to hide? It wasn't even like I could steal her horse and take off on it; the beast was loyal to one person only. I could only imagine that any attempt to steal Wraith would end with me trampled or, at best, thrown off her back into the dirt if I even managed to mount her.

"What? No witty comments this time?" she asked, the corner of her mouth quirking up in the closest I'd seen to a smile from her.

The expression made something in my stomach flip… I'd never been nauseated by someone else's amusement before, but I'd also never been captured for this long, or dragged through the Grimmaker Woods, or denied a micro-dragon, so it was truly an adventure of firsts. I still wanted one of those damn dragons.

"I didn't think you'd actually do it," I told her, wiggling my fingers, the nails of which were starting to get dirty. Another first. I scrunched my nose in disgust. "And you're enjoying it, no less."

"Don't flatter yourself. I just can't have you making a run for it while I bathe," she told me, her gaze trained on the intricate knot she was creating. I couldn't tell if she was cutting off the blood flow in my arms or if it was the sensation of her touching my skin that had me lightheaded… I was about to comment on the tightness of her bonds when I realized what she had said. "I don't think you'd get far, but then I'd have to run through the woods naked to find you, and that really seems like a pain in the ass, don't you think? Even with Wraith, I'd have to stop and get dressed; shockingly, she prefers I wear pants," she added. Wraith snorted.

I squinted at her in confusion. "We're in the middle of the woods where there are supposedly monsters that will eat you, and you're going to take a bath?"

Max looked up to meet my gaze after giving the rope a firm tug for good measure. She humored me with a far-off look that made it seem like she was truly considering my question. "Hmm, yes, I believe I am," she told me, very clear that there was no room for negotiation. It appeared that Max the Menace did whatever the fuck she wanted, even if it was confusing to me. Then, she guided me to a tree, instructed me to sit down on the side opposite the pool of water, and told me, "I'll get you some water. Hold on." When she returned, she'd filled the canteen with cold water from the pool and wedged it between my bound hands so that I could bring it up to my lips to drink. Before she left, however, she bent down in front of me and bound my ankles as well. A chill ran through my body as she yanked the rope snugly around my legs. "For good measure." The way she wrapped the rope and secured it was done with such care and attention to detail that I was left wondering how long she'd been doing this. Each movement looked second nature, graceful, and fluid, despite being an act of domination. It made me wonder, however, if she was always this nice to her captives, too. Sure, she called me names, but to make sure I was fed, to fetch me water, it seemed like an impressive level of care for someone she'd be turning over to be tortured or killed or posted up in the town square. It was hard to say what my fate would be when I still didn't know why I was being held hostage.

I watched her leave in bewilderment, and soon I was stuck staring off into the forest with a rather boring landscape to hold my attention. A couple of birds chirped somewhere above me, and the leaf litter rustled with a bug or mouse; it wasn't the most exciting way to pass the time. I took a couple of sips from the canteen before the sound of Max shedding her armor hit me; buckles hit the ground, one leather plate squeaked against another, and her array of weaponry fell onto the dirt in a pile of metal. I couldn't see her, of course, but I assumed all of her weaponry was on the ground, unless she kept a secret miniature knife or throwing star tucked behind her ear while she bathed. Was it smart for her to leave me tied up and herself naked and defenseless if there were dangers in these woods? When I realized that I was trying to picture the process in my mind, I squeezed my eyes shut; if I kept imagining her undressing, I'd eventually have to picture her nude body. It had been longer than I liked since I'd last gotten laid, but not long enough to begin romanticizing my captor, I told myself. I'd heard of that happening… *That's how they get you,* I told myself.

Wraith huffed nearby as if to agree with me, but then she wandered off, probably to drink from the pool while her person washed. There was a small splash from behind the tree and then the sound of laughter, like the tinkling of bells, wandered playfully into my ears. It was so sweet, so soft and delicate that I had to wonder if we were alone anymore. Perhaps we were encountering another novel mythical creature for me to add to my travel tales. A nymph of sorts, maybe? Max didn't laugh. I hadn't known her for long, but I knew enough to have believed in that statement. She wasn't a spritely young woman who giggled or made jokes; she was a hardened killer who found absolutely nothing funny aside from the subtle jabs she could make at me. But there it was again, a sound more joyous than anything I'd ever expected to leave her body… "Wraith, cut it out!" she scolded the massive horse between giggles. I wondered what I was missing. Perhaps they were splashing each other in the pool. In my mind, it seemed like a humorous sight… too humorous to miss out on, I thought, maybe even something I could make fun of later on if I could catch a glimpse.

But when I shifted my body around the tree after scooting like a sad, tied-up slug, the sight I came upon was not what I expected, just as the laughter hadn't been. The midday light trickled through the treetops and cast shimmering speckles of sun onto the ground and water below. The water in the pool and small, cascading waterfall was a translucent cerulean so blue that it almost felt unreal, like an image from a watercolor painting or a piece of stained glass… and there, in the pool, with her back to me, was Max. Her hair was damp, inky black with its wetness, and fell over her bare shoulders in a curtain of dark strands. The rest of her body was bare, so on display that it took my breath away; her flesh looked warm, golden and soft, the curve of her hips completely new to me in this light. I'd only ever seen her in full armor. Despite knowing that there was a shapely woman beneath all of it, seeing that figure for myself was disarming.

When she turned to splash Wraith, another laugh leaving her lips, I caught her unfiltered profile. I had yet to see Max without her hood on or pulled up around her neck or splattered with blood, either an opponent's or hers. Her eyes were creased in amusement, and her chest heaved with each burst of laughter, causing her breasts to bounce ever so slightly. They were small and round, her nipples a dusty rose, and the depths of my mind had me wondering how they'd feel rolled gently between my teeth. Even the way her lips were parted as she spoke to her horse had my own agape and panting. What delicious sounds would come from those voluptuous lips if I had my way with her? Could I have her begging? What would it be like to hear her utter my name not in disgust but in delight, in pleasure?

A distant snort from Wraith shook me from my stupor, and I felt found out despite no one else seeing me. I shuffled quietly back to my original position, but the canteen fell from my fingers and spilled on the ground in front of me. "Fuck." The front of my trousers were damp, too, but not from the water in the canteen; watching Max wash in the pool had left me so painfully hard that I was dripping precum. My head fell back against the tree, and I set my bound hands on my lap, cursing myself mentally and determined to say that I'd spilled my water on my lap if Max looked suspicious. She would be disgusted at the suggestion that I'd been watching her and not only that, but fantasizing about being with her. Me, her captive, the opposite of the type of person she would ever have interest in… and how pathetic of me to fantasize about the person who was hauling me off to my death for a quick payday? But even when I closed my eyes, I couldn't shake the image of her warm, wet body from my mind.

I was just lonely, that had to be it. At the castle, I had partners on a regular basis. I was used to getting laid regularly. This was just testing my body and had nothing to do with Max; any virile man like myself would get hard at the sight of any remotely attractive naked woman. It was biologically appropriate and only meant that I appreciated her body in isolation from the rest of her salty, domineering self. That was it.

Max's voice snapped me from my internal dialogue again, and I was surprised to hear it coming from the other side of the tree, where she must have been getting dressed. I had no idea how long I had been sitting there trying to regain composure. "Almost ready to go."

I could picture the warm rays of sun illuminating little water droplets on her tawny flesh, and imagined them dripping down the curves and valleys of her body as she dried off with a small towel she kept in her pack. My helplessly aroused brain told me that I would lap them up just to hold on to a tiny piece of her, to consume her in any capacity I was able. I mused at the thought of those droplets being replaced by sweat, sweat that I was responsible for, and when I realized I was getting carried away again, all I could do was bite out my response. "Great." No matter how fondly I saw her in my mind, I had still been left tied up by a tree by this woman, and not in a sexy way either.

Max was none the wiser. "All good back there? Need more water?" Her voice was muffled as if her face was covered by a towel as she dried her hair.

"Untie me, I need to piss," I lied, feeling twitchy and irate as I struggled against my bonds. I couldn't let her see that I was straining against the fabric of my pants from thinking about the way her ass moved in the shallow water of the pool… the way her raven pubic hair made a triangle that I wished I could bury my face in. The women in the castle were always bare, smooth and naked like they were incapable of growing body hair. But Max's, dark and obvious, lit something deep within me that was feral and ravenous. It wasn't right.

"Hang on," she told me. From behind the tree came the sound of her belt fastening.

"Now," I snipped, but was once again reminded that I had absolutely no authority in our dynamic. I was grasping at straws.

Max eyed me in suspicion when she rounded the tree and found the canteen on the ground in front of me. "Guess I'll fill this," she muttered, picking the container up and tucking it under her arm. It took everything in me to look away from her as she untied my wrists and ankles. Her damp hair spilled over her shoulders as she worked, and I could smell her, cold and clean from the waterfall. She wasn't wearing her blood-stained top anymore either, but instead sported a clean shirt that stuck to her still-damp flesh in a few places. "Well, go on then," she told me, gesturing for me to get up and run off as if she were shooing an animal.

"Give me some space," I bit out. "I've been sitting here so long my legs are numb. I know you've got super strength, but you don't want me to crush you if my legs give out." I was lying, I just didn't want to poke her eye out if I stood up next to her. When she backed away and rounded the tree again, I got up as quickly as I could without seeming like I was going to make a run for it, and headed farther into the forest.

She called after me, and I thought I detected a hint of concern. There was a certain hospitality in her offer that I had not expected, but I couldn't be bothered to stick around for a reply. "There might be time for you to wash off if you—"

I didn't slow down until I could no longer hear the waterfall, until I no longer smelled her clean skin – a sensation I didn't realize I was fixated on until I got some distance between us – and then I stopped, panting, my back against another massive tree. To my dismay, I was still so hard that my balls ached, and I realized that I'd need to return quickly before she came looking for me. I couldn't even think of the man-eating monster that was suppos-edly waiting until nightfall to eat me, hard dick and all. "You just need to let off some steam," I muttered to myself, irritation coursing through my body. "You've been abducted, you're being treated like a prisoner, you've got a lot of pent-up rage. It makes sense." The pep talk was not working. It didn't really make sense. I was lying to myself, just like I had lied to myself about being rescued soon, about needing to enjoy the adventure while it was in front of me.

I was still angry when I unbuttoned my trousers and fisted my cock, which was so stiff that just the contact of my palm caused my knees to buckle slightly. I didn't have time to enjoy any of the act, I just needed to handle it, needed to rid myself of the desperate thoughts I was having about Max just because she was the only woman within a hundred miles. I was angry when I found myself practically fucking my hand and when I came, shuddering as my prick jerked in my hand and spilled thick come onto my fingers. Her name slipped from my lips as I throbbed, and I bit my lip as punishment. "Ah, fuck, Max… so good." The metallic tang of blood filled my mouth, and to my dismay, it reminded me of her even more because she'd been covered in blood through so many of our interactions. That should have been a turnoff on its own, but it wasn't, and I hated myself for that. My heartbeat pounded in my ears as I tucked my still-stiff prick back into my pants just in time for Max to have found me again. How long had I taken? Longer than the average person takes to piss, apparently.

"Are you done yet? We need to go," Max chimed from closer than I had expected. The joy that she'd displayed while playing with Wraith in the pool appeared to have fizzled away; her voice was firm and commanding and had returned to her baseline of annoyance with my very existence. It made the position she had caught me in even more vile. As the post-rushed-orgasm calm settled over me, I felt rational thought return to my frazzled mind as well. I avoided the hand she extended me as I climbed onto Wraith, who once again shuddered as if there was something amiss in the woods. The sun was beginning to set in the distance. "I didn't realize how late it was getting," my captor added. Again, I wondered how long I'd spent alone in the woods before she found me. It hadn't seemed so close to sunset, but then again, I didn't spend all that much time outside.

I said nothing as we rode on through the woods. The taste of Max's name on my tongue as I experienced such an intimate act lingered and sent a tornado of confusion tearing through my mind. I wanted to brush it off, to let it go. After all, everyone fantasizes from time to time, even if it's an odd or inappropriate fantasy. People talk to themselves, say people's names. Not me, though; I had strict boundaries when it came to sex, and what had just happened was decimating several of them in a way that had me concerned for the remainder of the trip. I could only imagine the shame I'd feel when she finally turned me over to those paying her if I realized that I had some sort of crush on her. The trees swayed around us, the orange of the setting sun peeking through each branch, and I realized I had no clue how far we were from the tavern, nor did I have the desire to ask Max. I didn't want to speak to her, didn't even want to think about her. I closed my eyes and steadied myself atop Wraith, determined to hold on to Max as little as possible.

"I just can't, it's not you," I'd told the woman in my bed. I didn't remember her name, but she was stunning: tall, blond, and fit, with sparkling blue eyes. Her pussy was a tight, pink vise that had gripped me so hard a more functional man would've exploded, but when I wouldn't, when I couldn't, she let me know how disappointed she was. I tried to make up for it with enthusiasm throughout our encounter, knowing that I wouldn't be able to

deliver a grand finale on my end. I'd eaten her out with vigor, fucked her until I was certain she wouldn't be able to walk right for days, and yet…

"What do you mean, Auggie?" she later asked from the floor, where she pulled my cock out of her mouth to look up at me. I throbbed in her hand, where she'd been gripping it for what felt like hours. It was flattering, really, that she put so much effort into trying to make me come. She ran her manicured fingers over my legs, massaging each defined muscle, then kneaded my balls. It felt good when the tips of her nails traced along my flesh and left me with a chill. But I couldn't give her what she wanted. "The prince of Barrien doesn't wanna blow his load in my tight little pussy?" Before I could respond, she was running her tongue up my length again, lapping at me as if I were some divine treat, like my come would solve all of her problems. It was flattering, but did nothing to change the issue at hand.

"He does," I grunted, irritated with the malfunction of my body and also at everyone else's obsession with that single act. Couldn't people enjoy pleasure without climax? *"I do. I promise, I do. But I can't."*

When she finally gave up and left, I had an unsatisfying stroke alone, just to take the edge off. Every sexual encounter from then on had been the same. Men, women, all attractive, I couldn't climax with a single one. We'd fool around, we'd have fun, then they'd leave, and I'd handle things on my own. It almost became a competition among my sexual partners as if the person who could finally make me come would have some magical powers and as a reward, get an "in" with the prince of the kingdom. It never happened.

One perk to everyone's attempts was that I had lots of experience. But of all the sexual partners I'd enjoyed and appreciated, I never missed them when they left, never imagined them when I was touching myself, and I certainly never moaned their name. They always said mine, though. I could hear every whimper and cry of pleasure that I'd stored away in my mind. *"Auggie, August! Oh God, August—"*

"August? Hang on, we need to pick up speed," Max told me.

When my wits were about me again, we were thundering through the woods, which were now almost pitch black. The trees sped by us in a blur of dark trunks. It hadn't been that dark when I first got caught up in my own thoughts… I inadvertently gripped Max's waist a little tighter to hang on. Had the sun set quicker than expected, or had we waited too long? Wraith's hooves thudded against the forest floor, her massive rib cage causing my legs to flex with every panting breath she took. We were running from something.

Almost as if she felt my hesitation, Max added a breathless "Don't look behind you."

THE UMBRAL

MAX

I could've predicted that August wouldn't listen to me. He shouted behind me almost immediately in confirmation of that thought. "Max, what the fuck is that?" His voice was panicked, and I realized that he had been somewhere else mentally until I'd called for his attention.

"I told you not to look, you big idiot!" I yelled, unable to cast a glance back and show August just how annoyed I was at his continued defiance. "The sun went down faster than I expected."

"I looked! I looked! Oh shit, I looked, what the hell is that?" August shouted, his voice so loud that it easily penetrated my hood and the rushing wind of our speed. Suddenly, he seemed back to normal – as normal as one can be in the midst of a deadly pursuit – after whatever had happened during our stop in the woods. His strangeness following our stop had reminded me why I didn't bother with human relationships; they were hard to navigate, and people were hard to understand. There was no way he'd been that uppity just because he had to pee.

He still wasn't listening as he mused about the creature

pursuing us. "It's like a wolf, but it's..." His voice trailed off, but his frantic breathing was clear. The way he gripped my hips was alarming. Last I'd checked, we were keeping a good distance from our pursuer, but if he was that scared, maybe the distance had closed. I didn't want to lose track of the path ahead by turning around.

Accompanying the powerful force of Wraith's hooves was the sound of another set of feet. Unfortunately, they belonged to the creature I'd warned August about only hours before. How lucky that I could show him exactly what I was talking about. What a tour guide I was! "Huge, right? It's an Umbral!" When I had worried about other people taking my bounty from me, I hadn't considered the fact that he might be slaughtered by a wild Umbral to the point where I wouldn't even have a body to turn in. They were so big, in fact, that Wraith looked like an average horse next to one. The thought alone was scary; Wraith wasn't supposed to look "average" next to anyone.

This wasn't the first time I'd run from an Umbral, but this was the only place I had ever encountered one, and even as we sprinted from it, I could see it vividly in my mind without casting it another glance. It was a hulking wolfdog of gray and black that lurked in the shadows of the forest. Its paws, massive and lumbering, had thick claws, each the length of my hand, that left pockets in the soft ground as it ran. Worse than that, though, was its face: its narrow muzzle was lined with jagged yellow teeth, and its dual rows of eyes, bloodshot and crazed, scanned everything around it while it was on the hunt. Each eye operated independently, as if to provide it with a view from every angle. I'd never been unfortunate enough to be cornered or caught by it, but the legends said that its saliva, thick and putrid, would cause its victims to die a most painful death. That was as long as it didn't tear that victim to shreds with its claws or teeth first. I couldn't imagine that a beast that size would let a human body go to waste, especially with how little other game there was in Grim-maker Woods.

"Yeah, it's fucking huge! Wh-what are we doing?" August stammered behind me.

"We have to get to the tavern!" I tangled my fingers into Wraith's mane, dropping the reins, and tried to urge her on. I knew she must be tiring; she wasn't meant to sprint, and carrying the added weight of our additional passenger and goods was slowing her down. It would be one thing to lose my prisoner, but having my horse injured would be devastating. In fact, there would be no return from that, especially with how low my resources were already running. "Come on, girl, we're close!"

August was beside himself. I couldn't blame him. If you live a sheltered life, your first experience with reality can be disorienting, especially if that reality involves a bloodthirsty wolf the size of a cow. A very, very fast cow, but still… I wished August would shut up and let me focus. Instead, he rambled on and on in frantic indignation. "What good is a tavern? Can't this thing just eat buildings whole? Are you gonna buy it a beer and ask for a truce? Ah, shit, why does it have so many eyes? That's not right!" Any other time, I might've laughed a little at his panicked commentary. Maybe once we were safe in the tavern, we could look back on it, and I'd be able to tease him a bit. It was becoming one of my favorite pastimes.

"Stop looking at it, we're almost there! There's a barrier around the tavern. The Umbral won't be able to get in!" The lights of the tavern shone in the distance, glowing and warm, like a beacon calling us to safety. I could taste the cold beer, feel the plush warmth of a pillow beneath my head. We were so close. Hell, I could've sworn I heard the music of a raucous celebration emanating from the windows of the old building as if to say "get your asses in here!" I leaned forward to sink myself closer to Wraith's head, and just then, August's grip slipped from my waist.

He cried out for me as his body slid down Wraith's. "Max!"

I turned my head in time to see him sliding backward off of the horse's rear, his face a picture of panic. "Wraith, don't stop!" If we slowed down, we would all die; there was no way either of us was fast enough to haul August's body back onto the horse and get moving again with the Umbral already only feet from us. Instead, I'd have to figure things out while in motion.

The Umbral was closing in, a wild look in its eyes. Its rotten breath left its muzzle in sharp gusts. How long had it been since this creature had eaten? And how sweet would the supple flesh of a pampered prince taste after months of birds and other pitiful game? I couldn't let the creature find out. I managed to pivot in the saddle and catch August's arm just as he slid farther down Wraith's back, barely holding onto the leather of my seat with his fingertips. He was practically horizontal on her, his legs parallel with her tail and only inches from the Umbral's lusting mouth.

We were so close. I gripped August's arm like my fate was intertwined with his, like I couldn't risk losing him. I held on so tight that I feared his arm may pop from his shoulder if our ride got any bumpier, but a dislocated shoulder was undoubtedly better than death. Once we hit the boundary of the tavern, the Umbral would have to stop or be mortally wounded if it tried to push through. "Hang on, August, we're almost—"

The scream that left the prince's lips as the Umbral sunk its desperate mouth into his leg echoed through the forest like a crash of thunder. But before I could react, we slid into the barrier around the tavern, Wraith skidding to a halt only once the Umbral had screeched in pain and retreated. August and I slid from her back onto the damp forest floor, the light of the tavern windows illuminating us, but all I could see was the pain in my captive's face.

"Ah, fuck!" August screamed, curled into a ball and gripping his leg. His hands were already stained with blood and the thick, vile saliva that the Umbral's mouth had injected into his wound. The injury alone would be agonizing, but if the legends about the Umbral were true, the prince had never felt pain like the spit of the wolfdog before in his life. "It fucking – it fucking bit me, Max!"

I tried not to panic. I really, really tried. To keep my cool, I forced myself to look away from the prince's face; something about his agony made my own limb ache. I had to be calm, even though everyone knew Umbral saliva was lethal to humans and animals. Everyone. That wasn't a legend; that was fact. "It's okay," I lied, scrambling to my feet so that I could hoist him upright. Every attempt I made to move him elicited another groan or yell until he was finally leaning on me, and we hobbled toward the building. "I've got you." I was sweating. I was panicking. I gave Wraith a nod to tell her to wait even though she'd never go anywhere without me, whether I tied her up or not, and tried to escort August to the entrance of the tavern.

BEAST'S BREATH TAVERN

MAX

When I threw my body into the door of the Beast's Breath Tavern to shove it open, the sound of merriment in the form of laughter, glasses clinking, and music playing hit me hard. The pain in my shoulder from using it as a battering ram against the massive door, which was easily twice my height, would hit me later. The contrast between my situation and the joy being experienced within the tavern was stark. I somehow managed to drag August in, the weight of his large body oppressive and debilitating, as he drifted in and out of consciousness due to his pain. He muttered against my ear as I hobbled, but I couldn't make out any of what he was saying. Instead, I could only imagine the agony of the Umbral's venom seeping into the tissue of his leg and rotting away his muscles. I wasn't sure how far I could carry him, but at least we were inside and people could see that we needed help. I wondered then if I had yelled sooner, if I had sounded the alarm somehow, maybe we could have avoided this, but with the tremendous noise I knew no one would have heard me. If I had been lucky enough to get someone's attention, I don't think they would've done much but watch; our world was very much each person for himself, and a tavern full of other killers-for-hire was no exception.

When the innkeeper set her eyes, wide and concerned, on me from her desk at the entrance, I gasped out a plea as I struggled to keep myself and my charge upright. "Umbral. Help." It was almost as if the word itself caused a silence to settle over the bar, but in reality, people were starting to notice that I had come in carrying someone who was speeding toward death's door. Mortal injuries tend to put a damper on things, no matter how commonplace they are in a certain setting.

Juniper, the innkeeper and self-proclaimed "head bitch" of the Beast's Breath Tavern, was a tall, muscular woman. Every time I saw her, I was in awe of her size and power and had to remind myself that my size made me really good at my job. Hers made her good at throwing out unruly guests. Her auburn hair lay in two thick braids over the front of either shoulder, and her green eyes, vibrant like calcinite, saw everything that happened on her property. Everything. It made her an especially effective innkeeper and leader, but also gave her all of the gossip. If you wanted to know who was sleeping with who or which mercenary had the best jobs, Juniper would be the one to get friendly with. I don't know precisely when we began considering each other friends, but these days, months could go by without us seeing each other, and every time we reconnected, it was like we'd never parted. I wavered as I stood in the entryway, and she snapped her fingers at a few men drinking near the bar. "Gents, get this man into a room."

When two hulking patrons that I knew from my previous visits to the tavern – Florian and Dagon – took August from me, I found myself cautioning them. "His leg, shit, please be careful." There was no way I could get him into a room, let alone up onto a bed, by myself, but I desperately wanted to be the one handling him to minimize any further damage.

August screamed again, much to the dismay of the onlookers in the tavern, and my head spun. I had heard my fair share of people in pain, people begging for their lives, but for some reason, this man's pain filled me with inexplicable dread. As the two patrons carried him off, his head lolling in half-conscious agony, I remembered that I would have to pay for lodging no matter the circumstances. Nothing is free, not even when you're friends with the innkeeper. If Juniper let me stay without charge, I would owe her, and I didn't like owing people favors. I dug in my pockets and found them empty, realizing that my crystals were with Wraith. That was inconvenient for several reasons; all of my money was out in the open where it could be pinched easily, and I didn't have any way to pay Juniper without leaving August, who was in a dire condition. Not usually being one to rely on favors, I looked at Juniper in uncomfortable helplessness: not a feeling I enjoyed. "June, I—"

"Later." The innkeeper waved a hand and gestured up the stairs, where the two men were carrying August to a room for the night. At least, I told myself it was for the night, as if he were going to sleep and carry on in the morning. He would be okay, I lied to myself. We would get through the night, pack up in the morning, and carry on as planned.

I swallowed hard and forced myself to move, to follow them, despite every fiber of my being screaming at me to run. He was going to die. August of Barrien was going to die under my watch, and all of my plans were going to fall apart. All of my detailed, carefully thought-out plans... I mourned them already. As I ascended the stairs, Juniper clapped her hands at the rest of the patrons. "Carry on, folks."

I couldn't blame her. This was a place of business, and people wouldn't be cheerily making noise and spending their money if they had to see the reality of what was right outside the door. The last thing they wanted to see was a dead body or a body writhing in agony as it rotted away. Hell, I didn't want to see that either. Chatter and music started up again seconds later; the noise made my head buzz. Life tends to move on, with or without you.

Up I went. The halls of the tavern lodging were dark and cool, sending a chill down my sweat-slicked back. They were mostly empty, save for the occasional painting hung on the wall, each of which was knocked off-center by patrons slamming doors or moving too quickly down the hallway. At least Juniper had tried to make the place welcoming. When the men set August up in a room, they promptly turned and met me at the door. Their expressions did not inspire confidence.

Florian, a dark elf who I'd encountered many times at the tavern, raised an eyebrow at me. "How'd you get yourself into this mess, little menace? You know better than to race an Umbral." His voice was smooth, like the purr of a massive cat, and his gaze was just as predatory. The elf was tall, a solid foot more so than myself, at least, and built like every elf was: visually perfect, as if carved from stone, and sleek, which made him the ideal creature for our type of work. While other mercenaries could be stealthy when needed, Florian conducted himself as if his steps were lighter than air on a regular basis. His clothing, never dirty nor torn, was perfectly tailored to his broad shoulders, tight waist, and long legs. The elf's skin, a warm gray, was contrasted perfectly by the stark white of his long hair, which draped over each shoulder like a cascading waterfall. He was much, much older than my small human shell, and during his time, he had perfected the use of many different weapons. Florian was the type of being that everyone found objectively beautiful, because he was. Unfortunately, his cockiness often got in the way of his overall appeal to me. Florian was undoubtedly my least proud hookup; despite how enjoyable every time with him was, he was very full of himself. Had that stopped me from falling into his bed in the past? Definitely not.

I sucked my teeth in frustration at his sly commentary. "I do know better. It wasn't a race." I narrowed my gaze at him as if he should know better than to tease while someone was dying. I suppose that was another thing that made us so different from each other; I'd never once seen Florian express remorse for his job and the acts that he committed as a result. In fact, I'd seen him slit someone's throat, then turn and finish a meal, only stopping to wipe his hands clean. "I'm on a job."

"Well," Florian continued, "when your little pet dies, feel free to visit my room." He glanced back into the room for a second and then turned to me again, his stark white hair swaying as he did so. The movement stirred up what smelled like cinnamon, and I wondered again how the fuck this guy managed to be so immaculately put together at all times. I hadn't checked in a while, but I could guess that I smelled like sweat and horse shit despite having just bathed. I sniffed the air as subtly as I could manage… oh, and blood. "I don't envy him. It'd be painful even for an elf, but for a human… I can feel it radiating off of him, like his pathetic human weakness is rubbing off on me already." He grimaced, then shrugged before heading back down the hall.

Dagon – who despite being the exact opposite of Florian, found himself accompanying him on a regular basis – followed after him with a sympathetic glance. "Sorry, Max, hope it wasn't an important job." I almost stopped him to ask for help and advice when August let out another agonizing scream. There wasn't time. I knew that the other man would just tell me to hold his hand while he died. The patrons of the Beast's Breath Tavern had undoubtedly seen many of their friends and fellow wanderers mowed down by the Umbral. Most of them knew better than to risk traveling so close to sundown, but a good share of them had just been unlucky like August and I.

"How long?" I called after the pair, lingering in the doorway because I couldn't bring myself to step in yet. Once the door closed behind me, as it needed to, I would be trapped in there with him. Trapped with the passage of time, which slows to a crawl when a merciful death is around the corner... trapped with the stench of rotting flesh and the harrowing loneliness of being the only conscious person. I'd be trapped with the memories of watching my loved ones rot away before me and having to relive it all over again with this man.

Florian didn't even bother looking back at me, nor did he slow his descent of the stairs, when he spoke. "A couple of hours, maybe. He certainly won't make it through the night, little one."

August had quieted again, probably because he was unconscious, by the time I slid into the room and closed the door behind me. It was dark, aside from a candle that one of the men had lit at the bedside table, and August's still form lay on the bed, his chest heaving despite not being awake. His body was so restless that he appeared to be in the midst of a nightmare, but I knew that his body was simply rebelling against the flow of venom infiltrating his powerless human bloodstream.

I approached him cautiously, and my heart sank when I got closer to him. His face was pale and drenched in sweat, and each rasping breath left his parted lips in an angry gust. I searched the room to see what I had at my disposal. Like any other seedy tavern, there wasn't much: a bed with a banged-up nightstand; a wooden chair that was probably older than I was; a small table with a basin, pitcher of water, and a couple of washcloths; and a small, flickering fireplace. The chair had a couple of tattered blankets, the cleanliness of which I didn't bother to consider. It was nice that Juniper went through to fold the blankets after each guest left, but I could only imagine how many people had fucked, farted, or dropped dead on this particular batch over the years. I hoped that the washcloths at the basin were at least moderately clean. It was then that I realized that the rest of my provisions were still with Wraith, packed away neatly in my saddlebags from after my bath. I looked outside of the small window to see her pacing near the side of the building. Even though she was safe from the beasts of the forest, it was unlike me to leave her without our usual tie up and unpack routine for the evening. Our relationship was so symbiotic, in fact, that I felt dysregulated without our routine as well.

Though I didn't know how long it would last, August remained still and silent. If I ran, perhaps I could make it out and back before the pain woke him again. I only hoped that I wouldn't come back to find him no longer breathing or worse, screaming in his suffering. I cast him one last glance before bolting out the door and down the stairs of the tavern. And as my boots hit the main floor, I ran directly into Juniper.

"Sorry, Max," she said, calm and collected as if there wasn't a dying man in her establishment. It was probably a more common occurrence than one would think, and if anything, she was probably only hoping that we didn't leave blood on her floors.

"I'll be back," I told her in a rush. "I need to rack Wraith up and get my things."

June held up a bottle of murky gray liquid and used it to gesture toward the stairs. "I'll leave this by your door."

When I returned a few minutes later, I inspected the bottle and learned that it was Tuber Toddy[1], a highly potent, highly alcoholic concoction no doubt meant to take the edge off for August. It was made of dingy, sinewy root vegetable that was found only in the Grimmaker Woods, which made it this bar's claim to fame. It tasted awful, but we all found it particularly useful for blocking out painful memories... and memories in general. If we were lucky, it would keep him comfortable or, better yet, permanently knock him out so that he wouldn't have to suffer through the pain of his untimely death. I wasn't much for alcohol given the way my inhibitions tended to disappear if I partook a little too heavily. Juniper herself likely had some embarrassing stories that she would have loved to share with August. I eyed it for a moment before a groan drew me back into the room.

"August, I'm here, hang on," I told him, even though I wanted to turn and run. For someone who was responsible for a lot of death, I didn't like suffering. I didn't want to watch him thrash in pain. But I put the bottle down on the nightstand and unloaded my belongings onto the floor. As I sorted through all of my gear, I couldn't shake the image of my dying mother from my mind. We'd lost my father already when she fell ill, and Danny had been so small, maybe three or four years old. I locked myself in my mother's bedroom at one point, leaving Danny outside of the door with a small toy I'd made him. I didn't want him to watch our mother die... and it had been such a long, painful process that when I finally saw the light begin to fade from her eyes, I was determined not to leave the room until she drew her last breath. Her death had not been quick. Nor had it been quiet. Despite her attempts to shelter me throughout my life, she had been unable to mask the pain of her own passing. To watch your loved one beg and plead for you to help them when there's no help to be had, when you're nothing but a teenager with a gentle hand to offer... I bit back tears of frustration as I unpacked, angry that life had once again left me holding someone's hand as they crawled toward their grave. Back then, I didn't have it in me to put my mother out of her misery. How could I, a child at the time, do such a thing and then go out to face my sibling? I couldn't rationalize it. For whatever reason, the same idea seemed impossible in these circumstances with August as well. Why couldn't I be merciful? I didn't know.

"Hell, it fucking hurts," August groaned from the bed. I tossed the blankets onto the floor so I could pull the chair to his bedside and sit with him. I couldn't help but wonder if it was really comforting to have someone there while you flopped and flailed in pain. I was quick with a blade, I thought, and I could give him a relatively painless end rather than letting him suffer like this. But he was still lucid and not begging for death, so I told myself not to go down that path yet, wondering if I'd be ready to do it if his tone changed. I'd killed a lot of people, but this felt very, very different. I hated that.

"I know," I told him. That wasn't helpful. Hell, what do people even say to that?

"You do?" His glistening honey-colored eyes caught mine, and I saw real fear in them. The stark contrast between the August I'd been traveling with and the one before me made me feel sick. I wanted his pompous self back... his overconfidence, his comfortable-in-any-situation attitude. I longed for his foolish questioning.

"No," I confessed with a sigh. "But I can imagine. I'm sorry." I had almost reached out to grab his hand when I realized there was more I had planned to do.

"Stay," August croaked out as I rose from the seat. The way his hand raised from the bed to reach for me sent a pang of guilt through my icy heart. My mouth went dry. His palm would be clammy. I wasn't ready.

"I'm staying," I told him, my eyes darting around the room to avoid his searching gaze. "But I need to clean you up. I grabbed my bag and I have a few things—"

"It's okay, Max." The prince closed his eyes and let his head fall back on the pillow as if he had already resigned himself to his fate. I had never told him that the Umbral's spit was deadly, but perhaps the pain was so bad that he had no choice but to assume. Or maybe he had heard Florian's less than tactful commentary. When he arched his back into the mattress and stifled a groan, I forced myself not to look away. "Cleaning me up isn't going to do anything."

"Shut up," I bit out, searching through my backpack. I found a small vial of a potion Beatrice concocted for me before every long trip; I used it on a variety of wounds, but it likely would do very little to heal the Umbral's damage. Nevertheless, I set the vial on the nightstand, and the moonlight from the room's tiny window illuminated the liquid through its glass. "Let's try to get you a little more comfortable."

August chuckled, a weak, pitiful sound, before he winced in pain again. "Can't wait."

I uncorked the bottle that Juniper had left us and did what I could to prop August up well enough for him to drink it. When all he did was sip, I tried to encourage him. "It's nasty, I know, but it'll take the edge off. Drink." He didn't have the energy to protest. When I laid him back down, I took a swig myself. The room blurred momentarily, and I stifled a cough before trying to gather my wits. God, that was horrific, but I needed something to cope. I didn't heal people. I didn't take care of anyone except for Danny, Wraith, and myself. But this was different than any of those. "Come on, Max," I grumbled to myself.

August was shivering and sweating at the same time. I grabbed a washcloth from the small table and dipped it into the basin, then placed it over his forehead before moving to his leg. I'd been avoiding it, not because I was afraid of the gore, but because I knew touching it would only make it hurt more. I made quick work of his pant leg with the blade of my dagger, exposing the bite to the still, hot air of the room. It was deep and ugly, the divot of each individual Umbral tooth clear as day even with the limited light in the room. Not only that, but it stunk; the saliva of the monstrous beast was thick and bubbling and looked to be eating away at his flesh. I did all I could think to do, which was to grab another washcloth and attempt to clear as much of the spit away as possible. With each wipe, the fabric of the washcloth seemed to disintegrate a little, each fiber being eaten up by the hellish biology of the creature's venom.

August twitched and groaned, so I shoved the bottle of Tuber Toddy into his hand and propped it up in his mouth until I heard him gulp a few more times. Once his skin was as clean as I could manage, I uncorked the vial and doused the wound in what was left of my potion. I couldn't think about the fact that I'd be fucked if I got hurt any time soon. I didn't know what else to do, so I draped a blanket over him and settled myself into the chair. Then I watched him by the light of the candle, so focused on the rise and fall of his chest that I didn't recognize the sound of ever-so-light footsteps in the hallway. There was a knock at the door. Florian, checking in sooner than I liked.

"You in there, little menace?" the elf purred from the other side of the door. The way he spoke always sounded like he was on the hunt, and it made me feel like I should be hiding. Sometimes it gave me a thrill. This time, it made me want to punch him.

"Not now, Florian." I was bleary eyed and exhausted and had no argument left in me, especially not for someone as inconsequential as Florian Feather-foot.

Florian tsked at me through the wood of the door, suggesting I should be grateful for his mere presence. "No need to be hostile," he chided. "Just came to see if you need help carrying him out."

"He's still alive," I told him. I hoped that August was knocked out enough by the alcohol that he didn't hear our disrespectful conversation. How awful it must be to lie on death's door and hear people talking about what they'd do with your body when you finally kicked the bucket.

"Impressive. Well, you know where to find me when you need a hand." Then he paused, as if to see how much darkness was still left outside. "I give him another hour."

I wanted to scream, to tell him to fuck off, but I didn't have the energy. I couldn't let myself believe that we'd be carrying his body out soon. He'd made it this far – that had to mean something. And yet, when I pulled back the blanket to look at his wound again, it sizzled with the venom of the Umbral. The blanket itself was drenched with sweat, almost as if each droplet was his life force leaving his body. He'd be dehydrated soon, and if the venom didn't kill him, that just might.

I'd never had an opportunity so close before only to have it snatched from my grasping fingertips. Even as his chest rose and fell, I felt it in my heart that he was going to die, as much as my internal monologue tried to fight it. What would make August of Barrien so special that he could survive an attack that no one else ever had? It certainly wouldn't be the combination of Tuber Toddy and Savers Salve[2] that saved him, nor my exceptional nursing skills. As I sat there, his shallow breaths filling the room, I saw everything I had worked for slip away into the darkness. I would not be able to provide for Danny like I had hoped. Hell, I didn't even know if I had the crystals to pay for our lodging and resources that evening; what I'd earned us pawning off teeth from the tooth faeries had barely gotten us into the woods. I sniffled, then cursed at myself for even considering crying. The sight of

August's face again in the pale moonlight made my heart hurt. Was I only attached to this person because of what his capture had offered me? I wasn't sure. I reached out to stroke a sweat dampened curl from his clammy forehead and found myself grateful for his sedation; at least he wasn't screaming anymore. At least one of us would meet our end graciously. For me, starvation seemed likely, or maybe I'd meet my death attempting the next highest-paying job.

I thought of Danny, holed away in our home in the Wild Open, waiting for me to return with this bounty I had promised him. Things would change, I'd told him, they would get better, be easier. His dark eyes, the mirror image of mine, had looked so hopeful when I made those promises; no matter how many times I made them, he always seemed to have faith that this would be the time everything worked out as planned. I wondered how long he would wait before he realized I had failed and he was on his own. Very few people knew exactly where he was. Wraith knew how to get there, so if something happened to me, I had always planned to send her to fetch him. She was the third member of our small family.

August's shivering drew me from my daze again, and I stood, thoughtless but determined to leave him in the best shape possible before I went back down to the bar. I slid the dampened blanket from his body, then used my knife to cut his shirt – also drenched – free. Exposing his midsection gave way to his trembling abdomen, the muscles of which were tense from his frequent writhing. I was disgusted with myself when I realized I was admiring the way each ridge and valley of muscle looked, slick with sweat. I'd seen him shirtless before, prior to my capture of him, and back then, I'd found him too pompous to think anything of his physical beauty. I took the last washcloth and wiped his forehead again, his neck, his chest. I admired the way the action caused goosebumps to scatter along his flesh and sighed. I dried him. I pulled off his necklace, which had been twisted around his straining neck and digging into his flesh, and left it on the nightstand. I cleaned his wound once more, then covered him with a clean blanket. Before I left, I stroked his hair one last time and gave his hand a squeeze. His breathing was shallow. I only hoped that his last breath would come and go painlessly, but for whatever reason, I could not bring myself to sit there and watch.

My arrival at the bar downstairs was met with a curious eyebrow raise from Juniper, who I handed a fistful of crystals to. I was scraping the bottom of my pouch of money. A couple of loose crystals jostled around within the leather sack, and I wondered just how drunk I could get for what I had left. "For tonight," I told her. "Let me know if anything needs to be done around here. I wasn't planning on losing this job…"

Juniper regarded me with a nod, then let me drag my sorry ass over to the bar, where I plopped down in a barstool without a word.

The bartender, a bright-eyed young goblin with a knack for tricks, looked me over. "You're not looking so hot, Max," she told me as she tossed a glass into the air and caught it behind her back without looking.

"Not feeling so hot."

"Well, what'll it be?"

"Whatever's cheapest, Vorma," I told her, utterly defeated. I set my head down on the counter for a moment. Everything felt heavy. I rummaged in my pocket and plopped a lone crystal onto the bar top in defeat.

The goblin sniffed and turned to look at the wall of liquor with her hand on her hip. "Let's see… for a crystal, we've got… Gloom Glug[3] or Crum Chug[4]." She wrinkled her nose. "Not very fun, I know."

I stifled a gag at my options, knowing that enough of anything that gross would desensitize me to its nastiness and hopefully the sadness of my reality. I was about to pick the latter when Florian piped up from behind me.

"Now, now, no little menace of mine is going to be stuck drinking glug or chug this evening." Lord, he loved to hear himself speak.

I almost wanted to pound a can of either to make a point, but Florian was a resource I wouldn't dare reject. Money, connections, weaponry, he had it all. To turn down Florian was a foolish move for anyone in my field. Before I could interject, Vorma commented, "Well, buy her something better, then! Shots?"

"I think so," Florian told her, sidling up to me at the bar. His spicy perfume hit me before his voice did. "It's not every night Max the Menace chooses to drink, so I think we should give her something special."

"What a gentleman!" Vorma commented. I wanted to glare at her, but I couldn't blame her for going after tips, especially considering her target. Moments later, Vorma delivered a tray with a lineup of shots that were lit on fire; each glass was a varying shade of brown, and they got darker as the glasses continued, culminating in a pitch-black glass that immediately caught my eye. "A Flaming Flight for the lady!" she announced, setting it down directly in front of me.

"Thanks, Florian."

"My pleasure," he told me. Florian pointed a slender finger toward one flaming shot glass that sparkled like champagne, the flames of which glittered in the dim light of the bar. It was pretty, elegant, just like Florian, so I wasn't surprised that he was drawn to it. Perhaps the bar had even named it after him. "So, this one really has a nice undertone of—"

I held up a hand to silence him. "Which one is strongest?"

Florian scoffed and then composed himself again in time to point at the flaming black glass at the end of the flight. Others might have tolerated or even fawned over his poshness, but he should have known better than to be surprised at my directness and disinterest. I downed the shot without thinking and was sent immediately into a violent coughing fit, my lungs and throat burning. The pain was a welcome distraction.

"There are some things you really should work up to, menace. You know that, right?"

"I don't really care," I confessed with a sigh, completely bypassing his attempt at flirtation. "You gonna join me or not?"

Moments later we were both working our way through our own Flaming Flights. Florian hardly seemed affected by his, while the giggles were starting to sneak up on me against my will. Admittedly, it felt nice to surrender to the power of something else. The elf tossed each shot back like it was part of a dance, and by the end of it, he was still leaning casually against the bar top. I downed my final shot and grimaced as it slid down my throat, a tingly burning sensation that made my eyes water.

"Another?" I asked, about to flag down Vorma again.

"Not sure that's a good idea, menace," Florian told me, running his thin pointer finger, perfectly manicured, around the rim of one of his shot glasses. My gaze flicked from the finger to his face and back again. "Why don't we get you upstairs?"

I snorted, about to make a jab at him when I remembered exactly what was waiting for me upstairs. The dead body of August III, most likely. "Huh, yeah… I guess I should go check…" I murmured, sliding from the barstool to stand on the floor. The room spun a little, and I had to catch myself as the sting of stomach acid crawled up my throat. "I'm good, I got it. I'm good."

Florian gave me a look that said "I didn't ask" before taking my arm.

The crawl up the stairs was tedious, with Florian taking the brunt of my clumsy staggering and guiding me up. I knew he would've rather just carried me, but he had tried that once and met the end of my blade. He knew better, that nothing made me feel less like a menace than being manhandled. Once we got to the top, he tried to turn me to the right despite my room with August being to the left of the staircase, and I wiggled out of his grasp.

"Let me check," I said with a hiss, yanking my arm free.

"Fine, but seeing a corpse better not take you out of the mood." Nothing surprised me anymore. Not horny elves, not flaming alcohol, not tooth faeries, or Umbrals. That didn't mean that I wasn't annoyed by the way Florian thought with his dick and had zero regard for how it came across. The way he equated August III to nothing but a corpse made my stomach roll – though the alcohol was probably also contributing in some way – and I found myself leaning against the doorframe to steady myself. "Come on," he insisted, "deal with him tomorrow."

I didn't have it in me to fight him anymore, so I submitted, telling myself that anything would be a welcome distraction from the utter despair on the other side of that door.

Finally over my belligerent stumbling, Florian scooped me into his arms and carried me to his room. I told myself again and again that this was a resource I couldn't bear to lose, not with Danny's safety and providing for him on the line. One day, I told myself, I'd get to make decisions based on my desires and comfort and not my planning for the future and my responsibilities. I would have been lying to myself, however, if I told myself that submitting to Florian's advances was just for Danny... like I said before, Florian wasn't half bad in bed despite his obnoxious ego, and well, getting fucked into oblivion would be a very welcome distraction, especially once the effects of our shots started to wear off.

When he set me down in the doorway of his room, the familiar scent of his cinnamon musk overwhelmed me. "Does Juniper keep this room for you?" I mused aloud. "It's very... nice." It was. In fact, it looked like a slightly dingy version of what I imagined Florian's home – if he had one – would look like. How was this asshole pulling in enough money to have a standing room at the tavern and one that he'd decorated himself, no less? I stood in the doorway and glanced around the room, taking it in for the first time in a while; it had been months, at least, since we were at the tavern together and consequently, since I'd been in his room. Often, despite his better judgment, he ended up in mine. Florian liked things a very specific way, and bringing in strangers jeopardized that.

The room was aglow with floating candles, no doubt enchanted by someone Florian had done a job for at some point. On the bed, just as rickety and janky as the one in my room, there were fine sheets of silk that were laid perfectly and tucked in just right. I couldn't picture Juniper making Florian's bed, so he must have done it himself or perhaps he strong-armed Dagon into doing his housekeeping. The floor was spotless even though it had the same wear and scuffs as the other rooms in the tavern. Much like the room I'd been assigned, he had the same worn wooden chair, but somehow his fine elven clothing draped over the back made it seem more elegant. Finally, the table and basin he'd been given glimmered with water that must have had magical properties, and next to it, there was an array of liquids in shimmering glass vials. They looked like potions, but I knew better; they had to be various perfumes and lotions that were part of Florian's primping routine.

"I like nice things," Florian said coolly, sliding into the room behind me and shutting the door with a smooth click.

"I know." He'd never been a very flowery flirt. Was he calling me nice? I wanted to tell him to shut up and bang already, but I knew he'd be offended, so I went along with it. I exhaled slowly

through my nostrils and let my eyes flutter closed as he slid a hand
along the side of my neck and pulled me close. When his lips
pressed to mine, I mused internally about how, in the midst of a
lawless wasteland, Florian found time to brush his teeth so regularly. He tasted like cardamom, and I let my lips part so that he
could sweep his tongue inside of my mouth. I knew better than to
tangle my fingers in his finely combed hair, so instead I traced my
hand along his leanly muscled forearm before gripping it tightly. I
thanked the stars that I was drunk when he put a hand on my
shoulder and directed me to my knees in front of him.

Florian made quick work of his pants, which were laced at the
front with a fine leather cord that he undid with one hand, then
slid down. The elf didn't wear undergarments, which always
surprised me because he struck me as a satin panty kind of man,
and when he presented his cock to me in a manicured hand, it was
only half hard; it felt like the perfect display of his holier-than-thou
apathy. I slid the organ into my mouth, drunk enough to find pleasure in the fact that he smelled and tasted good. He was clean
shaven, not a speck of hair to be found on him, and as I ran my
tongue up the underside of his hardening member, he removed his
shirt. The act almost seemed as much for him as it was for my
viewing pleasure. Once he'd tossed it aside, he reached down and
stroked my cheek as I sucked him. It was obvious that he was more
focused on the act itself than anything about me, so I closed my
eyes; looking up at him involved a level of intimacy that simply
didn't belong in our relationship.

When Florian pulled me from the floor and directed me to the
bed, bending me over its side without any sort of input on my end,
I let my mind wander. I disconnected from the thudding of the
bedframe against the wall and Florian's lackluster panting. What
was August like in bed? I wondered if he was vocal, if he was
complimentary. I could imagine his husky voice biting out

passionate praise. Did he work up a sweat? Was he giving? What would the stubble of his chiseled jaw feel like between my thighs?

When my eyes snapped open in realization that I'd been thinking of August like *that*, I gasped. "Oh God!"

Florian didn't miss a chance to take that as a compliment. "I know. Pretty amazing, right?"

The rest of the night was a blur.

THE NEXT MORNING the pounding in my head woke me, and I couldn't bring myself to open my eyes. I could tell that Florian wasn't still in bed only because I could actually move my body in the ridiculously small bed, but the sounds of him moving around the room did not escape me. The tinkling of jars as he got ready for the day caused me to wince and pull the sheets back over my head in frustration.

"My, my," Florian commented. "Max the Menace, defeated by six shots and a good lay. I must say, I've never envied humans, and the existence of hangovers makes me even more glad to be anything but."

I groaned. "As pretty as your voice is, elf, it's not helping."

"Well, I need to leave. I'm meeting with some others from Emynor. You can stay here as long as you like, but don't mess up my room."

If it hadn't been so painful to move at all, I would've rolled my eyes.

"And don't forget to take care of your friend in your room or you'll be racking up a bill over a dead body. Not the best way to manage your money."

Everything came rushing back to me then, causing my head to throb even more. I couldn't bring myself to reply to the elf before he left and instead spent the remainder of the day wishing that I could disappear. As comfortable as Florian's accommodations were, I couldn't hide there forever. I had obligations: a horse to feed, a body to bury, work to find. Staying in Grimmaker to ride my relationship with Florian as far as it would go didn't seem like a sustainable option, but at least I hadn't burned that bridge the night before.

WHEN I EXHUMED myself from the depths of Florian's sheets, I forced myself to make the bed. It wasn't nearly as immaculate as it had been when we'd arrived the night before, but I hoped my blow job skills would earn me a bit of forgiveness on that front. I pulled my clothes off the floor and dressed in silence, then ran my hands through my hair in an attempt to make myself look presentable; my fingers caught on several tangles, and I surrendered, pulling my hood over my head before I slipped out of the room. The elf's interest in me occasionally confused me if I thought too long on it – he was undeniably perfect as far as appearances went, and I, a human, had to be the complete opposite. Perhaps it was a novelty for him to sleep with a human. I didn't care enough to dwell on it for too long.

June gave me a curious look when I made it to the main floor of the tavern, and I stopped her commentary before it could begin by putting a hand up. "I know. He's not good for me," I told her, not ceasing my walk to the massive front door of the building as I spoke. I turned so that I was still facing her, walking backward, as I added my next few comments. "He's an asshole. I can do better. Yes, I know, my horse needs to be fed and I need to get the dead body out of my room. I'm on it. Thank you, mother."

She scoffed, then looked back at her ledger with a wry smile, but left me alone. Juniper had always been a good friend to me, much better than any sort of mother figure, and our good-hearted ribbing kept me sane. I hoped she knew that.

By the time I was done with Wraith, who gave me a stern head-butt as a reprimand for everything I'd put her through, the sky was already beginning to darken with the end of the day. I wasn't sure how it had gotten away from me so quickly, and the hair on the back of my neck stood on edge as I imagined the Umbral pacing the perimeter of the tavern's barrier. Would it come back now that it had a taste of the prince's blood? Or perhaps it half expected me to throw his body to it, as a reward for finally catching its prey? I shook my head to erase those thoughts; I would never desecrate someone's remains like that. Then, the survivalist in me chimed in. "Never say never," I told myself. "You also say you'd never eat another person to survive, but who knows? Stranger things have happened."

The steps to the top of the landing were a million miles tall. My legs fought me with each stair, and still, my mind berated me for my failure. I'd let my captive die. I'd lost my chance at a windfall that would've set Danny and myself up for a good long while. I'd have to clean up a dead body, and dead bodies were stinky. I'd let Florian come on my butt cheeks. The list was never-ending.

I rolled my eyes – finally – and slid into the dark room again, holding my breath until the door latched behind me. When I was inside, I pressed my back to the door and squinted into the dark room until my eyes adjusted and I could make out August's figure. It didn't smell like death, surprisingly. In fact, all I could smell was the stale sweat that had been there when we'd dragged our tired asses in the night before… that, and the lingering astringent odor of the potion I had put on my travel partner's leg before leaving him.

Then, it happened. August's chest rose and fell. I blinked more times than I could count, then steadied my gaze again. Was my grieving brain playing tricks on me? Would I step closer to see his dead face, mouth wide with his final horrified gasp? My throat filled with the threat of vomit, and I forced it back down.

He was still breathing.

He was still breathing!

I gasped and ran to his bedside, unsure what I was expecting to happen next but beyond elated and unable to stifle my hungover, unmasked emotions. I took his hand in mind, and when I found it still warm, pressed my forehead to it, and cried. Ah, shit, I had left him here, and he was breathing, and I hadn't been taking care of him at all. The night before, I'd been concerned about his dehydration, and then I proceeded to leave him alone for half a day thinking he was rotting into the crappy tavern mattress!

I sobbed against the back of his hand before gathering the willpower to stand and get my shit together. When I got up, I stood and looked at him for a few seconds longer to make sure I hadn't imagined his breathing.

Down the hall, there was a small cabinet of items for guests of the inn, including but not limited to: more half-cleaned blankets and washcloths, some cheap essentials like leather shoelaces, and glass bottles of water. I grabbed a few washcloths and some water and hurried back to the room before Florian reappeared, looking for round two. One bottle went into the basin, so that I could get August cleaned up again, and the other came with me to his bedside where I tried to dribble a stream of it into his parted, chapped lips.

"August, you big idiot…" I chastised him as I tried to get his unconscious self to drink. In reality, he'd done nothing wrong, but I'd gotten so used to picking on him that it was almost a comfort at that point. His lips moved a little, and he took in some drops of water. I didn't stop until I saw him swallow a few times.

He grumbled when I pulled the bottle away. "So rude…"

"What?"

"Rude… I thought you were starting to like me…" he murmured, nearly inaudible.

I wanted to laugh, then cry, then laugh again. A feeling of relief like I had never experienced before washed over me. "Shut up and drink," I told him, bringing the bottle to his lips again. He took a few more sips, but then stopped responding. I watched his chest rise and fall, much more consistently and calmly now than the night before, and then began to clean him up again. The state of the wound on his leg was still bleak: a festering, sweltering hole in which I could see the muscle of his calf. Given what I knew about the Umbral, I didn't know how he was still alive, and I wasn't sure how long he would continue to be. Nevertheless, I cleaned his leg and wrapped it with the shreds of a blanket. I didn't have any more Savers Salve, so water was my only resource. I thought back to Florian's room, which I'd last surveyed in either drunken or hungover stupor and wondered if I'd seen any medical supplies there… Not likely, with Florian's magic and elven healing abilities.

Next, I wiped August's brow with a damp cloth and then dabbed at his neck and chest until he was no longer sticky with dry sweat. Sometime later I found myself sitting at his bedside, stroking his now-dry curls thoughtlessly as I watched him breathe. I had completely checked out, and when I looked at the window, the darkness of dead night stared me in the face. My stomach dropped. August hadn't stirred in hours. He was still breathing, but only just.

When I stomped down the steps to the bar, I was seething. Rage bubbled in me so furiously that I felt my blood about to burst through my veins. "How come no one has killed this fucking thing yet?" I asked, with no regard for my volume, once I was among the other patrons.

A few men laughed nearby, almost as if I were telling a joke. Vorma raised her eyebrows behind the bar, then poured another patron a drink without saying anything.

"What's so funny, shithead?" I whirled on one of the men who was amused by my outrage, a tubby dwarf whose name I had never bothered to commit to memory.

"You think you can kill it?" he said with a grunt before bringing his beer back up to his mustached mouth. "You're in a tavern fulla folks stronger and more experienced than you are. If anyone coulda taken it down, they woulda already. But if you think you're somethin' special… go on ahead, little lady." The curled ends of his red facial hair dipped into the foam of his drink, but he didn't seem to care. I had fallen into a strange role at the tavern and in the mercenary community whereby most people knew how skilled I was, but never let the fact that I was a woman, and a small woman at that, be forgotten. Most men at the tavern regarded me as an equal when it came to drinking or sharing stories, but when it came down to competitiveness, they all thought they could do better than me. Not only that, but they also simultaneously seemed to think that they could flirt with or bed me, even though Florian had been the only exception to my "no banging other killers!" rule. This dwarf obviously just saw me as a small child with a blade, and as I stood there, I imagined using that blade to slide the mustache off his smug face.

I scoffed. "I don't do anything for free, especially not things I'm good at… and especially not for a bunch of lazy assholes who won't do it themselves. Why should I improve your life out of the kindness of my heart?" I also wanted to tell him I didn't need his permission to go kill something, but I tried to reel in the onslaught of emotion that August's waning life force had shoved onto me.

"Improve my life?" the dwarf scoffed. "I'm pretty comfortable right here." He sipped his beer, then wiped his mouth with the back of his thick, hairy arm. Now his arm hair was covered in beer foam. He could've burped and farted then, and I would not have been surprised by just how comfortable he appeared.

I groaned, letting my head fall back, when I realized I'd have to explain things to him. "You can't tell me you've never wished to travel through Grimmaker without racing the sun. But maybe you like risking your life every time to enter the woods," I told him with a shrug. The circumstances had left me with very little filter. These men knew what I was capable of, knew my reputation. It was in their best interests to at least let me try, especially if it came at a nominal cost to them and no risk. Worst case, they'd get to watch me die from the comfort of the Beast's Breath barrier field.

The men chatted amongst themselves, some of them laughing their drunken laughs or eyeing me with amusement. But when all was said and done, one of them piped up. "I'll throw you fifty crystals if you can do it." He tossed a small leather pouch onto the bar top, which landed, then toppled over, spilling its contents onto the counter. I caught one of the crystals that nearly rolled off the surface and flicked it back into the pile.

It wasn't enough. I needed 20,000 to make the dent I was hoping to. Regardless of what was realistic, I just couldn't shake the number from my mind. "Who else? I'm not risking my ass for fifty measly crystals." It wasn't measly, though, it was a good bit. I'd ripped out my own tooth for a bowl of cabbage water and some grain for Wraith.

"Thirty from me," another said with a grunt, a handful of crystals spraying across the counter next to the existing pile. They glittered in the dim light of the bar.

Vorma watched the money pile up as hungrily as I did. "I'll throw in ten," the goblin offered, digging in her pockets to share some of her tips. It was a generous move on her part. "Wouldn't mind taking my smoke break without that thing staring me in the eyes. Come on, boys. Is that all you can do?" She winked at me as she egged the others on.

A few of the other patrons chipped in after some deliberation: an impossibly polite troll who offered another forty; two short, thin men who offered fifty together if it would save them from dealing with the Umbral; several others who chipped in a couple hundred combined; and then…

"Little one, if you take down the Umbral all by yourself, I'll give you whatever you please," Florian said coolly and surprised me by appearing at my side. When had he returned? I must have missed it while I was giving the entire bar a rallying speech. He leaned against the bar top on his forearm and eyed me as I stood there, chest heaving with rage and nerves. "Five hundred from me."

I bristled at his cockiness, but forced myself not to react too harshly. It wasn't enough, but I would take it, especially since it was the best paying job I'd be able to find outside of necromancing August. I tried not to think about his withering form upstairs. It also occurred to me that I felt much better taking Florian's money this way than by letting myself be a booty call for whom he occasionally bought things. The sum was more than I'd ever made from killing a beast, but to be fair, this would probably be the most dangerous beast I'd ever killed, paid or not. It wasn't like the dragon, which had only earned me two hundred crystals despite burning Wraith's mane clean off, or the cyclops, who just needed a good talking to in order to stop killing villagers for their organ meat. I didn't get paid for the latter, obviously.

"I'll even throw in another night of passion," Florian added, and I groaned internally as I was bombarded with memories from the night before. I was such a sloppy drunk that it was hard for me to understand what Florian had really gotten from that encounter, and yet, if it made him want to help me, then maybe he could have another messy, drunken romp in the hay.

"1,000 total," I told them all without wavering. "You have until I gear up to figure out how you're going to reach that number if you want the job done." It was a pittance in comparison to the opportunity I was losing as August wasted away upstairs, but I kept telling myself I needed the money. I danced around my feelings of a need for revenge. Yes, I wanted revenge against the beast for taking away the opportunity I'd hung so much on, for taking away my ability to fulfill my responsibilities and provide for the person who needed me. That was it, I told myself. August of Barrien was just a means to an end, and while his suffering was disappointing, I would have been distraught to see anyone injured and in agony like he was. Could I not mourn the loss of life without caring whose life it was?

I had just turned away from the group and was preparing to assess my equipment when Juniper caught me by the arm. "Max, what are you doing?" I couldn't avoid the concern in her gaze; she knew me well enough that she must have known I wasn't joking. But then again, when had I ever been the joking sort? Juniper had known me through all of my intensity and madness, especially considering the lengths I was willing to go to for Danny and my promises to him.

I set my jaw and looked her in the eyes. "June, if I die killing this fucker, you better make sure to gather those crystals up and send them to Danny, okay? Don't let those greedy assholes take it back. Give it to Wraith and tell her to go home. She'll take it to him."

"Maxine, you—"

"Since when do you call me Maxine, *Juniper*?"

Juniper narrowed her gaze at me. "Since you make stupid decisions like agreeing to go kill an Umbral in the middle of the night. Max the Menace is smarter than that."

I pushed back. "Promise me you'll get it to him if I can't myself."

Juniper released me, then folded her arms across her chest and narrowed her eyes at me.

"June. Promise," I told her. "Besides, don't you think this would be good for business? I'd say more people would be likely to visit your tavern if they didn't have to worry about being eaten alive on the way."

She let out a groan of defeat and nodded. That was the end of it. I could trust her. Now I could deal with the matter at hand. When her gaze flicked to the fireplace in the common area of the tavern, I followed it. There, barely visible in the dimness of pipe smoke and flickering candles, was a crossbow almost as big as my entire body. It was heavy and dusty, not having been moved or so much as wiped down for many, many years. The piece, intricately carved with the head of a ram, was part of a legend that I'd heard more times than I could count; everyone in the tavern knew that the ram's head crossbow was said to have taken down an Umbral many, many centuries ago and that it, with its final bolt, would be the thing to defeat the last Umbral. The Umbral that now roamed the Grimmaker Woods.

The legend said that there used to be many, many Umbrals in the Grimmaker Woods. Too many, in fact, and because of their dense population, their food sources eventually began to run out. As the Umbrals died from starvation, the remaining monsters turned to hunting travelers, who needed to use the woods after dark to get from one city to another. Most magic proved to be useless against the Umbrals, so a generous elf, June's great-great-great-grandmother – Juniper's own elf content was quite diluted by now – took it upon herself to build a tavern in the middle of the woods as a stopping point for these travelers. With the help of many of those travelers, they equipped the tavern with a barrier that kept those inside safe overnight so that they could resume their travels in the morning unscathed. Only those who left the tavern or didn't make it to the tavern before the sun set would be vulnerable to the Umbral's fierce need for prey and its bubbling, toxic venom.

The last time an Umbral was killed, however, the mercenary who took it down brought its body back into the tavern to celebrate. They stripped the body, not daring to use any of the fur or meat for their own purposes lest it be as dangerous to consume or wear as the beast's saliva, but they kept the Umbral's bones. One of the tavern regulars, Blorn, used his woodworking skills to whittle the bone into a massive sharp crossbow bolt, still filled with the rotten marrow of the beast. The bolt sat loaded into the crossbow, primed and ready for action whenever someone was ready to exterminate the species for good. As far as everyone knew, the Umbral that chased travelers back then was the last remaining monster of its kind, desperate to kill and keep itself alive. We had no clue how long their life expectancy was, though, so without interference, that particular wolf could very well carry on forever.

I scoffed. "It's just a legend. Besides, I don't even think I can carry that thing." My musing didn't stop me from eyeballing the weapon, though. Part of the fun of having violence as your job is that you get to experiment with different weapons. Knives, swords, maces, bow and arrow, I'd messed with it all, including a much smaller, much lighter crossbow back on the Isle of Wyrms. Back then, I had used it to pierce the hide of a particularly volatile griffin. I could still recall the sound of the arrow slicing through the air at top speed and the sickening crunch of it landing a blow in the beast's hide.

June's eyebrows shot up in surprise. "Legend or not, I can't see any living creature surviving a blow from that bolt. You're telling me that a wolf is gonna make it if you send a giant crossbow bolt made of bone sailing through its forehead? Come on." She shrugged and turned away, leaving me alone with my thoughts. Despite my extensive experience with killing rare, monstrous creatures, I had not given much thought to how to take down the Umbral. All I knew when I stormed down to make the deal was that it needed to die and that, if I didn't act then, I'd likely lose my nerve. Once daylight rolled around, it would be gone for another day, and I wouldn't stick around to wait for it. A glance at the clock told me I had only a couple of hours before the sun crept into the forest again, so I was running out of time for my nerves to talk me out of my promise.

"Oy, 2,500 crystals!" one of the men from earlier shouted to get my attention. I was stunned that they'd come up with more than my initial request.

"Worst case, we get a free show," the nameless dwarf added, starting on another pint of beer. He slurped it with indifference toward the entire event, and I found that I didn't really care what he thought would happen.

The pile on the bar top glistened in the hazy tavern light. It was a far-off number from the payload I'd expected to be taking home once I forked August over, but it would be useful; it would make an even bigger difference than the measly number I'd demanded at first. Despite knowing how dirty each of those crystals was, part of me wanted to bury my face in them.

As I stood in the entryway of the tavern, I checked my belt for every possible weapon I had thought to load up: two daggers, a sword, three potions of varying effects, rope, and then some. I had as many weapons and as much skill as anyone else, so it occurred to me that the only thing that had been standing in my way for all those years was fear and being willing to take the risk. Many big, strong men had tried and failed, but I did happen to have a couple of tools they didn't; my size, speed, and now way more motivation than I'd ever had before. I couldn't outrun the Umbral over long distances, but I was lithe enough to maybe keep it from guessing my next move.

"Any last requests, little menace?" Florian purred from behind me. He brushed my hair from my neck and put a hand, cool and slender, on my shoulder. I forced myself not to shy away from his touch.

"Yeah, pull that crossbow down for me." I had just tightened my belt to accommodate the extra weight of all my weaponry, and I turned to face the elf. The look on his face suggested he was holding back a laugh, but I didn't have time for his teasing. "Crossbow or nothing, I'm afraid. The rest I can handle on my own, I just can't reach that damn thing."

The elf grumbled, but returned moments later with the crossbow, loaded with the only suitable bolt in sight. I said a silent prayer that I wouldn't have to use it and that, if I did, I would have a miraculously good aim for a weapon I had never wielded before: not likely. All I needed to do was kill the beast, though, even if I died with it. That gave me a lot of options of how it could go down. I took a steadying breath and wiped my nose on the back of my sleeve when I felt my eyes glaze over with exhausted tears. I wasn't crying. I didn't cry.

I looked back at June, who gave me a nod and crossed her heart with her finger. I couldn't bring myself to glance at the staircase, knowing what was at the very top. It was that very desperate realization that caused me to push ahead toward the door of the tavern.

---

1. Tuber Toddy: strong root liquor, murky, tastes awful but will get you drunk quickly. Great for distracting you from the pains of existence.
2. Savers Salve: general first aid, used for cuts, scrapes, and other minor injuries. Can disinfect serious wounds like an Umbral bite, but cannot heal them.
3. Gloom Glug: cheap dark beer, has an earthy aftertaste.
4. Crum Chug: cheap pale beer, undertones of urine.

RUMBLE WITH THE UMBRAL

MAX

"Hey! Wolf!" I yelled as I clinked out into the open space surrounding the tavern. Wraith eyed me from her spot on the side of the building and whinnied in a way that suggested she was worried about who would feed her if I died like an idiot. I didn't blame her, but two thousand five hundred crystals would make sure she and Danny both got fed for a good while to come. She snorted and went back to eating as I walked around the perimeter, making my presence known.

Meanwhile, the windows of the bottom floor of the tavern were opening, and the men who'd sponsored my attempt were pulling up their chairs to drink and watch. I had promised them a show, after all. The dwarf from earlier had a prime viewing spot, another frothy beer in hand. Did he do anything else? He seemed to be a staple in the bar, just drinking and trash talking, yet even with all of the alcohol he didn't seem any less lucid than earlier. I couldn't dwell on my audience for too long because the Umbral soon lumbered into view, pacing a ten-foot stretch of the barrier where it could keep its eyes on me. And boy, were those eyes weird; even from where I stood near the building, they were obviously darting every which way, triangulating its audience and zoning in on its prey. Now that I could see it, I felt a bit less confident. The thing was massive. If I got any closer, we'd be staring eye-to-eye; I was small, and it was freakishly large. Its head was easily the length of my torso. It snarled, flexing its toes against the wet dirt of the forest, and a long, thick glob of spit fell from its waiting maw onto the ground next to its feet. A thin wisp of smoke sizzled out of the spot where the saliva had fallen, and I cringed at the returned imagery of August's decaying leg wound. Still, he lay upstairs breathing when all of us had been certain he would die. If not for the money, perhaps I would still put up this fight just to be as tough as his constitution had proven.

"Go on, girl!" one of the men yelled from their window side seats. "It ain't gonna come to you, no matter how bad it wants to!"

I threw a middle finger up to the window, patted my weapons down once more, then hoisted the crossbow over my shoulder to carry it. I only had one bolt in the heaving monster of machinery, so I'd have to save it for later, but I needed to bring it past the barrier so that I could actually use it. When I got to the magical barrier, the wolf and I stared at each other for a few moments in curious observation. Did it know it was going to die? Or did it think I was sacrificing myself because I hadn't let it eat August? A peace offering perhaps… but no, it couldn't be so foolish. I threw the crossbow through the protective field, and it landed in the dirt next to the Umbral, who didn't flinch.

"You're a cocky bastard, huh?" I asked the wolf, annoyed that it was so confident since landing a blow on my travel partner.

It sniffed at the air as if it could smell my fear. Maybe it just wanted a taste of something less gamey than the usual big, lumbering men who traveled through the woods. I unclipped a bottle of potion from my hip and rolled the smooth glass between my fingers, admiring the way the liquid inside looked like a brewing storm. Beatrice called it "Storm-in-a-Bottle[1]," which was easily her least creative potion name. She said that its magic came from lightning striking all of the ingredients as they were mixed together in her cauldron. If the Umbral couldn't be distracted by me prepping my crossbow to kill it, I'd need a way to distract it so I could actually get into the woods and engage it. Otherwise, I'd step outside of the barrier and be killed in an instant.

Step.

Chomp.

I could see it clearly in my mind.

For a moment I considered bringing Wraith with me and using her speed to help me lead the Umbral on a chase, but I knew better than to risk the only other being who knew how to get to Danny. She also probably knew better than to walk out into the woods with me at night, and her massive size made it so that she wouldn't do anything unless she was fully on board. In fact, she could easily avoid letting me mount her by side-stepping any of my attempts. She'd done it before.

When I launched the Storm-in-a-Bottle, it crashed onto the ground next to the Umbral, not far from my crossbow. Again, the creature didn't even dignify my action with a flinch or a turn of its head. Instead, it licked its lips – the wet squelch of which made me queasy – and kept staring me down. The liquid from the bottle began to bubble, and within seconds, the wolf was surrounded by what looked like a miniature storm: blinding swirls of black and gray clouds wrapped around it, effectively covering it from view but also restricting its own view. A crack of thunder emitted from the swirling mass, and I used my chance to step out of the protective bubble, then darted across the clearing to get farther away from the beast. When it finally emerged from the fake storm, sopping wet, it shook its fur off and stalked toward me. It snorted, sending droplets of water shooting out of its flared nostrils, and walked in my direction with a ferocity in its gaze that I hadn't expected.

"Come on, pup. It's just a little water," I teased.

It growled.

I drew my sword.

When the beast lunged, I rolled away, my fear getting the best of me. I couldn't risk a single bite, or I'd be done for, and I wasn't confident enough to know that it would land on my sword if I stayed put. We faced each other again, and this time, when it made a move for me, I forced myself to jab in response and landed a slice on his chest. The creature howled, the look in its eyes almost surprised, and a rush of confidence came over me. This time when I lunged, the wolf sent a paw straight at me, and I only barely managed to dodge it as I backed into a tree. "Shit shit shit," I berated myself, then turned to climb it as quickly as possible, scrambling to sheath my sword as I moved. I'd landed one blow and was already retreating. As I did so, knowing that the Umbral couldn't climb after me, it sunk its claws into my foot, and I let out a scream of anguish. Searing pain coursed through my body as I attempted to shake the beast loose, and when I finally did, it took my boot with it. I scrambled farther up the branches, the pain from my new wound only tempered by the adrenaline that kept me climbing, and when I settled on a sturdy, high up branch, I stopped to rest.

The Umbral circled below.

I yanked off my sock as I sat there, staring down the enemy below, and looked at the massive puncture wounds that had penetrated one side of my bare foot through the other. I yelled, angry that I was already down after only a few moments and angrier that I could literally see through my damn foot. It burned. Blood dripped down from my spot onto the forest floor, and, as if to add insult to injury, the Umbral lapped it up. When it looked up at me again, its nose was tinged pink. It licked its chops.

"Think, Max," I scolded myself. The crossbow was within sight, but much too far away for me to sprint for, given our current configuration. It was an unpleasant realization, however, because shooting the damn thing from a tree would have been ideal. I'd have to get back to that weapon somehow.

The Umbral took a seat at the base of the tree, almost as if to say he'd wait however long it took, and I angrily threw my sock down at it. It glanced at the shredded wad of fabric, huffed, then looked back up at me again. Its yellow eyes had stopped going every direction and instead were all pointed directly up at me, where they settled in great delight. I could understand the look in its gaze because it had probably been on my face before... There are times when you get so, so hungry and have spent days, maybe weeks, waiting for your next filling meal. Then, when you finally get paid or get wherever you're going to or manage to take down some big game yourself, there's that time when you're waiting for the food to be prepared or brought out to you, and even though you're still hungry, starving even, you know you're about to be fed. The thought alone can tide you over, fill your belly just for a bit. The smell of the food or maybe a little taste from the ladle, much like the lick of blood the Umbral had gotten from me, keeps you excited, but patient.

The sound of the bar patrons chatting floated through the trees toward me, but did nothing to distract my opponent. I was running out of weapons. My sword, which I'd dropped in my scramble up the tree, glinted on the ground near the base of the trunk. I felt around my belt, then the strap on my leg, and found that I only had my knives left unless I could get to the weapons on the ground. I didn't have anything more in the way of distracting potions. So, while the Umbral was staring right up at me, licking its lips, I yanked a dagger from my hip and sent it sailing down toward the creature's side, where it landed with a hearty crunch. The creature wailed, much like it had when it ran into the barrier the night before, then rolled onto its side to attempt to pull the blade out with its mouth. It couldn't, but it continued to try, lunging at the protruding handle over and over again.

When I jumped, and I had to jump, I landed right on my injured foot and bit back a scream before scrambling toward the crossbow. Each step was agony, twigs and branches and rocks lodging themself into the open wound of my sole. I realized then that putting my sock on or at least tying it around my foot probably would've given me a better chance. Nevertheless, I ran toward the crossbow, and as I approached, the Umbral's whimper and huff followed me. I had wounded it, sure, but only slightly, probably not much more than an annoyance. My heartbeat pounded in my ears, and the spectators from the bar, suddenly unsure of what they had signed themselves up for, went quiet.

The Umbral's steps were close, almost lazy, as if it were playing with its injured prey. Just as I reached for the crossbow, it lunged and rolled me onto my back, where it stood over me and stared me down with its dirty, yellow gaze. Its breath was hot and acrid, and my eyes watered in response to each gust of poisonous fumes it blew my way. My arms were pinned by its massive paws, and I grasped at the ground next to me, the wood of the crossbow grazing my fingers as I reached. I had a feeling I was going to die, but with the crossbow so close, I hoped that I could at least take the beast down with me.

A yell sailed through the air. "Max!"

---

1. Storm-in-a-Bottle: creates a storm, complete with thunder, lightning, and rain, to use as a distraction. Its magic comes from lightning striking all of the ingredients as they're mixed.

MORNING LIGHT

AUGUST

I woke to the first tendrils of morning light trickling onto my face in a room I barely recognized. It was nothing like waking in the kingdom of Barrien, but it was better. Light streamed in softly through an open window, and with it came gentle warmth. When I followed the small beams of light, they settled on the bare shoulder of the woman lying next to me in bed: Max. Her raven hair was sprawled across her pillow like a lion's mane, her chest rising and falling slowly with sleep. I propped myself up on my elbow and watched her for a while, amused by the small smile that crept onto her fair face as she dreamt. When her eyes flickered open, their dark brown deep and illuminated, she rubbed the sleep from them. "What are you staring at, you big idiot?" This time when she said it, though, she smiled. It was a term of endearment, not annoyance, and when she pulled me onto her in a playful embrace, I melted into her.

What actually woke me from my sleep was the sound of an unfamiliar yell, but when I opened my eyes, there was no morning light. Instead, the room was pitch black, with the sad wisp of smoke from a burnt-out candle floating in my vision.

I winced as I sat up, but found that I could breathe at least. After blinking repeatedly to let my eyes adjust to the darkness of the room, I recognized some of its contents. My necklace shone a little on the bedside table, where it had been carefully set aside. Max's bag was in the corner; the room even smelled a little like I remembered her smelling by the waterfall. How long had I been out for? At least I wasn't in the wrong room.

A groan escaped me as I hauled myself up off the bed, then peered out the window. There, in the dim light of the tavern's windows, just outside the glowing barrier of anti-Umbral magic, was Max. I watched her sprint in horror until I realized that no one was going to help her and she was destined for a fate similar to mine. Personally, I had no idea what had compelled her to face off against the beast, nor did I have time to ponder that question. Instead, I scrambled for the door and searched for the stairs. When I finally found them, my leg was aching, so my descent was more of a controlled fall from top to bottom. I stumbled into the lobby of the tavern, front desk and bar nearby, and settled upon a group of men by the windows watching the event unfold like a show. They murmured to themselves and sipped their drinks as if watching a claw-ball tournament, and a pile of crystals sat nearby on the bar top, waiting to be claimed.

I rushed to the front door and hauled it open, stifling a groan as my leg throbbed, but not before the woman I assumed was the innkeeper shot me a confused look. I was weak. Depleted. Hell, it felt like I shouldn't be alive, let alone walking around. I glared at the men by the window, then shouted. "Help her, you assholes!"

One of them scoffed at me. "Psh, no way. We've got a wager going."

"Yeah, mate, if she kills that thing before she bites the dust, we won't be out any crystals!" another commented, raising his beer in mock celebration.

"Not to mention a significant decline in mercenary competition," another commented with a shrug. "Don't tell her I said that if she makes it, though. She'd never let me live it down."

Nearby, a lanky elf watched silently, his arms folded over his chest. He regarded me with a raised eyebrow before looking back out the window. "Rules are rules. She's supposed to do it on her own if she wants the money," he said coolly, but that was all he offered. Useless.

Still holding the door open, but only barely, I shouted to my travel partner just as she was pinned beneath the hulking beast. "Max!" What good was that? I had no clue, but my sense of urgency was on fire, and I'd effectively lost all of the wonderment I had during the initial part of our trip. My memory was foggy, I was aching, and Max was inches away from the gaping maw that had nearly disassembled my leg.

Max the Menace looked at me for a moment, shock streaking her fair face, as she fought to hold the Umbral off and reached for her weapon on the ground. The last thing I wanted to do was get near the wolf again, but I ran. I sprinted as well as my damaged leg could carry me and slid past the barrier of the tavern in time to shove the crossbow into Max's hands. The events of the next moments passed me in a flash. Max met my gaze briefly, but then she grabbed the crossbow and sent a bolt straight through the Umbral's head. The creature itself didn't make a sound of pain or defeat. In fact, the only sound that sailed through the air was the sickening crack of the air splitting the monster's skull and then shattering out the other side of its head. A thick spurt of blood squelched from the open wound of its cranium and streaked the ground as if to say "it's over." Then, the Umbral froze and collapsed on its side, causing the ground to tremble with the impact of its mighty frame.

The forest went silent, and my vision swam as if I were in a dream. Max lay there panting, and I, too, fatigued with the new strain on my hardly healed leg, gasped for air a bit as I lay next to her. Finally, I looked at her, frustrated that she had put herself in such a near-death situation and for no good reason as far as I could tell. "What the fuck were you—"

Before I could get my question all the way out, she was on me in a way that transported me back to my brief, sweet dream. She wrapped her arms around me as if we were old friends who hadn't seen each other in years and hugged me so tight that the air left my lungs. When I pushed through the shock of this change in approach to me, I hugged her back. What the hell had happened while I was down? I sighed and realized that she was burying her face in my shoulder and trembling.

"Don't scare me like that again!" she chastised me, her face still pressed against the crook of my neck. Had I not known better, I would've thought we were lovers and I had been hit with a case of amnesia… or perhaps I was a famed war hero, returning from battle. I let my mind settle there briefly instead of facing the truth.

"Me… scare you?" I guffawed. I tried to pull her from me, but when she didn't budge, I ceased all efforts. I found that I wanted to lie there with her regardless of the circumstances. I didn't want to think. "Listen, Max, you're going to have to—"

Once again, my attempt at gathering information was cut short.

"Someone buy this woman a drink!" shouted one of the men from the bar, all of whom were pouring out of the tavern and into the open area in front of the building. Many plodded over to congratulate Max, who hastily got to her feet and helped me up, but then let go of my hand as if she hadn't just been holding on to me for dear life. I stood there dumbstruck until the innkeeper pulled her aside.

"Now you have to take those crystals to Danny yourself, huh, Max?" the innkeeper commented. The mention of this person, Danny, who I'd never heard of before caught me off guard. It didn't seem like the time to ask about him, but I wouldn't be able to forget that there was another person behind Max's motivation for money. Her husband, perhaps? A child? All this time I'd viewed Max as someone only out for herself.

Max nodded, but didn't say much else aside from casting me an occasional glance. The innkeeper meanwhile kept eyeing me and added, "And we'll have to talk about him before you go."

"Sure, June," Max agreed, voice tired and low.

A few of the men gathered up the lifeless form of the wolf, while the others ushered Max inside. I followed behind, though none of them knew who I was. I felt a responsibility to keep a close eye on Max, if only to determine why she was acting so strange. Max was wounded and shambled over to the building with her torn boot in her hand. I wanted to help her for reasons I couldn't place, but her body language suggested she suddenly wanted nothing to do with me. When we were all settled in at the bar, the men who had only moments ago been betting on her death were now cheering her on and buying her drinks. I watched Max as I sipped a celebratory glass of beer.

The lanky elf from earlier was shockingly handsy with her and wrapped his arms around her in the way she had me only moments before, but her enthusiasm in response was non-existent. Was this Danny? No, that didn't make sense. Danny was definitely not an elf name. "Not bad, little menace," he told her where everyone could hear. "Now you've got your prize money and your prisoner back." He looked at me momentarily, his gaze narrowed in curiosity. "Though I'm not sure how you survived."

I was also unsure. I shrugged and sipped my beer, unable to stifle the unease bubbling within me when the elf wrapped an arm around Max's waist. Why did I care? I didn't, I couldn't. Apparently, I'd survived just to continue along the path of being turned in for a reward. Should I have been thankful for that?

A SLIGHT DELAY

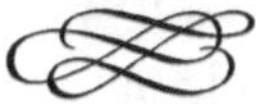

MAX

"Thank you, but we really ought to get some rest before we travel out again in the morning," I told the crowd after swiping the crystals off the bar top and into my pockets. I didn't trust them not to go back on their word if I didn't act fast; moments ago they'd been content to witness my demise. I plucked the last few crystals off of the counter and shoved them into my pocket, careful not to miss a single one with how hard I had worked for them.

"Now, now, you don't want him to die on the road after all the work you put into keeping him alive, do you?" Florian's voice, smooth as ever, had me on edge. He was prying. Why now, when he could've gotten way more information from me when I was drunk the night before? He must have sensed my irritation because he added, "If you don't let him heal all the way, he's not going to be in very good shape once you get where you're going. Where is that again?"

"Oh yeah, Max, tell us all about where you're headed next… oh Great Umbral Slayer!" Vorma chimed in, happily filling my glass without question. She was sweet, she really was, but she didn't see the ulterior motive in Florian's questioning the way that I did. Mercenaries only looked out for themselves, as proven by my relationship with Florian, and if he was asking questions, it wasn't because he wanted to get to know me better. Either he was trying to figure something out because he didn't trust what I was saying, or he thought that August might be worth stealing right out from under me.

Florian leaned in closer to look at both my prisoner and me, his sky-blue gaze inspecting the prince closely. He sniffed the air around August with zero regard for the strangeness of his behavior. "It's interesting – you had an odd feel about you when you arrived, you know, half alive. It's gone now."

"Yes, I imagine people do feel odd when they're about to drop dead," August said confidently. Not many people could stand up to Florian without doubting themselves, but then again, not many people were as bullheaded and optimistic as Prince August III. I would never admit it aloud, but I was glad to see some of his attitude returning.

"Afraid it'll have to be another night, folks," I told them all, patting my pockets once more to ensure they were still sufficiently full. I downed the drink Vorma had poured me out of courtesy, then left the glass and two crystals for her on the counter. When I turned to August, I found that it was hard to look him in the eyes. I couldn't tell if it was the sheer strangeness of everyone talking about him right in front of him or the fact that I had just seen him on death's door only hours earlier, but it felt odd. "Come on, let's get you back to bed."

"What? No 'big idiot' at the end?" August put a hand to his chest in mock anguish. I wondered briefly if his brush with death had him feeling invincible. "You wound me."

"I will if you don't come along." I gritted my teeth and lowered my voice as I leaned over to him. "You don't want to be left alone around this crowd, believe me."

Thankfully, someone else in the group caught Florian's attention and preoccupied him while we slipped away. Because August seemed okay to walk on his own, I led the way toward the stairs, past the entryway and front desk. When the adrenaline wore off, the pain in my foot would probably make me as unsteady as my captive. For now, though, I was okay. We didn't make it far, of course, because Juniper was standing there, perusing her ledger and doing whatever it is that innkeepers do at their front desk. "Pretty lucky," she mused aloud, still looking at the book on the counter in front of her. "Never seen anyone survive a bite from an Umbral."

August opened his mouth to speak, and I shook my head discreetly. I trusted June, but I didn't trust August not to share more than I wanted him to. Not only that, but I was still piecing together how exactly he had survived the unsurvivable, and I didn't want anyone to get there before I did in case they uncovered something that would put yet another damper on my plans.

"Huh, yeah, lucky," August grumbled finally. "Must be one of those magic potions that Max carries around that did it."

I groaned internally.

Juniper offered us a small smile as we ascended the stairs. When August slipped and I caught him without thinking, a twinkle shone in her eye. "Must be," she commented, turning back to her ledger. "You'll have to let me know what Beatrice cooked up for you this time, Max."

"Sure, June," I told her again. Great, another person looking at me a bit too closely for my liking. My stomach grumbled as we approached the stairs, and I looked back at June. "Any chance you can send a bit of food up? I haven't fed this man, and I'd hate to starve him to death after he just came back to the land of the living."

When we made it back to the room, I latched the door and leaned against it, then let myself slide down to the floor with a sigh of relief. I hadn't bothered to ask how long we should stay – Florian would have known. "Two days," I told August finally, rubbing my tired eyes with my hands.

"What?"

"Two days, and then we're gone. Two days for you to rest up and get your strength back, and then we're leaving. Even with the Umbral gone, it's not smart to linger here." I wasn't waiting for a response, but when the room went silent, I looked up at August, who was standing in front of me. "What?"

"You're going to have to tell me at some point," August said, folding his arms over his chest in a way that made me want to dig my boot into his wounded leg.

"You know, it's a bold move of the near-dead hostage to be making demands," I blurted out, unable to stop myself from being mean in an attempt to cover up whatever the heck was actually going on in my head. Whatever it was, I didn't like it. I considered dragging my sad self over to Florian's room, but knew that would be an entirely different type of trouble. My muscles ached when I hoisted myself to my feet and looked up at August again, shockingly glad to see his dark eyes open and staring back at me. The way those deep pools of golden brown, like bowls of freshly ground cinnamon, sucked me in was alarming. Unsettling. But they were so warm and right. I swallowed hard and wished I could reset my brain so that it didn't have those pitiful, wandering thoughts that were no doubt a byproduct of almost watching the man die. "Two days, prince charming. Get some rest."

"There's only one bed," August remarked without missing a beat. He didn't look away as he spoke.

I smirked. "It's okay. There's a floor. I'll take it this time since you're injured." I didn't think I would be sleeping much that night, not with the adrenaline of killing the Umbral and seeing August upright and alive again. If anything, I could nap during the day when he woke.

I took a step over to my bag, and the sensation of putting weight on my single bare and injured foot caused me to yelp in a way that immediately embarrassed me. "Shit."

August crossed his arms over his chest again. "Shit is right," he scolded me. "You're hurt, too. We'll have to take turns."

"It's fine."

"It's not fine. Sit down," he instructed me. I complied and took a seat in the rickety chair next to the bed. The room still smelled of proof that I hadn't imagined August almost dying; potions, blood, sweat, it was all there. He hobbled around the room, taking stock of what we had left, and I wondered if he'd ever dressed a wound in his life. The prince of Barrien probably had someone to do that for him at home. He glanced at the empty potion bottle on the floor. "Any more of that?"

I shook my head. "No, but it's really alright. It didn't bite me. I'll be okay, it just needs time to heal… and now I really need that new pair of boots."

August eyed me curiously, then pulled the basin off of the small table and uncorked an extra bottle of water I'd left beside it. "Well," he began, lowering the basin to the floor in front of me and placing my foot into it. It was an oddly intimate act. "Your prize money from killing that wolf ought to help… not to mention my bounty." Before I could reply, he continued speaking. "I may not have been totally here, but I watched you bandage my leg."

"Oh." My breath caught in my throat as I pictured him watching me through hooded eyes as I wiped down his bare chest. I couldn't think of anything to say, so instead I just watched him in return as he poured water over my foot. I sucked in a sharp breath at the contact and the sensation of water running through a hole in my foot, but bit my lip to stop from making any other noise. He rinsed my foot again until the muck of the forest floor was gone, showing no distaste for the blood and dirt that was covering his hands by the end, then dried my foot with a dry washcloth. Then, he tore the hem of his shirt to make me a bandage, which he wrapped around the arch of my foot without a single word. The way he moved the basin and set my foot gently down onto the floor again left me feeling more open and vulnerable than the treatment of a wound should have. I wiggled my toes and gave him a small nod. "Thanks."

"Sure."

THE NEXT FEW days passed in a silence that should have been strained, but wasn't. We alternated turns of who got to sleep in the bed and who slept on a pile of blankets on the hard floor. We ate. We rested. I spent a lot of time with Wraith, outside and away from the patrons of the bar, but not so long that I couldn't keep an eye on August. I suggested that he not tell anyone his business or his name because the other mercenaries couldn't be trusted, just like me.

Then, we set off for my homeland: the Wild Open.

THE WILD OPEN

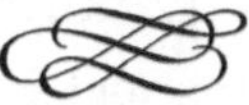

MAX

It's strange when your homeland is a lawless open wasteland. Part of you feels allegiance to that wasteland, and the other part knows you could get murdered there at any moment. Complexities aside, I had missed the Wild Open, so when our journey took us there, it was a relief to be back in familiar lands. We wouldn't be passing by my home, thankfully, but we would be traveling through areas that I knew like the back of my hand. It was set to be an easy leg of the trip, and the Wild Open had no treacherous beasts quite like the Umbral, so as we set out on our way, I was feeling decent. We had rested, and August had recovered as much as two days would let him, which was far more than anyone had expected. I was also riding the high of slaying a notorious nightmare creature, winning a wager with a bunch of filthy male mercenaries, and – though I wouldn't let myself dwell on it – the relief of August's survival. The sun shined brighter, and everything felt clear and open. August was even back to asking his questions, which would have annoyed the ever-loving shit out of me had I not just gotten close to actually watching him die.

"How do you know your way around the entire continent?" he asked, as content as he'd ever been on the back of Wraith. I wasn't sure if something had shifted between us during our time in Grimmaker, but if it had, no one had addressed it outright.

"Well, for starters, it's my job," I mused aloud, unable to come up with a clever joke about how sheltered August's life was. It wasn't really, at least not anymore; his brush with death had earned him some unspoken respect from me, though I could never let him know that. "Also, I live here. Well, I live everywhere, but my home is here."

August shifted behind me, and I could picture him holding his hand flat above his eyes as he searched the distance. "Where? I'm not seeing a house that really screams 'Max.' No moats, no piercing spires, no…"

"Dragons guarding the entrance?" I offered, smirking to myself beneath the cover of my hooded cowl.

"That would be cool, but I pictured more like… demons? Wings still, yes. Intimidating, horrifying at times…"

"But no fire? I'm shocked."

"That's the thing," he said. "They don't even need fire. They're just enough on their own. That, or the heat of your everlasting rage is enough."

"Ah, yes, that makes sense." I chuckled to myself. "You won't ever find it, moats and all, though, so don't waste your time."

"Why not?" August asked, and despite being prepared for the question, it caused the hair on my body to stand on end. It felt personal, prying, invasive for him – or anybody – to ask more about my home.

"I'm protecting something special there," I said simply. Danny was something special; he was the last little bit of a family I had left, and I owed him a safe, loving life because of what we'd been through with our parents. "Guarding it from the harshness of the world." I half expected a jab about how I couldn't possibly have much to protect given my lack of values and feelings, but the jab never came. We carried on.

We spent the next few days traveling across the Wild Open. Our trip was mostly silent, aside from communicating about necessary stops and occasional curiosities from August which eventually grated on me once more. Because the Wild wasn't teeming with nighttime-only horrors, we were able to camp most nights. During the day, however, I was swiftly reminded about my need to keep both of us fed and alive until we got to our destination, which meant that I should take any jobs that came my way. The 2,500 was useful, but if I wasn't careful, it could be used up easily by two people on the road; I wasn't used to having to care for two people and a horse on such a long trip. However, after defeating the Umbral, I felt ready to tackle anything. For some reason, the thought of getting my 20,000-crystal reward for August popped into my head less and less over time. Ever since I'd seen him nearly drop dead, the thought of putting a price on his surrender made me feel sick to my stomach. Don't get me wrong, that was still the plan, I just couldn't think about it.

With Wraith moving at full speed and us traveling by ourselves with no need for conversation, little sleep, and food only when we needed it, we could make it from the Beast's Breath Tavern in the middle of the Grimmaker Woods across the Wild Open in two weeks. But with August, especially since he was still nursing a healing wound, we had to stop much more frequently. My own wound was minimal enough that it didn't put a damper on our travels... either that or my tolerance for the discomforts of travel was simply higher than August's. Not only did he whine if not fed on a regular basis, but his highness required a full night of sleep and was very, very curious about each and every thing we passed. The Wild Open also contained tens of smaller communities that governed themselves, so traveling through the Wild meant that you had to ensure you knew where you were going and which communities you were going to encounter; not all of them were welcoming to people from other parts of the Wild.

About halfway through our trip through the Wild, we set up camp in a small wooded area with a nearby river. I had used this spot many times to rest safely as well as fill my canteens. The wooded area also generally had rabbits and small birds that I could usually catch and kill for a small meal.

"Did you hunt in your kingdom?" I asked August as I unpacked Wraith's saddlebags and set her up for the evening. I was still making do with a boot and a half, so I slipped my shoes off whenever I had the chance and gave my injured foot a chance to rest.

"For fun, sure," August told me as he set up the blanket and jacket I'd given him as a sleeping spot. I found a spot to sit and sharpened a stick with one of my blades.

"You never used what you killed?" Judgment slipped into my voice again. I wasn't very good at hiding it. Perhaps it was a defense mechanism. I had to find flaws in August in order to feel better about the fate I was going to resign him to when we hit Emynor.

"To be fair, I don't think I ever successfully killed anything." He laughed a little. He seemed genuinely amused at his own flaws for some reason. He didn't take offense to my criticisms and prying questions the way I did. "But the little things that my hunting partners killed usually went to the dogs, I think."

I smiled to myself as I imagined August riding a horse through the woods after a squirrel. He was refined due to his upbringing, but it seemed there would always be a part of him that was a bit of a lumbering oaf. He didn't strike me as graceful or stealthy, certainly not like Florian. Florian could stand so still that he would become part of the woods, then reach out quickly as a bird flew by and grasp it in his hand; even the bird would be amazed – confused, horrified, yes, but amazed as it met its quick demise. Unlike humans, elves had a lot more time to sit around and wait for their prey to come to them.

"How about fishing?" I mused aloud after some silence, thinking that the nearby stream might be a good chance to vary our diets a little. Fish were a pain in the ass because their bones were annoying and they weren't very substantial, but I hadn't seen many small critters around since our entry into the wooded area. Meanwhile, my stomach grumbled.

"Fishing..." August mulled over the idea as he plopped down near what would soon be our fire. "No, I haven't tried."

"There's a first time for everything, I suppose," I told him. I quickly sharpened a second stick to use as a spear and gestured for him to follow me, much to his dismay. He still hadn't regained his speed since his injury, and it took him a moment to get standing again, but I was already off toward the stream I had noticed. It felt wrong to wait on him, to baby him as if he couldn't take care of himself, and I figured that keeping him alive, fed, and out of harm's way was as much as I could be expected to do. I already had enough responsibility as it was, and with how vocal August was about his other needs, I imagined that he would pipe up if he needed anything else.

"First time for what now?" he called after me, hobbling through the trees in what sounded like a less-than-graceful manner. Twigs snapped, and I was certain he hit the ground at one point, but he must've gotten back up because he kept commenting through his exasperation. "Surely we're not relying on me for tonight's food! We'll starve!"

The stream nearby was beautiful: a coursing vein of crystal blue that snaked through the woods. I closed my eyes at the edge of it and inhaled deeply, the sound of the rushing water immediately centering my usually restless brain. It was nice to be back in familiar land, where there wasn't a surprise around every—

"What the fuck is that?"

My eyes snapped open at August's elegant commentary, and I found him crouched over, hands on his knees next to me as he caught his breath. He was pointing toward the water.

"That's… a bear," I managed before a burst of laughter escaped my lips against my will. "You've never seen a bear?"

The creature looked at us briefly before returning to its spot pawing at the water. It narrowly missed a fish that swam by and huffed in frustration.

"First of all, no, I've never seen a bear," August said, standing upright as if to defend himself. "Second, isn't it going to eat us?"

The bear looked annoyed.

"No." I laughed again. I wished I could stop, but the fact that this man continued to amaze me with just how little of the world he had experienced had me highly amused. To think he'd never even seen a drawing of a bear in a book was outlandish to me, but if I had been in the same position, seeing one in real life would've been a shock to me, too. Still, I laughed. It felt novel and strange, but with each giggle, the fresh forest air filled my lungs, and I felt more aligned than I had in a very long time.

"Third," August added, reaching over and placing his palm on my forehead without warning. "Is that laughter? Are you sure you're well? This is very unlike the Max the Menace I know."

I didn't mean to, but I froze immediately at the contact. I glanced up at his hand, broad and rough, and then met his gaze. Again, I was rendered speechless by our closeness but also by the fact that we were face-to-face. When riding, I had our position to shield me from being so directly in front of him and the fact that I always had my hood up, but now…

"Max? Seriously, are you alright?" August swallowed hard, so hard that I could see his Adam's apple bob, and removed his hand. His tone had changed so abruptly that it drew me from my daze, and I returned my focus to the rushing water beneath us.

"It's, um, pretty straightforward," I told him, attempting to move on as if time hadn't slowed for a moment. "Just try to aim for where the fish is going to be, not where it is, when you throw your spear." I could feel August's gaze on the side of my face, so I busied myself further with a demonstration. I pulled my arm back once I spotted a fish I wanted to claim, then took a steadying breath and sent my makeshift spear flying. It made immediate contact, and I grabbed the fish from the water, then pulled it from the stick triumphantly. "Like that."

The bear across the water sniffed at the air, and with a sigh, I relinquished the fish to it by tossing it to the bank across the stream, where it was consumed almost immediately.

I could just imagine the look on August's face behind me, so I added, "Consider it a peace offering. Alright, your turn. Don't let us starve!" For whatever reason, I couldn't bring myself to look at him, so I just stood there until he found his place next to me. His presence following our intimate and overwhelming eye contact was daunting; often I forgot just how much bigger he was than me because he often acted so foolish, but when I was met with his ability to be intense, it was staggering. We stood in silence until I found it in me to speak again. "Find one you want to try for."

"There," August said, voice calm. He didn't gesture toward the water, but I assumed he had his eye on a particular target. Thankfully, the fish in the stream seemed frequent and plentiful, so he would have many opportunities before the sun went down and we were forced to go to sleep hungry.

"Now get it."

He let the spear loose into the water, and it planted itself firmly between the rocks at the bottom of the river, the fish swimming around it as if it were another part of the stream. I plucked it from the gravel and handed it back to August before he could lament his failed attempt.

"Again."

The man grunted, then steadied his gaze on the water again. He threw the spear. It plopped into the water, and I grabbed it again before it floated by.

The sun was beginning to set, and our spears were taking on so much water that I wasn't sure they were sharp enough to hit anything when August flopped onto the bank in frustration. "This time you'll get it," I told him confidently.

"Good one," August said with a groan, glaring at the water as if it was nature's fault that fish weren't just flinging their bodies at us for consumption. "Why don't you just catch us fish for dinner? It would take you all of ten seconds!" He threw his hands up.

I set my jaw. "If I catch a fish tonight, I'm the only one eating it," I told him, finally forcing myself to look in his direction. "What's the point of all those muscles if you can't use them to launch a stick into a fish so you can feed yourself?"

There was silence as I realized what I had just said. I was pretty sure that the bear had taken off as well when it realized just how awkward my commentary was.

"All those muscles, huh?" August asked. He raised his eyebrow. Of course. "If you like them, you can just say—"

"Shut up. You know what I mean," I bit out. "What's the point of having a personal trainer if you can't do anything functional with your body?"

"It's for the ladies. Sometimes the gentlemen, if they're the right kind."

"Well, pretend you're trying to impress a lady and kill a fucking fish to show her that you can survive on your own!" I scowled at him and held out the spear for what felt like the twentieth time at least. "I'm getting hungry."

When August grabbed the sad, wet stick of wood from me and hoisted himself to his feet, not complaining about his leg, I stood back. The whole exchange had my face bright red, and I was glad to have his attention directed elsewhere while I tried to calm myself. Since when did I make comments on prisoners' physiques, least of all Prince August III? I berated myself internally as I stood there and watched him with my arms crossed.

Again, he spotted his target swimming through the water. This time the setting sun had darkened the surface a bit. August aimed his weapon, the reliability of which I was starting to doubt, took a deep breath, then hurled it forward with a grunt of power that almost resembled a roar. When the wood made contact with its target, effectively killing dinner for us, August stood there in shock.

"Well, grab it before it floats away!" I gestured at the water in a way that added a "big idiot" comment without me having to say it, and August sprang into action, stomping into the water without a care. He grabbed the stick, fish still attached, and held it up in the air.

"I did it!" he exclaimed, waving his still slightly alive catch in the air. "How's that for a 'functional body'?" He flexed his free arm, and I forced myself to ignore the way the fabric of his shirt strained against his bicep. The sound of a few threads straining and snapping was not lost on me.

I turned on my heel to head back to our campsite, then shouted back to him. "I don't suppose the muscles know how to cook a raw fish?"

"Where are we headed next?" August asked between bites of slightly burned fish. Despite the effort it took him to kill and cook the fish, he seemed pleased with his accomplishments for the day. I was, too, but couldn't compliment him because of how I'd misspoken earlier. Instead, I ate my share in contented silence, my only wish being for a pinch of salt.

"The End of the Road," I told him from across the fire.

He stopped chewing, his eyes immediately going wide. "That's it? We're almost there?"

I shook my head, then picked a fish bone from my teeth before answering him. "No, that's what the next stop is called. We still have a while yet."

I didn't miss the relief in his expression, but I couldn't tell if it was simply because his handing-over was put off or because our trip together would last a bit longer. Perhaps some of both.

"Good, then I still have some time to escape," August said before taking another bite. He didn't meet my gaze.

MERMAIDS DON'T HAVE FANGS

AUGUST

We spent several more days in the Wild Open, and despite her attempts to be as mysterious as possible, I learned more and more about Max as we traveled. I wasn't sure why, but she forced me to catch our meals each evening. It didn't make sense to me given the fact that either Emynor or Barrien would feed me, either as a prisoner or a prince. It didn't matter, though, because I enjoyed those small glimpses into her life and I got the feeling that she had not shared them with many others before.

On our tenth night in the Wild Open, I volunteered to attempt spearing a fish again and wandered, on my own, down to a small lake that we'd passed on our way to that evening's campsite. Max looked suspicious of me when I suggested it, but she let me go without much of a fuss, aside from insisting she would find me if I didn't come back fast enough. I thought back to what had happened in the woods near the waterfall and nodded in agreement, telling myself not to take too long.

The lake was much more wide open than the river had been, so it was difficult for me to see fish within it. I pulled off my boots, rolled up my pants as far as they would go, then waded in and stood in the shallow pool for a few moments, waiting to see if fish would approach me once the water stilled. The coolness of the water was a relief to my still-aching leg. As I waited, I admired the view, the setting sun reflecting brilliantly on the water's surface. The old me would not have found joy or peace in such a scene, but life had forced me to slow down and see only what was in front of me. Moments later, however, the scene changed before my eyes.

The water's surface, previously still and reflective, rippled in the distance. The movement in the water came closer and closer to me, but for some reason I didn't take it as a sign that I should turn and leave. Perhaps it was just a large fish approaching me and I'd have something truly impressive to bring back to Max for dinner. Since I'd been responsible for all of our evening meals, I was starting to get hungry; it would be nice to have something a bit more substantial than what I had managed to catch so far. I stood still, then lifted my hand to aim my spear at the water where the ripples continued, hoping that I would be able to see past the reflection of the setting sun and into the water so I could be more effective with my dinky weapon. When the surface of the water broke a mere body's length away from me, however, I couldn't stifle my gasp.

"Hello, weary traveler." The voice invaded my brain before the face of the person whom it belonged to had fully left the water. It was smooth and sultry, unmistakably feminine, and when I was face-to-face with its owner, her voice continued to appear in my mind without passing through her thick, shapely lips. "What brings you to my lake?"

My mouth went dry as I surveyed the woman before me, who was, for now, beneath the water aside from her head and shoulders, which were bare. What was she doing so far out in the water?

How had she stayed beneath the surface for so long? Her skin was pale and smooth, water from the lake sliding off of it as if it was repellant. Her long, silky hair fell over her shoulders in a curtain of flaxen strands, and her eyes reflected the colors of the water beneath her: green and blue and inky black.

"Your lake?" I asked suddenly, struggling to find words as the woman floated only a few feet away from me.

She nodded, then rose a little further out of the water, exposing her ample bare chest, which immediately caught my lonely gaze. It had been so long since I'd been this close to a woman aside from Max, and this one was quite lovely. My mouth watered. "Yes, I'm Serena," her voice told me again inside of my mind. "I live here, but it's not often I get a visitor as handsome as yourself."

I couldn't tear my gaze away from her as she swam closer, her lean, pale arms slicing through the water like a blade. She paused a bit and floated on the surface, eying me in a way that was both flirty and a little dangerous. There was a twinkle in her eye that I couldn't quite place, but I told myself it was interest and nothing more sinister. She was curious about me… she liked what she saw. Who wouldn't?

"Handsome?" I asked aloud, somehow flustered by this water nymph, though I had spent a great deal of my life taking compliments from women. "I'm flattered that you think so. Why don't you come a bit closer so I can admire you more?"

A giggle fluttered into my mind, and the woman rolled through the water onto her back, exposing her bare midsection to the sky. My gaze raked her form, and as I took in her breasts again, then her navel, I was shocked when it landed on the start of a scaled tail. The transition between human flesh and pearlescent scales was flawless, one melding into the other without a clear line of where they would separate. Of course, a mermaid. What had I been expecting? "Do you like what you see?" she asked, her eyes still glued on my face.

"More than I could possibly put into words," I admitted to her. I bit my lip without thinking.

The woman smiled, her lips still pressed together, and her hair floating around her in the water. The thin wisps floated toward me on the surface. "So, tell me, what brings you to this lake?" she asked.

"Just trying to catch some dinner. You see, I'm traveling, just passing through," I told her briefly. "With a companion." Surely the suggestion of me being a captive prisoner would not be attractive to a mermaid, whose stunning wholesomeness gave me pause. Did mythical creatures care about morals? Probably... at least mermaids, who seemed like the most wholesome of non-human creatures, would.

"A companion?" The woman's voice was slightly more serious now. I had hoped that she would be able to snatch a fish from under the water and hand it to me, if nothing else, but the tone of our conversation seemed to change.

I tried to respond, but was cut off. "Yeah—"

"August, where are you?"

"There she is now," I told my mermaid friend, jerking my thumb behind me toward Max's voice, which wasn't nearly as soft or sweet. "Kind of a wet blanket, though."

It was as though the sound of my traveling partner's voice had enraged the mermaid, however. She immediately turned over the water and was upright again, her wet hair sticking to her bare shoulders and chest, and her stare now intent and focused on my face. The way she had her eyes locked on me made me feel slightly uncomfortable, but I chalked it up to her extreme interest in me. Perhaps she was lonely, just like I was. I found that I couldn't tear my focus away from her, so when the dull thud of Max's boots came stomping into the clearing by the lake, I didn't turn. "What do you want, Max?" I called back to her. "I'm a bit busy!"

"Yes," the mermaid purred in my mind, encouraging me. "Tell your companion to wait for you somewhere else. You're my handsome traveler, not hers."

A chill coursed through my body. "You don't need to act jealous, Max," I told her without turning to look over my shoulder. It was so unattractive when women got clingy like that. Besides, she had her lanky tavern elf to flirt with and whoever the hell Danny was. The least she could give me was one last hurrah with a beautiful woman before I was locked up forever in Emynor. "I believe this lovely lady just wants some time alone with me before I catch our dinner. What's the harm in that, Max? Don't be so uptight."

"Not a good idea, August," Max scolded me. "I mean it! Believe me, I know better than you do about this stuff."

Irritation found me and snipped back at Max. "What are you talking about? You've got your elf at the tavern, why shouldn't I be allowed to have a little fun? She's great!"

Max scoffed. I could hear her sloshing into the lake behind me as she spoke. "That's only because you haven't seen her fangs yet!"

"What fangs? Mermaids don't have fangs!"

"This one does!" Max yelled, her grip on my shirt tight enough to begin dragging me back to shore. I couldn't tear my gaze away from Serena, however, and as I was yanked through the water against my will, the mermaid transformed again. Her mouth, which had made my own water with desire, finally parted. Her grin was impossibly wide, cracking at the corners where it then caused her entire head to split in half as she unhinged her jaw. I could no longer see her nose or eyes, only a gaping maw that was filled with, as Max had said, fangs. They were massive, long and sharp, with stringy saliva hanging between each one. No wonder she hadn't spoken with her mouth; the sight was a total turnoff.

"Ah, fuck," I groaned, both hating that Max was right because I would never live down the shame and hating the fact that the only woman interested in me in several hundred miles just wanted to eat me.

"I wouldn't advise it!" Max snipped.

My captor had just pulled me onto the pebbled shore of the lake when a horrific screech filled the air, and I looked over to see the mermaid flopping its body into the shallow edge of the lake, reaching for me. "Come back, handsome traveler!" it screeched in my mind. "I'll show you a good time!"

We made our way back to camp sopping wet and silent, not to mention without fish. Food was scarce during the next leg of the trip as well, though Max's judgmental glares would've stopped me from eating even if we did have food.

THE END OF THE ROAD INN

MAX

The End of the Road Inn was not named by someone creative; it was an inn at the end of one of the long main roads between the kingdom of Barrien and the kingdom of Emynor, where I was headed to surrender August to the highest bidder. Whatever happened to him after he left my charge and I received my pay meant nothing to me. Nothing at all. This had become my mantra whenever my current job's mission popped into my head. Surrender August. Get crystals. Return to Danny. Be comfortable. I'd stayed at the inn on numerous occasions during my travels, often enough, in fact, that they knew me by name.

"What can I do ya for, Max?" the innkeeper, Seymour, asked as we clunked our way into the entrance of the building. His one good eye looked me up and down, as if he were inspecting me for a mortal injury. It was probably a surprise to him every time I showed up still alive and moderately well. Well, as well as a life of crime could leave one. Whereas Juniper was like a sister to me, Seymour was perhaps a weird, estranged, but caring uncle. I'd say father figure, but I couldn't really recall much about my dad anymore, so I didn't have a great point of reference. Hell, Seymour may have been someone's actual dad. I had no idea. What I did know, however, was that Seymour's dad was a cyclops and his mom was a human, which explained him having two eyes but only one good one.

"Just one night," I told him as I tossed a few crystals on the well-worn counter. The wood was rife with ridges and knife marks. "And grain? For Wraith," I added, dropping one more crystal into the pile as I racked up the bill. I'd tied my girl up outside like I always did. I was hungry, too, but Wraith was the one carrying our miserable asses all over the place, so snacks for myself would have to wait. Once we got paid our reward money, we'd eat like royalty. If we didn't get paid, we'd just have to eat the royalty we were hauling around. Then again, I thought about the wound in August's leg and decided against cannibalism as an option.

"Aye, I'll take care of your girl," the innkeeper assured me. Wraith liked the staff here, which was saying a lot. "Got an apple waiting for her, too." That couldn't hurt.

My stomach growled at the mention of an apple. It had been a long time since I'd had a piece of fruit. "Thanks, Seymour."

I was settling the arrangements for the evening when the old man looked over my shoulder, his foggy eye wandering the other direction, and jerked his chin at August, who was glancing around the inn as curious as ever. Given the context of his last stay at an inn, I half expected him to be a bit more reserved. Perhaps even scared. No such luck, of course; a healed August was an annoying and nosy August, apparently. "Two more crystals if you want him locked up." The End of the Road Inn had what resembled a makeshift jail, where folks like myself could pay to have their captives securely handled for the evening so they could rest without worrying about escape. Beast's Breath didn't have one because no one in their right mind would make a run for it through those woods, though that had likely changed with the recent defeat of the Umbral. Normally, I'd consider taking Seymour up on the offer, but August Theodoric was a highly wanted man. It wasn't beyond thieves and mercenaries to steal bounties from each other, and this wasn't one I could afford to risk. Even the way Seymour looked at him had me feeling uneasy; we were all just trying to get by, and I couldn't take it personally if that meant people putting their best interests over friendships. I stood by the assumption that he had not yet been recognized, however.

I looked from the innkeeper to my charge and back again. "Nah, he'll have to stay with me. I trust your people, but I don't trust him not to give them a hard time." That was a lie on both counts.

Seymour grunted, then tossed me a worn and rusted looking key. "Suit yourself. We only got a room with one bed left, though." He eyed both of us again before flicking me a silver coin in return and gesturing over to the bar. "Ya look thin. Mary made stew earlier. Tell 'er I said there's a bowl for ya on me." Okay, maybe he was a father figure after all.

I rubbed my face in exhaustion and looked toward the bar, which was brimming with patrons. I would need something if I was going to get through the night with this idiot. "Thanks again, Seymour." I'd need something stronger than stew, but it would be a start.

The stew was hot and filled with chunks of some sort of mystery meat as well as some other floating unmentionables that I assumed must be edible at the very least. I slid it toward August as we took seats opposite of each other in a booth. When he didn't immediately start eating, I gestured to the bowl again, nudging it a little closer to him. "Come on, I know firsthand that you haven't had anything warm to eat in weeks. That sad little fish in the woods was hardly a meal."

"If I haven't, you definitely haven't," August replied, narrowing his eyes at me. "Why are you being so nice?"

"I can't turn you over on death's door. Eat." Before he could come up with a snarky comeback, I excused myself from the table. Ugh, why was I being so nice? I made it one step before turning back to him. "If you leave, I'll kill you. You know that." He didn't answer, but at this point it was less of a threat and more of a way for me to remind myself of my role in our arrangement. I could kill him. I think. But what a waste that would've been after saving his stupid life.

I made my way over to the bar and flagged down the bartender, who poured me a pint of ale without question. I had just taken a sip of the foam off the top when he leaned on his forearms across the bar. They were littered with an array of scratchy black tattoos, supposedly depicting all of the lives he'd taken. From where I stood with my beer, I could see a stick figure decapitating a giant snake. I had no clue if that had actually happened, but I made a mental note to get a cool tattoo to emphasize my Max the Menace persona; maybe I'd seem tougher.

"How's Danny?" he asked, ignoring another patron who was vying for his attention. If there was one thing about Arvin, it was that he made you feel like he was actually listening to you and cared about what you had to say. His focus and seriousness gave him an entirely different energy than Vorma at the other tavern.

I eyed him over the rim of my drink, a little surprised at his question, which seemed to come out of nowhere. He knew better than to talk about my brother so casually and in such a crowded space. "Not sure, but I haven't heard anything. I'm on a job, haven't been home in a while."

He nodded, then suggested, "Maybe you should swing by home before you finish your job, ya know?"

My heart suddenly began to race and my blood pumped loudly in my ears. Before I could ask why, he had turned to serve someone else. When I turned around to look for my charge, he was no longer at the table. I would've called for him if I hadn't known it would draw unwanted attention to us; what other outcome could yelling a wanted prince's name yield? Besides, just as I opened my lips, the strumming of a lute filled the stifling air of the inn, and all space for conversation was lost.

Someone cheered the bard on in the distance.

When I finally spotted August, he was dancing with a young woman whose breasts were on the verge of spilling from the top of her dress, which looked to be hanging on by a thread. I rolled my eyes; it seemed he had a type and a way to find that type regardless of our setting or my threats. I wasn't put off by the woman, but rather August's incessant pursuit of women like her and the deadly mermaid even when he was in the midst of being turned over to a warring kingdom. I folded my arms across my chest and leaned against the bar, only changing my position to take a swig of my drink and then resume watching them. August twirled the woman in front of him, his still-healing leg not putting a damper on his dance moves. The woman was lovely, if I let myself actually appreciate her rather than criticize her for her association with my prisoner. When she spun back toward August, she landed in his arms, and he lowered her with a graceful dip, the likes of which I had no idea he could manage. I couldn't help but admire the twinkle in his eyes when he laughed and the look of contentment on his chiseled face when she wrapped her arms around him and they swayed together. He was the type of person who needed physical closeness. I couldn't shame him for that, even if I did feel uneasy whenever he was too far away from me. I had to keep an eye on him.

Our trip so far had not been easy, so I didn't interrupt August's continued dancing with the woman from the bar. Instead, I returned to our table and sipped my beer in quiet observation. I tried not to be too obvious while still making it clear to other patrons that August was with me; if they knew who I was, they knew that he wasn't just a travel companion. Eventually, the music slowed, the drinks stopped being poured, and the company at the bar fizzled out. Patrons, ranging from tipsy to downright belligerent, made their way to their rooms for the night. August and I were among the last to do the same, and though his dance partner attempted to steer him toward her own room, I was able to reel him back in and toward our accommodations for the evening.

Our room at the inn was small and dingy, as was every room in that godforsaken shack, and I loved it. It might've been the fact that Prince August Theodoric III would've felt like he was crawling out of his skin in such a place that kept me so smugly satisfied, but I wouldn't admit that out loud. I had likely stayed in each one of those rooms at some point, and the place had become somewhat of a second home to me. The only saving grace was that the sheets were probably clean and there was a lock on the door; even though I loved some components of the Beast's Breath Tavern, it had none of those amenities. The first thing I did, however, was push the heavy wooden dresser in front of the door. I liked The End of the Road more than the Beast's Breath Tavern for lodging, but this place was unmistakably more dangerous when it came to other human-like creatures. No bloodthirsty wolves, just bloodthirsty people.

August stood back and watched me lazily, making absolutely no attempt to assist me in making the room safe. Perhaps he was secretly hoping that a nicer mercenary would come steal him from me after my decision not to lock him up with the rest of the captives. Or maybe he was just bitter that I hadn't let him run off with his new girlfriend; for all he knew, though, this one had fangs as well. "Who's Danny?"

I froze. Every hair on my body stood on end as the name tumbled from the prince's lips. It wasn't a name he was supposed to know, just like it wasn't a person he was supposed to know the existence of. I turned to him with narrowed eyes. "Come again?" My tone was icy.

"In the woods, the innkeeper mentioned Danny after you took down the Umbral. And this evening I heard you talking to the barkeep about someone named Danny. Who is he?" August's gaze was serious, deep and focused as he looked at me. I didn't like the idea of him knowing who Danny was, nor did I like the idea of him eavesdropping on my conversations. After all, why did he care?

Not much set me on edge, but the mention of my brother was one topic that could send me into an instant internal panic. I hid it to the best of my ability, but still found myself wanting to go off on August for even mentioning the name. It was none of his business. I wondered if Prince August had ever experienced a single troubling thought prior to our adventure. "What's it to you?"

Suddenly, August shrugged, then plopped himself down on the bed and began examining his fingernails. I couldn't tell if his sudden apathy toward the situation was genuine or not, though. "Figured I would've heard about a husband by now, if you had one… I mean, at first I thought you were with the elf guy at the tavern, but then you hardly even said goodbye to him. Just didn't picture you as the marrying sort, you know."

"I'm not. I'm the murdering sort," I told him, returning to arranging the room so that I didn't have to stare at his pompous ass while he interrogated me. Who was in charge here anyway?

The more I'd tried to show him grace in our arrangement and to humanize the prince, the more he seemed to take advantage of my kindness.

He ignored my joke, and in the moment, I felt some of the most distaste I had for him in our entire trip. I should've been happy for us to be returned to a state of separation, without the joking and comfort that had me doubting my decision to continue with my job. Instead, I felt a pang of discomfort that I couldn't quite place. He continued his prying. "So Danny isn't your husband then. A boyfriend, perhaps?"

I whirled on him. "Again, why does it matter who Danny is? And why are you assuming you get the bed?"

August continued his musing, only choosing to acknowledge my questions when it served his train of thought, apparently. He was seemingly unfazed or maybe even pleased with my irritation. I had a short temper, sure, but it usually took a lot for someone to get under my skin. It seemed to be a skill of August's, however. He pried further. "Maybe Danny is a woman? Danielle, then?"

"Not a woman," I said with a sigh.

My captive looked up from his hands in shock, as if I'd just denied some secret truth about myself. "Oh come on, no judgment here. I've slept with all sorts of people."

I groaned, entirely unsure why I was humoring this jackass with an explanation. "It's not about judgment or some... I don't know, discomfort with my sexuality, August. I'm not married, and Danny isn't a woman." I rubbed my face, then grabbed my backpack and tossed it on top of the chest. "As for who you've slept with... I know you have varied tastes. Or are you forgetting the night I captured you?"

"Now that you mention it, the details of that night are a bit foggy. Perhaps it has something to do with the potion you threw into my room, therefore knocking me and my guests completely unconscious for hours?" He tapped his chin in mock thoughtful-ness. "Or did you also hit my head on the castle wall on the way down? Hard to say; the whole night is a bit of a blur."

I couldn't help but laugh, and immediately, I scolded myself for being lulled into a casual, humorous conversation with him again. How did he keep doing that? "Didn't seem like there was all that much to protect in there, so I may have taken some liber-ties with getting you to the ground. No broken bones, though, right?"

"I suppose not." He inspected his arms, his forearms flexing under the thin fabric of his shirt, as if he were still determining his answer. "Not as far as I can tell, at least. You really should be more gentle with royalty, though."

"The instructions for your delivery didn't indicate the condi-tion in which I'm required to deliver you… concussion, no concus-sion, gaping Umbral bite, as long as you're alive it's all the same I suppose…" I mused aloud, pulling a length of leather cord from my bag. I turned to him again and shrugged. "They don't care, and neither do I, aside from the fact that broken bones might make you even more insufferable." The way I could lie through my teeth impressed me.

There was a moment of silence as August considered my state-ment, which had effectively ruined the light mood. "Are you sure about that? You fed me earlier. It would probably be cheaper in the long run not to. Not to mention the fact that you've ensured my comfort throughout our trip, whether you want to admit it or not." He met my gaze again, almost as if he were daring me to say that I cared about his survival.

I didn't. I couldn't. The second I started to care about someone whose surrender I'd make money off of, I was screwed; there weren't many other ways for me to make the money I did, the money I needed to. I wasn't exactly willing to give the matchmaker career path another try. This had to work, whatever weird way I was feeling about it aside.

"What do you know about budgeting, August?" I put my hair into a loose braid as we talked, then tied it off with the leather cord. My appearance wasn't really a big point of concern, but my hair had a mind of its own. I knew the answer to my question. Did he even know the value of the crystals of our continent?

"Nothing." August shrugged, then kicked his boots off and let them tumble off the edge of the bed unceremoniously. I imagined that he had a maid to pick those up back home in the castle. If I thought about it too long, I wanted to throw him off the bed and teach him what it was like to be anything but royalty, but instead, I didn't comment on it.

"Right, so if you have any sense of self-preservation, I'd shut up, eat the stew when it's offered, and don't tempt me with mentioning broken bones." The floor was hard, but it wasn't anything new to me. People often ask me how I sleep when my job is kidnapping and killing people. I slept like a rock and woke up in the exact same position I had fallen asleep in.

DANNY

MAX

The next morning, I woke to August's snoring, his limp hand hanging over the side of the bed into my space. I swatted it away and threw one of his boots at him to wake him, then we packed up in silence. Well, mostly silence.

"What are you doing?" August asked in alarm when I turned away from him and yanked my shirt over my head to change.

I tossed my old shirt – it was dirty and had a few blood splatters from hunting in the woods – into my bag on the floor in hopes that I'd at least be able to let it air out at our next campsite if I couldn't wash it. If we were staying at the End of the Road any longer, I would've taken advantage of Mary's generosity and let her do my laundry like she often offered to. Otherwise, it would be the next stream or creek. "Changing…" I told him over my shoulder. "I might not be a princess, but I prefer not to smell like ass for too long."

"But… I'm right here," August mused aloud. "And your shirt is off."

I groaned. "Then turn around!" Did everything need to be a

conversation? He'd obviously seen a woman in various states of undress before, and I had no clue why this was any different.

The room was silent until I heard the floor creak with his movement, which took several seconds longer than I expected. I pulled the new shirt, probably the cleanest thing I owned, over my head and got to work fastening all of my armor on top of it. My armor and accessories were worn, a mess of griffin leather that an armorer on the Isle of Wyrms had made for me many, many years ago. It served its purpose, but because it was custom made for me, I had to be sure that my body didn't change much over the years. One of the things I wanted to do with the reward money was get myself a new set. And the new boots. If August had been known by others based on his appearance, I might've invested in armor for him, but so far we hadn't seen any attempts to swoop in and snag or kill him.

I'd never introduced my kid brother and reason for my line of work, Danny, to anyone, and certainly not to one of my captives. But when the bartender once again urged me to check on him, I couldn't argue. I had to stop home on our journey. I tried asking Arvin for more information, but all he could tell me was that he'd heard "whispers" around the inn that led him to feel like I should go check on my brother. The fact that we were going off whispers didn't inspire confidence, but then again, there was no reason for people to be whispering about the person I tried to keep secret, so I was forced to look into it. Another delay.

Leaving Danny home alone was a gamble – he was only ten years old, and ten-year-olds don't know much about taking care of themselves – but I couldn't very well bring him on the road with me, where he was more likely to get into trouble or get both of us killed. My little brother was a bright kid, but he was still a kid; he didn't know how to blend in or keep quiet. He had managed to learn what was required to keep our household running while I was away, but beyond that I tried not to burden him with more responsibility than necessary. He deserved some sort of childhood. It was always my hope that, once I hit a windfall like the one I expected from the job with August, I could be home more often and allow Danny to really live his childhood… to play, laugh, and be carefree. We both needed that to heal the wounds in our hearts. Losing our parents had done a lot of damage to me, but imagining what it had done to my baby brother made me feel sick if I let myself think about it.

I hadn't told August where we were going or why and preferred to let him believe that Danny was some old flame that mutual connections still asked about. Perhaps I could slip into my house, see that everything was okay, and then return to our trip without any further questioning. I didn't believe that August was keeping track of anywhere we went either, but our home in the Wild Open was very secluded and for good reason; I couldn't think of a more wanted target than a successful mercenary or an easier way to threaten one than to get ahold of their family.

We set off toward my home later that morning, and as if on cue, August began with his questioning even before he had fully mounted Wraith. "The ferry's next, yeah?" Was he counting down the days until I turned him over?

"Sort of," I said, not bothering to look back at him lest I over explain like I'd formed a habit of doing lately. "We need to make one stop first."

"Ah," August said with a grunt, settling in behind me. "What will it be this time? Wolves? Mermaids? Tooth faeries? Always an adventure with Max the Menace."

"Nothing quite that exciting, let's hope." I clicked my tongue in a way that only meant one thing between Wraith and me: head home.

CAPTURED

AUGUST

*P*risoners really should have better rights, especially if they don't really know why they're being imprisoned. For example, if I was respected enough to not be tied up during our trip – though Max continued to threaten to do so – shouldn't I also be allowed to know where we were going? Was I not part of the team, so to speak? I grumbled to myself as we took off from the End of the Road Inn, where I'd had a better rest than the last lodge we'd stayed at, and found the patrons to be significantly more attractive as well. Don't get me wrong, the goblin bartender in the woods was a real gem, but not much to look at. Similarly, the elf there had been rightly stunning, but the way he looked at Max and sometimes me had me on edge. I couldn't figure out why. And jeez, who the hell was Danny? I'd now heard the name multiple times and been given next to no information about this apparently important person in Max's life.

The speed at which Wraith took us to our "one stop" and the seriousness in Max was alarming. Well, not the latter. Max had been undeniably serious during our entire time together, aside from the laughter I'd somehow coaxed from her by the river. That laughter had sent something through me that I couldn't place, just like it had when I heard her playing with Wraith by the waterfall. This last time had been different, of course, because I was the reason she was laughing. The sound had rivaled the most beautiful music I'd ever heard, and the burst of warmth it had sent through me was so intense that I had questioned if I'd been struck in the chest when it happened. What would she think if she knew about that? If she knew about what had happened after her bath in the falls? As we rode, I wondered if this was some sort of sick trick of the mind where I was coming to appreciate my captor, to identify with her despite her being the undeniable reason for my upcoming demise. I thought often of the fact that she had dressed my wound and stayed with me after I was bitten in the Grimmaker Woods... thought of the way she had gone out and killed the beast when she thought I was on death's door. I wasn't totally stupid, though, despite what Max may have thought; I knew that much, if not all, of her motivation was the money she'd get for my surrender. But there was something in the way she'd hugged me after she killed the Umbral that said she was glad I was alive, and not just because she would get reward money for me.

But this, this was different. Max was stiff as we rode, anchored to Wraith in a way I hadn't seen before. Normally she was comfortable on the horse, upright but sitting casually, the reins in her hand almost inconsequentially loose. We bolted across the vast land of the Wild Open, Wraith's speed causing my leg to ache as it jostled against her side. I said nothing, though, due to the severity of Max's tone and posture. This wasn't just a little side quest or errand. No, something was wrong. She was worried.

Miles went by without Max checking in. She didn't ask if I needed to stop, didn't point out a spot for us to fill our water or find something to eat. Eventually, I began to tire, but then we delved into a darker patch of woods where our pace slowed almost instantly. My captor reached over her shoulder, her first acknowledgement of me in hours, and handed me a strip of cloth. "Put it over your eyes."

"Pardon?"

Max's tone was clipped when she insisted, "You heard me. No time to joke around. I can't have you seeing where we're going."

I bit back every clever comment about kinks and surprises that I could think of and dutifully fastened the strip around my head. It felt like I'd be in trouble otherwise. The fabric smelled like Max's clothing. I hated that. It seemed every little detail was on the path to derail me and my focus, which should've been figuring out how to eventually escape. Shit, I'd really just been going along with the plan this whole time, even going so far as to put on a freaking blindfold while my captor led me through the woods.

As if Max could sense my internal dialogue, she added, "It's not about you. This is about keeping something important to me safe and private."

The air around us went mostly silent as we moved. No birds chirped, no critters rustled, and all I could hear was Wraith's cautious stepping and the consequent rustling of leaf litter as she walked.

"How much longer?" I asked, my voice like thunder after so much silence. I almost apologized. When she didn't reply, I asked again, more quietly this time. "Max?"

"Hush," Max scolded me. Before I could argue, she pressed something into my palm with one of her hands: a knife. "Just take it. This doesn't feel right." Her voice was low, cautioning. I gripped the weapon, not totally sure what she expected me to do with it, but concerned that she was giving her captive a weapon. How much trust did she need to have in a captive to arm them? Either that or she felt like she wouldn't be able to protect me herself, and the risk of me turning on her was low enough that it was worth it. Despite my formal training back home, I did not like my odds of beating another monster or mercenary with nothing but a boot knife. Personally, I'd had my share of life-or-death experiences on this trip and did not feel prepared for another. A chill ran through Wraith, and I froze, wishing I could remove my blindfold but also fairly certain I wouldn't want to see exactly what was happening.

We stopped. I didn't speak. I knew better. But when I heard Max draw her sword, I gripped the handle of my knife and wished Max would let me see what the fuck was happening. Above us, the branches of a tree creaked as if under pressure.

Then there was the sound of an arrow being drawn.

"What do you want?" Max said with a snarl that intimidated even me. "Show yourself."

By the time I thought to yank my blindfold off without Max's permission, she was gone. The sound of thundering hooves in the distance faded faster than I could've anticipated, and I was left sitting on Wraith, in the middle of nowhere, with nothing but a knife and a horse who was on the verge of a nervous breakdown.

"Fuck."

PLAYTHINGS

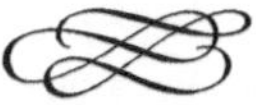

AUGUST

The way that Wraith screamed when we both had our wits about us was something I would not soon forget. "You're stressed?" I asked her, totally beside myself, as if she would be able to respond. "Get in line, girl! What the hell just happened? You didn't think to, I don't know, use your giant hooves to stomp whoever took her? You couldn't bite it in the ass with that big mouth of yours?"

Wraith's ears flattened as she glanced back at me over her shoulder.

"Okay, okay. Think." I slid forward on her back so that I was comfortably in Max's saddle, which was heinously small compared to the size of my ass, and picked up Wraith's reins. In any other circumstances, I knew she wouldn't listen to me; for example, if I had tried to leave Max and take Wraith for my own devices, I was certain I wouldn't get her to budge. I didn't doubt that she'd send me flying through the air if I attempted to push her. This seemed different, though. "I don't know what your magic words are, horse, but we gotta go."

She huffed, almost as if to question my judgment. In the end, though, I didn't really have a choice. I could get off of Wraith and walk – where, I didn't know – or we could try to find her person. "Let's go!" I told her again, irritation seeping into my voice. The longer we waited, the farther away she would be. "Go find Max!"

I wasn't prepared for the way that Wraith's tremendous lurch into action would practically send me flying backward, but I managed to stay on her back and right myself eventually. I didn't know where we were going, couldn't see or hear whoever had snatched Max right off of her horse's back, but it was clear that Wraith had some idea of where her person was. Maybe horses had some sort of dog-like sense of smell that I didn't know about.

When Wraith slowed a short time later, I could only guess that we were approaching a stopping point. Soon, a small building came into view. It was tiny and rundown and looked like a spot that might be used for a hideout, but not a general living space. A horse was tied up outside of the establishment, and Max's gear, including her belt with sword still attached, was lying on the ground out front as if they'd waited until their arrival to strip her of her weaponry. Despite her strength and skill, the thought of Max being captured and stripped in any way made me so uncom-fortable that it took a snort from Wraith to bring me back to the present. She paced in the woods near the building, keeping us covered in the shadow of the trees as if she were showing me our target. It was clear she knew her size and that getting any closer would give us away.

I slid off of the horse, landing in the soft dirt of the forest more quietly than I'd expected. The beast watched me closely, her onyx eyes following me as I stepped closer to the building, dipping behind a tree every few steps. I didn't have a plan. In fact, all I had was a knife and a limp and some strange allegiance to the woman who was trying to make money off of my bounty. It didn't seem like enough to save her from whatever the hell was happening in that building, but when Max's scream echoed through the woods, I decided I didn't need a plan.

Even when she was screaming in pain, I learned Max was filled with rage. "Let me go!" Her voice was a command, not a plea, and when I looked in through a dirty, cracked window of the building, I came upon her tied to a chair in the center of a desolate room.

"Uh, we just caught you. We ain't gonna let you go," grunted a big orc who stood directly in front of Max. He had a round belly that hung out from beneath his armor, and he looked like the type who could send someone like me through a brick wall with very little effort. Based on his commentary, however, he wasn't the brightest creature and was just there following orders from someone else. He looked confused by Max's demand, his bushy, single brow furrowed as he looked at her.

Max groaned and let her head fall back, her raven locks cascading over the back of the chair she was tied to. Hold up, why was I looking at her hair? "It's a thing people say when they've been captured, you fuckhead!" She shifted against her bonds, clearly more irritated by the exposure to asinine commentary than actually being tied up. "What do you want with me anyway?"

"You're taking all the high paying work, missy," a voice came from somewhere else in the room. "It's always 'Max the Menace this' and 'have you heard about Max?' and 'we don't want you guys, Max will do it and for half the price and faster, too!'"

"You're mad because I'm better than you," Max said plainly, not a hint of fear in her voice. "You're going to kill your competition."

"Uhhh, yep." The orc nodded. He had a club in one of his clunky hands, and he leaned on it as if it were a cane, then stumbled a little when it slipped against the wood of the floor.

"That seems kind of boring, doesn't it?" Max asked. "Not very creative."

"See, that's the thing! We're not going to kill you just yet. We'll make sure to have a bit of fun with you first. Best of both worlds, really," the man in the corner told her. My skin crawled at the comment. I couldn't take it lightly when men suggested "having fun" with bound and compromised women.

Max blew a gust of air upward, sending her hair flying out of her face as she eyed the captor who remained in the dark. "What kind of fun? So far I'm feeling pretty bored."

"Come on, you should know as well as anyone that people like us" – the tip of a blade poked out from the shadows and pointed between the three of them – "do what we do because it allows us to get paid for what we enjoy: hurting people."

"I don't like hurting people," Max said, her tone suddenly switching from teasing to dangerous. I realized it was true. I had yet to see Max garner pleasure from hurting anyone. "I'm just good at it."

"Oh, brother, and she doesn't even like hurting people! She does it from the goodness of her heart," the person from the dark commented, his tone sarcastic and annoyed. "Can you believe that?"

"Uh, no, I guess not, Striker," the orc said with a shrug. Goodness, he was really struggling to follow along. If Max had thought me an idiot, perhaps she would reconsider that title now that she'd met the orc. "Well, maybe? She did say that…"

"I find that hard to believe given your reputation, Max the Menace," the shadowed captor continued, dismissing his partner's commentary. "I don't think you'd be so good at it if it didn't give you a little thrill."

Max groaned again, wiggling in her seat, as if to say "get on with it already."

"What's got you in such a hurry?" the man in the corner hissed, then finally stepped out toward her, revealing himself. Striker was obviously human: average height, average build, a sharp, pointy nose, and black hair combed to one side. He looked like nothing extraordinary aside from the arsenal of weaponry he had lined on a belt around his waist and the cool, calloused air about him.

"I was in the middle of something when you interrupted," Max told him harshly.

The captor laughed, a shrill, irritating noise that made me hate him even more. "Ah, yes, Arvin said he'd come up with a story to send you this way. Good man."

From where I stood, I could see Max grit her teeth at the mention of her bartender friend. I supposed he wasn't so much of a friend any longer. She didn't respond to the man's comment and instead bit out, "So much exposition! Are you gonna beat me up or what?" Despite the seriousness of the situation, I had to stifle a laugh; even tied up and being threatened, Max had zero tolerance for the ramblings of other people. I would've at least tried to humor them and put off the inevitable beating, I thought. Oh, shit… the beating. I was supposed to be figuring out how to rescue her! I put a closed fist to my forehead, willing myself to come up with a plan while Wraith watched me from her spot in the brush.

I slipped away from the window and back to the front of the cabin where the man and orc had left Max's belongings. Once she was freed, she would want it all back. In the meantime, I could use her weapons to help get her. I loaded up her armor into one of the saddlebags on Wraith and then sorted through her weaponry. She didn't have much in the way of potions anymore, but her sword and the other small daggers she usually kept on her could be help-ful. I tucked them away where I could and returned to the window to find a sight that made my blood run cold.

As I peered through the glass again, I saw the man standing in front of Max, his fists balled in anger at his sides. She was laughing in his face. "I thought you said you were good at hurting people!" she taunted him, then spit directly at her captor. What came out of her mouth was pure blood, which landed on the man's cheek with a splat and then slid down onto his shirt. He had punched her while I was gone, hard. Her lip was split, and more blood was dribbling out of her mouth. Perhaps she had even lost a couple more teeth, which would undoubtedly join the molar that she had yet to magically reattach to her mouth.

"You little..." The man looked from Max's amused face to the blood on his shirt, which would surely stain. "Drog!" he then called to his partner, the orc, and turned away from Max to speak to him. I couldn't make out what they were saying.

Max laughed again, her head lolling to the side. Then she caught my gaze through the window. Her eyes widened and her laughter trailed off as she shook her head at me. I was fuming, but she mouthed: *not yet.*

I wanted to. I wanted to listen to Max, with all of her worldly knowledge and extensive experience in situations like this. After all, who knew how many times she'd been captured and then freed herself? But when the man turned back to her again, I could see the spiteful, sickening glint in his eye from a mile away. He poised his knife in front of her, and with a few quick slashes, had cut Max's shirt from her torso, fully exposing her chest. I'd only just watched her put that fabric over her body, and there it was, shredded and hanging by her bound shoulders. Her chest didn't heave; instead it stayed still with her caught breath. The last time I'd seen her bare like this, she'd been happily bathing by a waterfall. It hadn't been my sight to see then, but it felt even more wrong now, and I was sickened at the thought of this man seeing her so vulnerable and on display. He brought the blade down to the closure of her pants when my body overrode my brain, and I sprinted to the front of the cabin. I needed to get the men away from her, no matter the cost, even if it meant going against Max's wishes. She had, of course, told me to hold off prior to being violated by her captor, so maybe there was some wiggle room for me to make my own decisions.

I tried to spook the horse out front, but when it blew me off without a care, I took one of my blades and nicked it, which caused the creature to let out a loud neigh.

"Drog! Go see what that is!" Striker yelled from the cabin, thankfully momentarily distracted.

The orc chimed in with his predictable, oafish commentary. "That's a horse."

"Go see what's bothering the horse, Drog!"

I hurried to the porch of the cabin, then stood by the door out of sight. It was easy to hear Drog coming with his graceless, lumbering steps, and as he stomped out the front door, I caught him with an arm around the neck. Even though he was much bigger than me, my height helped in our brief physical struggle. Without thinking, I tightened my hold on his neck until he went limp and let him fall to the floor on the porch of the cabin. He would probably live; it was the man I had it out for.

I slid into the cabin to find the man still looming over Max and the laced-up fronts of her pants no longer laced; he had taken his knife and cut each cross section so that it was undone. The soft flesh of her lower belly was exposed, and he'd cut her there, too, a shimmering line of crimson obvious even from across the room. I didn't need to think too long to imagine what he planned to do once she was fully naked. The thought alone left me blinded with rage. I stood in the doorway, chest heaving with hateful breaths, and my teeth grit so hard they might've cracked.

Max looked alarmed. She was probably certain she could still handle herself just fine, and maybe she could, but we wouldn't be waiting around to find out. Not today, I told myself, not ever.

"Oh my, is this your blindfolded travel partner? I had assumed he was just a plaything," Striker mused aloud, looking me over. He turned back to Max briefly. "I thought you worked alone, Max the Menace."

"I do," she said through gritted teeth. "I don't have a partner."

"Shall we tie him up, too, so he can watch you become *my* plaything? What do you think?"

I held my blade so tightly that I could hardly feel my fingers.

"You don't need to do this, Aug—" Max began to say.

Striker was mid-turn back to me when I crossed the cabin in a few short strides and plunged the blade into his side, burying it to the hilt. My heartbeat pounded in my ears as the man groaned in pain, then slipped off of my knife and onto the floor, clutching his side. I watched him lie there, twitching a little until he stopped moving altogether. The rest of the room may as well have disappeared as I watched the last breath leave his disgusting body. I was shocked at how quickly the ordeal had started and finished, but could not have felt more relief in knowing that the scum on the floor would never be able to touch Max again.

"Shit." When the room returned to view following my emotionally charged outburst, Max was watching me with an expression I couldn't place. I sidestepped the puddle of blood leaking from my now-dead victim and untied Max without another word. She stood, too proud to cover her barely clothed body, and stormed out of the cabin, leaving me in the wake of my own destruction. Was she mad? I didn't understand. Sure, I had defied her instructions, but the man and his sidekick were about to assault her, then probably kill her. I couldn't have just stood by and let that happen, and for Max to believe I would made me feel sick; did she truly have so little trust in me? I stood there for what must have been several minutes, staring down at the lifeless eyes of the man who had almost killed Max, almost violated her before my eyes, and felt no shame. Should I have?

I found her outside by Wraith where she was rapidly shedding and replacing her ruined clothing while muttering something to her horse. I couldn't make out what she was saying, but she caught my eye as I approached. She discarded her torn clothes in a pile on the ground.

The blade still hung loosely in my grip when I tried to explain myself. "Max, I—"

"Don't." Max pulled her shirt over her body, then began replacing her armor piece by piece. I wondered when she'd request her weapons back. Was she afraid of me? Did she think I would use them against her?

I swallowed hard, then let the knife fall from my fingers to the ground as I watched her. "Don't what? I know that was… a lot, but I had to—"

She was so quick to respond that it nearly knocked the wind out of me. "This doesn't change anything, August."

I stood in open-mouthed shock for a moment before regaining the ability to speak. When I finally replied to her, I was frantic. "The hell it doesn't! We're out here risking our lives for each other, and it doesn't change anything? I can hear it in the way you say my name. You're not going to turn me in."

"I have to." Max didn't look at me when she spoke. She fastened her pauldrons, wincing a little as they rubbed over parts of her flesh that had been cut by her captor. Part of me ached to reach out, to soothe them, and I could no longer bring myself to resent those feelings. I had spent weeks stifling them, shoving them deep inside of me until they were weighed down with rage and jealousy and irritation. I didn't have the energy to keep them there any longer. But letting them come to the surface only meant that Max's hateful response cut deeper when she told me, "You saving my ass only means I can do it quicker."

My mouth fell open again. "What?"

"I would've escaped eventually and found you. You know that."

So cold. Icy. Frigid. Her words set me on edge. "Doesn't the fact that I came in and risked my life for you mean anything?"

Max looked down, tightening her last bit of armor and replacing her weapons. She bent down to grab the blade I had dropped before sticking it back into the strap on her thigh. "It doesn't change the fact that this is a job. It's my job to turn you in." The fact that she could just carry on, could just cut me down while dressing as if it were nothing, left me feeling hollow.

"Tell me why, then." I crossed my arms over my chest in indignation, a stance I used a lot back in my home kingdom.

"Why what?"

"Tell me why you're turning me in. The money? There are other ways to get that. You're gonna march me to my death for some fucking crystals? Tell me you feel good about that decision after the weeks we've spent together," I told her. "Look me in the eyes and tell me."

"The weeks we've spent together?" The look in Max's eyes didn't match her tone, but she pressed on with her blatant disdain. I had spent so much time trying to shove those thoughts deep down inside of me and now, with her admitting that it meant nothing to her, I felt like there was little left to lose. My life was already spoken for, so why not? "This isn't a fucking slumber party, August."

"Tell me why, Max."

WARRANTS

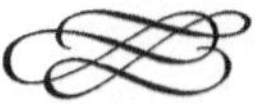

MAX

"You want to know why?" I spat, maddened by August's audacity. I'd captured him. We'd been on the road for weeks, and somehow, somewhere in his daft mind, he still thought he was in control. He still thought he was seconds away from being rescued by his royal family and handed over for a small fee. Or maybe he just thought he would charm me out of our arrangement, that I'd set him free out of the goodness of my heart because we'd become buddies. The seriousness of the situation, which involved his potential torture and death, seemed beyond his grasp. I glared up at him, daring him to keep pushing me.

August's gaze was dark and serious, with none of the humorous undertone he'd maintained during the first leg of our trip. "Yes! We're days away from you turning me over so yes, I'd like to know what I've been accused of. In fact, I can't believe it's taken this long!"

"Great," I bit out. I kept my eyes locked on his as I reached into my pocket and fished out a folded, tattered square of parchment that I'd been carrying around for months, ever since I started planning the capture of August III of Barrien. "Let's find out together."

"You haven't read it yet?" August's eyes were wide in surprise, in disbelief. How many times had he looked at me that way during this conversation alone? I didn't need to know what I was capturing someone for; I wasn't the law. I was a hired hand. That was all.

"I don't read beyond the name, bounty, and drawing if there is one," I told him. That had always been a rule of mine; I even avoided gossip about kingdom politics and other bounties. I'd looked at August's picture, sure, so I knew who to look for, but that was it beyond his name and the amount I'd be working for.

"Why the hell not?"

"It's not my job to form personal opinions about the people I capture. I don't get to pass judgment on them like that. I turn them over to the highest bidder, and they can let their own opinions fuel their decision making from there on out. If they end up being a royal dumbass during my time with them, then I typically judge them on that alone." I set my jaw hard as I looked at him; he had been a royal dumbass, and I wanted him to know it. I began unfolding the parchment, and August reached for it, but I turned away to block him with my shoulder despite the pain that came with moving. Between the cut my most recent captor had inflicted on my body and the injury in my foot which was still healing because I'd sacrificed my first aid potion for August, I was a walking wound. "Back off."

"No." August set his jaw and closed in on me. "I deserve to see it myself." He reached around me once more, and again, I held the paper out of reach. Unfortunately for me, he had me backed up against a tree, the base of which was wider than I could run around on short notice. When I looked up at August III, I kept my chin up and met his gaze with no fear in mine. It didn't matter that he was towering over me, that he was finally attempting to use his size to his advantage. I wouldn't let him overpower me. "Hand it over." His voice was dark and low, almost as if he believed he could intimidate me into submission. It seemed wrong of him to attempt to overpower me after what he had just rescued me from. I mentally gave him a pass because of how cruel I had just been to him. I hadn't heard this tone from him before, but I also hadn't seen him kill someone in cold blood before, so this part of our trip was certainly a learning experience for all.

"Back off," I repeated, louder this time. "Or neither of us will get to read it. What it says doesn't change the fact that I am delivering you to Emynor and claiming that bounty." I wondered momentarily how long it would take me to chew and swallow the parchment and if the effort alone would be worth how much it pissed August off.

August didn't budge. I was shocked that he'd lost his playful nature so suddenly and when he grabbed my wrist, pinning it to the bark of the tree with rough fingers, I gasped. I looked from my hand to his face and back again. When he spoke, it was as if he was trying not to yell. "I deserve to see what I'm being held captive for and what nominal fee has you willing to drag me across the continent, perhaps to my death." He plucked the paper from my clenched fist and unfolded it in front of me, but the spot where his hand had gripped my wrist tingled with sensation. His eyes darted across the page.

I folded my arms across my chest and waited, but was anxious to hear what it said. Perhaps I had avoided it for so long because I didn't want to know what was written on that paper. Maybe I had seen something in his eyes, in that stupid drawing of his stupid face, that made me want to believe he couldn't have actually done anything so terrible. I wanted him to be good… and the more we traveled together, the more I wanted to set the poster on fire and forget whatever he had been accused of. But there we were, with the truth at his fingertips and close to being aired. I didn't feel ready, but still I asked, "Well, what is it?"

The man's voice was hollow as he read from my crumpled parchment aloud. "Prince August Theodoric III – wanted by the kingdom of Emynor for his involvement in the mass genocide of the elven race within the city of Emynor and the deaths of over one thousand elves at the hands of his royal decrees. Reward for live delivery: 20,000 crystals."

My eyes widened, but August didn't budge.

"I didn't even know we were at war with Emynor." He spoke as though in a trance.

"I didn't hear anything about war," I said bitterly, snatching the paper from his trembling hands. Rage coursed through my veins, at the fact that he'd committed such atrocities but also that the information had been forced on me. I didn't want to know. I was supposed to be impartial, to do a job without inserting myself and my feelings into it. But that option was now long gone; now I had to react accordingly. "I heard genocide. Slaughter. That's not just war."

When August's gaze finally met mine, his normally golden eyes looked pale and shaken, like all warmth had been sapped from them. How dare he? How dare he act surprised that he'd been found out and that he was going to be held responsible for decisions he had made? "I didn't know," he said finally, his voice trailing off.

"The hell you didn't! It literally says you signed decrees that led to this! Have you ever even been to Emynor? Have you seen what's happening there?" I scowled, then shoved him away from me. The feeling of him so close to me, so close that he was cornering me, made me sick. "I can't be near you."

"N-no, Max, you know I haven't," he stammered as he took a

few unsteady steps back. "I don't even... I just sign the papers, that's my job!"

"Did you ever even read the papers that you sign, you twit?" I was shaking, rage coursing through every inch of my being.

As much as I wanted to believe that there was good in this man, especially with the tiny moments we'd shared, I knew then that it was impossible. Perhaps it was hypocritical because I was responsible for the death of many people, but the fact that he'd scribbled his name on some royal documents and that act alone had led to the death of thousands was inexcusable. Not knowing that he'd done it made it even worse. Did he just sign whatever was put in front of him and then return to his lavish, comfortable life? He'd never seen the spirit drain from the eyes of those he was responsible for killing, aside from the man inside of the cabin. I knew, based on what I'd heard in my travels, that the elves of Emynor had been treated brutally... and it wasn't just criminals and convicts like my victims were. No, the attack on the elves included everyone: the young, the old, the innocent. Based on the little I knew, it wasn't for anything worthwhile either. The elves were being slaughtered because they were different. How very like humans to destroy everything they couldn't understand.

When he didn't respond, I knew the answer. "Then you deserve everything that's coming to you," I said finally, the emotion draining from my voice. "I can't believe I... it doesn't matter. You have to see what you're responsible for."

"What about your quick stop here in the Wild?" August asked, still staring blankly at the parchment in his hands.

"It was a trap," I told him, grabbing my blade from the ground where he'd carelessly dropped it. I would need the rest of my weaponry back from him, too; he couldn't be trusted. The fact that Arvin had contributed to a setup that had me worried about Danny and almost cost me my life would have to be addressed another time. Perhaps after I had delivered August to Emynor. When he didn't respond, I snatched the parchment back from him and shoved it into my pocket as a reminder of why I had to stick to my plans. "Leave my weapons. Go get that other horse before the orc wakes up. It's time to go."

THE FERRY

AUGUST

The rest of the trip to Emynor was bleak. We didn't speak. The horse we had stolen wasn't nearly as hardheaded as Wraith and was convinced easily enough to follow Max and her horse, but it felt strange being so far from her. When we boarded the ferry and Max shelled out the additional crystals to bring the other horse along, I realized that we had stolen the creature solely because she couldn't stand to be near me; it was worth it to her to use up a precious resource so that I wouldn't be touching her. I couldn't blame her for that, nor could I blame the way she had hated me from the start of our relationship. What redeemable qualities could I possibly have if I would sign away the lives of thousands without even caring?

THE KINGDOM OF EMYNOR

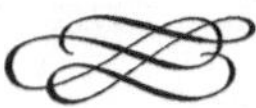

MAX

I'd never been to the kingdom of Emynor. I knew where it was, like I did with all kingdoms and cities in the continent, and I'd heard about it from Florian. He wasn't from Emynor, but he had joined together with the Emynorians in an attempt to protect their people, despite having "no side" as he claimed. According to Florian, Emynor had once been a thriving city of beautiful architecture surrounded by lush nature. What we saw upon exiting the ferry, however, was nothing of the sort. I'd given August one of my cloaks to wear because, despite the size not being quite right, we needed to keep him undercover. The actual castle of Emynor was surrounded by soldiers of Barrien, I'd learned on the ferry, who were patrolling the city and keeping its elves "in line." Actually getting into the castle would be a task in itself, and if any of Barrien's soldiers learned that I was transporting their prince, I'd be in big trouble. That was, if they even knew that their prince was missing, which remained to be seen when we were last in Barrien and the surrounding areas.

The city was desolate. I could not have imagined, based on

Florian's description, the amount of destruction we would come upon. Buildings were ruined, broken down by not only lack of care but active vandalism; windows were shattered, corners of once magnificent structures had crumbled under the weight of cannon fire. Even the homes of the common folk living in the surrounding city had seen better days. Many front doors looked like they had been broken in, and garden beds had been abandoned. Animals roamed the small streets of the city, but not nearly as many as one would expect from a thriving civilization. Were there no chickens being kept in yards? As our horses quietly made their way down the path winding through the town, Wraith stepped on something that let out a splintering crack, and when I looked back, I realized we had crushed an abandoned children's toy: a small wooden animal that was now a pile of shards. There wasn't an Emynorian in sight, only the occasional Barrien soldier walking by, bearing the symbol of their kingdom – a buzzard – the sight of which made me want to strangle my captive.

"It's there," I told August, pointing at a graying castle in the distance. "Just keep your head down until we're inside." He didn't reply. It was almost a relief. We hadn't spoken since our fight in the woods, and not hearing his voice only made it easier for me to distance myself from him. Despite days having gone by, August also hadn't taken any of the food I'd offered him, nor had he asked me for anything, silently or otherwise.

We were probably halfway through the surrounding village when our plans were derailed, as they seemed to have a habit of doing. It was the sound of a screaming child that hit me first and caused Wraith to stop in her tracks. The other horse, who we hadn't bothered to assign a name, huffed as he bumped into Wraith behind me.

"Mama!" the small voice screamed.

Then, there was another cry. A woman this time. Undoubtedly Mama. "Please, no! I'll do anything!" she screamed.

We didn't have to move any further to see what was happening because a Barrien soldier angrily burst from the front door of one of the small homes near us, dragging a young child of maybe three or four by the arm. The little boy screeched, thrashing in his captor's grip, and reaching behind him for his mother, who was racing out of the building behind them.

"Please! I'm begging you!" the woman screamed again, following close behind the soldier. "It's okay, my darling, it's okay," she assured the little boy, whose fair skin was bright red with his panicked screaming.

"Mama, please! Mama!" the child screamed again, pulling as hard as he could against the soldier's grip to reach for his mother. His dark curls were wet with tears and sweat and stuck to his small head, his pointed ears a sharp contrast against them.

When the soldier whirled on her, finally acknowledging her begging, he raised a staff with a glowing green tip toward her. Of course, why else would the kingdom of Barrien spend so much manpower on mining calcinite if not to use it on the one race it was most harmful to? "By order of the prince of Barrien," he barked, his thick helmet obscuring our view of his face, "this boy is our property now. If you'd like to keep your life and his intact, I'd suggest you stand down and tell your filthy elven brat to shut up!"

The woman flinched at the sight of the staff and immediately fell to her knees in front of the soldier. She reached out, grabbing her son's hand, and bowed her head. "Please, no, don't hurt him."

I swallowed hard as I watched, knowing that August was watching, too. These were the horrors that Florian had told me about, but I could not have imagined them even in my worst nightmares. I wondered what they would do with the child, what they needed young elves for, but couldn't dwell on the thought for too long because the sound of August's boots hitting the ground caught my attention. Before I could register what was happening, he took off toward the scene in a sprint. "Aug— ugh, wait! Don't!" I slid off of Wraith as quickly as I could and took off after him. He was going to ruin everything, and for what? One last attempt to prove that he was a good person despite all of this being his fault?

"Let him go!" August boomed as he approached the home of the elves who were being accosted. I was grateful when I caught up to him and saw that his hood was still up.

The soldier turned sharply, still gripping his young captive's wrist with no care. "Who do you think you're talking to?"

I grabbed August's shoulder in an attempt to pull him back. "Don't mind us," I responded. "We're just passing through."

"Then I'd advise you to mind your damn business," the soldier barked. "This area belongs to the kingdom of Barrien now, and I'm carrying out the prince's orders."

I tightened my grip on August's arm, but he shook me off and moved closer to the group. He seemed to waver a little as he closed the gap between them. "Surely you don't need this boy," he said. If I hadn't known better, I would've thought he was fighting back tears. "What'll it take for you to release him?"

The mother looked at us with hope glistening in her tired eyes, and I knew then that this scene would pan out even more unfortunately than it had started. The look on her face suggested that she had tried everything.

"Crystals? We can get them. Just please, let this boy stay with his mother. He's just a child, he's done nothing wrong!" I'd never heard August of Barrien beg nor stand up for anyone but himself before.

The little boy's lip quivered as he fought back more tears.

"You think you can bribe me?" the soldier scoffed, offended. "I should kill them both here for your meddling!"

The mother screamed. The boy cried again. She never let go of his tiny hand as she looked up at the guard and pleaded, "Don't hurt him. I'm begging you. Please. Take him, he'll be good, just don't hurt him."

I tried to drag August away. He wouldn't budge, but he didn't speak.

"Be quiet, Heath," the mother told her boy, stroking his tiny face with her free hand. "Be good. Be good. I'll be with you again." And when the soldier dragged the boy off, still glowering at us, his little hand finally wrenched free from his mother's.

We stood in silence as the woman sobbed on the ground outside of her home. There was another small toy near her, half-buried in the dirt where the young boy had probably been forced to abandon it and come inside. I wanted to comfort her, but we couldn't stay. I spun August around to face me, his huge form fighting each movement, and looked up into his cloaked eyes. "We need to go."

"I did this," August said, looking down at me with a horror in his gaze I could never have imagined. The pain in his face, so clear despite its shadowy veil, made my chest ache. His jaw was clenched in anger, heartache that I couldn't quite place. I couldn't imagine how it felt to hear that such horrors were being committed in his name, under his rule, because of decisions he had made. It didn't matter right then if he knew he was making them or not. He was the prince of Barrien, and he was responsible for this.

I couldn't stop myself when I replied, "You didn't know." He had told me that, though, hadn't he? "You would not have signed those orders if you had known." He was stupid. A big, stupid, idiot. He had been careless, yes. But he hadn't known that this would be the result of his carelessness. If I had learned anything about him during our time traveling together, it was that he had been exposed to very little during his life, and because of that, he was the perfect, clueless cover for whatever his parents had been using him for. Sure, he was an idiot, but he wasn't a monster. The pain in his eyes said it was impossible that he would've wished this hurt on anyone. "But we need to go."

"Where?" he asked. "Where could we possibly go?"

I swallowed hard. "I don't know. Away, before they realize who you are." I reached up to brush a glistening tear from his cheek, which I hadn't seen creased with a smile in days. I wouldn't have been surprised if he never smiled again. The thundering sound of hooves echoed somewhere down the path we were on. "We need to go," I said again, pulling his sleeve back toward our horses.

Before he turned to go with me, he looked at the elven mother, who hadn't left her spot on the ground in front of her home. "We'll get him back," August told her with the same confidence he had when he used to speak about his own exploits. "I promise you." We didn't stick around to hear her response, and honestly, I had no clue what the hell August was promising her. How could he say that with the state of Emynor? We'd only just gotten here, and already we were probably wanted by the soldiers thanks to August's bold move. I couldn't blame him, but I also didn't know what he was thinking.

The sound of horses became louder as I dragged him back to Wraith and instructed him to get on her behind me. We would be faster together. We'd have to leave the other horse.

"I have an idea!" August yelled behind me as we took off back down the road.

"Keep it to yourself until we get to the ferry, you big idiot, or we won't make it alive for me to hear it!"

IT TOOK us a long time to catch our breath after boarding the ferry and even longer to find the gall to look at each other and speak. The absolute terror and sadness in the elven mother's eyes would not leave my mind for many, many days to come, especially when I imagined the little boy as my own younger brother. I felt sick. I felt empty and full of rage at the same time. I wished Florian had better prepared me, but I could also understand why he hadn't; despite his callousness, he cared enough to know how much the description would hurt. Not only that, but when I asked about Emynor he had no idea I was going there. I'd kept the job and August's identity a secret in order to keep Florian from stepping in and taking over. He may have killed August himself had he known that was who I was transporting.

After continued silence, August jumped into his idea without any introduction. "If I have enough power to sign decrees that can lead to that" – he gestured into the distance where the shore of Emynor faded away – "then I must have the power to reverse it."

"I doubt it, since you didn't even know that was happening to begin with. It seems like they're using you as a cover," I thought aloud, not considering how painful that suggestion might be. After what we had witnessed, I didn't know if I had the emotional energy to censor myself, especially because my feelings toward August were still so at war with each other.

"As a prince, maybe not," August mused, still staring off. "But if I were king…"

I laughed. "You think they'll let you waltz in and make that happen?"

August shook his head. "No, but when is the autumn equinox?"

"Soon," I told him, not understanding the correlation at all. I chewed on a piece of dried fruit that I'd stored away in my saddle-bags at one of our stops. "Two weeks, maybe a little longer."

"Can we make it back to Barrien by then?"

"If we don't stop at all, maybe," I told him honestly. "There wouldn't be any time to heal from wolf attacks or do many side jobs, which we'll need in order to get by. Why?"

"There's a masquerade ball then, in Barrien, and my parents always use it to make big announcements."

"You think they're still going to hold that ball even though you're missing?"

August shrugged, and sadness radiated off of him in oppressive waves. "I don't think they care that I'm missing. I'm sure no one has been informed. The soldiers in Emynor didn't seem to know that the prince they're serving was kidnapped." He swallowed hard. "Besides, no one knows what I look like, and it's a masquerade. It would be easy to create a stand-in for me."

"Sure." I nodded, going along with his story for the sake of humoring him. Wraith huffed nearby. "Right?"

The prince was unfazed by our skepticism. "Just like it would be easy for me to sneak in undetected."

"Okay," I mumbled, still chewing. "So you're going to… what? Walk in and announce your new plans? Plans that go against everything they clearly believe in."

"We're going to go, you and I," August told me, popping up from his spot on the deck of the boat and beginning to pace.

"Uh huh, I can't dance," I commented, imagining myself in a ballgown. Not a good look for me personally. I also didn't see how I'd suddenly gone from capturing August for a bounty to planning to help him overthrow a kingdom, but I didn't mind. If not knowing how to dance was the biggest issue, maybe we could work with it.

"I'll teach you," he said, glancing at me with a nod that said "obviously." "And we're going to announce my coronation."

"Sure, right, of course."

"In front of everyone, where they can't take it back or play it off like I'm being foolish."

"Right, they'll love that." I nodded, imagining the look of an entire royal court when the prince drops a surprise coronation on them. "And if they resist somehow?"

"I'll figure that out."

"It's a great goal," I told him, standing up to join him in his animated pacing. I put a hand on his shoulder to stop him so that he would be forced to look me in the eye and slow down. As much as I could appreciate his large scale of thought and his desire to undo everything that had been wrongfully done in his name, it was a stretch, especially for someone who had thus far been kept out of actual royal dealing aside from when his signature was required. Not only that, but the logistics of getting back into Barrien, let alone into a royal masquerade ball, were not promising, especially given that we were across the continent. "It's admirable, really. But I don't—"

August's gaze was fierce, his jaw set hard, when he promised me, "That little boy will be back in his mother's arms, Max, if it's the last thing I do."

THE END OF THE ROAD, AGAIN

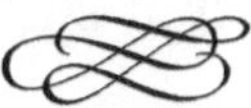

MAX

"This shithole again," August said with a grunt as we entered the inn.

"Hey, this is my favorite shithole. It's also the only shithole with vacancy on this side of the river, so you'll have to deal with it unless you want to sleep in the woods," I told August. I rummaged in my pockets again for a few of my remaining crystals, then tossed them on the counter as I'd gotten used to. I wasn't sure why I was trying to lighten the mood with jokes. Things weren't great. What we'd been through was not great. But while it was shocking and new for August, it was pretty commonplace for me and the people it was happening to on a regular basis. It felt okay for me to joke. Meanwhile, he looked like his world was crumbling. "One shithole – I mean, one night, Seymour."

"Only got one bed, Max." This time Seymour didn't bother looking up from his ledger. I wondered if he thought I'd gotten lost or forgotten where I was taking my hostage; I usually only passed through once on any particular job. In reality, he probably didn't care. Hell, he hadn't even noticed us calling his inn a shithole.

"Yeah, yeah, fine. Can't afford two anyway." I waved him off, my exhaustion finally setting in. I could sleep wherever as long as I was somewhat horizontal. We'd made one bed work before, we could figure it out this time. In fact, it probably wouldn't be the last time we'd have to scrounge to make lodging work if we were traveling all the way back to Barrien. He didn't mention any favors for Wraith this time, but I knew that she'd at least be tied up and fed for the night.

Before we dragged our fatigued asses up to the room, I made a stop at the bar to confront my old friend, Arvin. Despite the chaos and heartbreak of the recent leg of our trip, I had not forgotten the run-in with his people on my way to check on Danny, nor had I dismissed just how close they'd come to my home in the Wild Open. The closer they'd gotten to the house, the closer they were to Danny. I had to know if I should be worried about his safety; mine was one thing, but I had a responsibility to Danny. Arvin knew this, so the fact that he'd disrupted our trust for who knows what kind of payment had me on edge. It was impossible to truly trust anyone. "Go on up without me," I told August, tossing him the key. I didn't bother to see if he caught it, but it probably looked like a pretty cool exchange if he did. If not, it wasn't like we could appear to be a more disjointed pair. When I approached the bar, Arvin automatically stiffened at the sight of me. Ah, yes, he hadn't quite been expecting me, though, had he? I was supposed to be dead in a ditch somewhere.

"Hey, Max," he addressed me, but his nerves were obvious in his expression. He looked from me to another patron and busied himself with preparing their drink order.

"Hey, Arvin," I responded in a mocking tone. "Surprised to see me?"

"Now why would I be surprised to see you at the bar of your

favorite inn?" he asked, still far more focused on the drink he was pouring than the person he was speaking to.

I pulled up a seat at the bar and set my knife down on the worn surface. It was a common enough sight; patrons of the bar were often in the same field of work as myself and kept their weapons close by. Only Arvin would see it as a threat. "Oh, man. What a great question. I think—"

"You know why, you stupid fuck," August cut me off, and before I could protest, he was sitting beside me at the bar. Without even looking at him, I could tell that he had a wild look in his dark eyes. The events of that day had undoubtedly left him feeling like a loose cannon. I stifled a groan and told myself that we really needed to seem like a united front for this to be at all intimidating. I kind of liked August's emotional reactivity, but still... Arvin may have known why, but August didn't.

Arvin's tone immediately changed, and he looked annoyed at my traveling partner's audacity. "Yeah?" He folded his beefy arms across his chest and looked August over as if to challenge him. August was big, but Arvin was bigger, and he'd seen a lot more in the way of fighting; the man was covered in tattoos and scars and was used to throwing unruly patrons out with one hand.

August, in all of his bullheaded bravery, didn't miss a beat. I suppose he didn't have much left to lose at this point. "Yeah, you heard me!"

Oh, for fuck's sake, August. "Yes," I interjected. I kept my voice low when I added, "And if you don't want us making a big scene in front of the entire inn or better yet, slitting your throat in your sleep, I need you to answer my next two questions honestly."

Arvin sneered.

"I swear I'll do it, Arvin," I told him. "This is one job I'll do for free, as a little gift to myself. A treat, even. I'll do it, and I'll love it. I don't care if it means I don't have a favorite inn anymore." A shitty bed and shitty beer meant nothing when it came to getting my point across, especially if that point was related to Danny's safety and the privacy of my home.

The patron Arvin had just served looked over at us with a grunt. "Ya good, Arvin?" I recognized him as another bounty hunter. Maybe he knew the lovely Striker, too. What fun.

Arvin nodded and brushed him off, then moved closer to me and leaned on the bar top with his hands. The surface groaned a little under his weight. "What do you want?"

I looked at August and jerked a thumb toward a booth. "Wait for me," I told him. I was relieved when he complied, but didn't know how long it would last. When I turned back to Arvin, I spoke quickly and kept my voice low. "I need to know how much you told them about Danny and the house. Do they know where it is?"

Arvin shook his head. "No, of course not."

Rage bubbled inside of me. "What do you mean 'of course not'? You led me into a trap under the guise of my little brother being in danger. There is no 'of course not.'"

"That wasn't personal. It was just business. You know I wouldn't put Danny in danger," he argued. "I only told them the path you'd be taking, not where you were headed. And believe me, Max, you'd have done the same for the price they were offerin'."

"I don't give a damn about the price, Arvin. This is beyond personal. Trying to have me killed is putting Danny in danger. Who do you think is going to take care of him if I'm dead?"

Arvin tried to argue. "Max, I —"

"You think he can take care of himself, Arvin? He's ten years old." I gripped the handle of my knife with a trembling hand. It was difficult to force the image of my little brother from my mind, alone and wondering why I hadn't come back to take care of him, to check on him, to tell him that everything was going to be okay. I shoved the thought into the back of my mind, away where I kept all of my horrific fears like the image of the little elf boy being ripped from his mother's arms, and tried to detach myself from it when I asked, "Were you gonna go out there and explain to him why he's gonna starve to death because you had me killed for a few crystals?" I couldn't cry in front of all of those bounty hunters, but the thought made me want to.

Again, he opened his mouth to protest. "No, I—"

"Shut the fuck up," August butted in, once again overstepping. I hoped he hadn't heard the details of our conversation.

"No, you shut—" Arvin told him with a glare.

"No, you shut the fuck up!" the prince practically yelled. Our only saving grace was the high volume of the bar and the fact that most people probably thought he was just another drunk patron. Part of me wished he would go back to his old self and get distracted by some lady with her tits out so that I could handle the threats on my own.

We're both going to be killed tonight. I can just feel it. "Both of you, shut the fuck up. August, stand down. Arvin, you pull this shit again, and I will cut out your eyes and feed them to you, okay?"

"No seasoning! No salt, no pepper, nothing! Just eyes," August added, looking mighty proud like he'd actually contributed.

Arvin shot him a glare that caused me to seriously question the effectiveness of my threat, but I had clearly lost control over the situation. The best I could do was make sure that Arvin knew I was serious on the way out. Even though he didn't know exactly where our home in the Wild Open was, he knew enough to tell people where my path was, and that, as far as I was concerned, was too much. Perhaps it wasn't safe to let him live. I'd have to sleep on it and decide in the morning.

I didn't trust any drink Arvin would pour me from then on out, so we left the bar without partaking. We made our way upstairs and into our room, which looked unsurprisingly exactly like every single other room I'd stayed in there, and went to bed without really speaking. It was my turn to sleep in the bed, thankfully, and I was grateful for the luxury even though it was just an under-stuffed mattress, thin pillow, and sheets with more than a few holes in them. I was so drained from the day's events that I barely managed to shed my weaponry, and my head had hardly hit the pillow when I drifted off to sleep.

IT WAS LATE, the candle on the nightstand having burned out long ago, when August's scream roused me from my sleep. I sat up with my heart racing. The room was stifling hot because we'd been trying not to open any windows; it was a habit I'd picked up as both a mercenary and someone responsible for the safety of other people. It had been different at the Beast's Breath Tavern when I thought he was on death's door; if someone broke in and tried to steal him from me then, it didn't seem like it would've mattered. But now, even the smell of August's panicked sweat lingered in the air. When he spoke again from the dark, his voice was pure agony. "No... no, don't! They didn't do anything, I didn't know!"

I scrambled from the bed in time to hear another patron hit the shared wall and throw a variety of curses our way from their own room, but the sound alone did nothing to rouse August from his sleep. "August!" I half-whispered, half-yelled at him, searching the nightstand in desperation for another candle. I didn't want to step on him, but I had to wake him up as quickly as possible. We couldn't afford to be kicked out of our only option for lodging because of a bad dream. It would be many, many miles to the next safe place to rest, which no longer included the Beast's Breath just in case Florian was on the lookout for us. "It's just a dream… wake up!"

A choked sob escaped from wherever he was in the dark. "Please, please stop! This isn't right! You can't do that!" I had never heard him cry. Not even close.

"Oy! Keep it down with your kinky shit!" the patron in the room next to us yelled. A loud bang followed, and it sounded like they'd thrown something at the shared wall, perhaps a boot or a belt, that clanged to the floor loudly.

When I couldn't find a light source, I gave up and slid onto the floor next to a thrashing August, whose makeshift floor bed was in full disarray, his blanket tossed to the side and tangled around one leg. By the light of the moon peeking through our cracked curtains, his pained expression was clear. His dark hair was plastered to his forehead and neck with sweat, and his chest, bare from stripping down for sleep, was heaving with labored breath. He thrashed again, still asleep, as if he were fending off an invisible attacker, and the chain of his necklace jingled. I reached over him to pin his arm down before he hit the wall or nightstand. The last thing we needed was a complaint; I had a reputation and relationships to uphold, and if we were called out of our room for a confrontation, we were risking our safety even more. When he didn't calm down, I shook my head and climbed atop him to pin his arms down with my thighs.

I could tell he'd opened his eyes only by the light of the moon reflecting from the window onto them. They really were like little pots of honey, glistening and warm, but this time they were terrified. "Max," he whispered, barely audible amidst both of our panting.

"It's okay, August. It was just a dream," I told him with a tenderness I'd only ever used with Danny before. The world had been too hard to draw it from me in anyone else's presence, least of all a captive prince, but now I couldn't stop myself from feeling for him.

"A nightmare," he corrected, squeezing his eyes shut. A stray tear squeezed from one eye and slid down his flushed cheek. "A horrible nightmare. It was so vivid."

I reached out and brushed his hair from his sweat-slicked brow before I could talk myself out of it. It was nice to stop thinking about what I should be doing and just do what felt right... and with the fog of recent sleep, I didn't have to argue with my brain. "It's over, it wasn't real." I slid down to release his arms and found myself on his lap, but disregarded the strangeness of our positioning.

"It's not over. It's happening right now... because of me." His gaze contained a depth of rage and self-loathing that I never would've associated with the prince of Barrien. The expression on his face was so far off that I could almost see the reflection of the horrors we'd witnessed just the day before replaying over and over in his mind. Was he imagining Heath, the little boy, who was undoubtedly alone and afraid at that very moment? Had he seen the mother's face in full view like I had? Did he recall the pale-knuckled grip she'd tried to keep on her son's tiny hand? Even with the things I had seen in my job, it took a lot for me to shake the vision from my mind. It was only thanks to my sheer exhaustion that I had avoided being haunted in my sleep like he was.

"You can't change the past," I told him seriously, believing every word; I wasn't one for sugarcoating, nor did I have a reason to do so for this man, a prisoner of mine for whom I was supposed to have no attachment or sentiment. But I also wasn't a total monster and felt that I could be objective about most things. He'd shown that day that there was a heart somewhere under that pompous exterior. "And you're working on changing the way things are now. That's all anyone, including yourself, could hope for in these circumstances."

We sat in silence, the room filled with our breathing only, until I realized that I still had him pinned beneath me. I'd had plenty of people in this very situation, but only briefly before I shackled them or knocked them out and loaded them up onto Wraith for delivery. When I realized I'd been straddling him for so long, heat rose to my cheeks, and all of my self-assured comfort went out the window. "You should… get some sleep," I finally choked out, leaning sideways to grab the edge of the bed and swing my leg back over August's body. Perhaps if I didn't say anything about it, we could pretend it never happened. "I think we can risk cracking the window a little bit if it's too warm in here… I can lie under the sill to keep watch, and you can take the bed. I know how hard the floor can be on your back. This might be the last time we have access to a bed for a while." I was rambling. Since when did I give a shit about this man's comfort, even if I was a human with feelings? He'd spent his whole life on a plush mattress. Surely a few more nights of sleeping on the floor wouldn't kill him.

I was blindsided when August gripped my thigh and pulled me back on top of him, locking eyes with me so intensely that I struggled to gather my thoughts. "Stay," he said. And before I could respond, he pulled me down into a kiss. The gesture had none of the cockiness, none of the belligerent force that I'd come to associate with August of Barrien. His mouth was soft and gentle, and when I pulled away, we stared at each other breathlessly for a moment. "The bed or the floor, I don't care. Just stay with me."

"Okay."

His lips slanted over mine again, his tongue lapping its way into my mouth, and he tangled his fingers in my hair as he pulled me further down on top of him. His arms, rugged with muscle that I'd avoided staring at before, held me captive against his body until he traced his hands down my sides. My head spun in response. When he held me so tight that I winced at the pressure against my still-healing wounds, he withdrew in an instant and apologized against my lips. "Max, shit, I'm so sorry."

"It's okay," I told him, returning his hands to my body. "Don't let go." I wanted to kiss him again, but something about the way his face looked in the moonlight gave me pause. This was not the prince I had kidnapped; I had to believe that, or being in such a position with him would go against every standard I held for myself. The way his eyes looked desperate for comfort, for under-standing, and for forgiveness ran a stake through my heart. He didn't know. He couldn't have. Even as ignorant and disconnected as I had once thought him to be, he wasn't a monster; he would not have stood idly by when such horrors were done in his name. Now, more than anything, I could see he was desperate for comfort. I wanted nothing more than to be the one to give it to him. When I pressed my lips against his again, he took me in gratefully.

"I need to be part of something pure," he told me between kisses, and I knew he meant me. As violent and ruthless as I was, I had been honest with him from the start, which was more than anyone else in his life could say. At any given moment, he had the same information I did, no matter how painful. "For once in my life."

I nodded, then sat upright on his lap to pull my top off. It joined his shirt somewhere on the floor. I'd never been insecure about my body, but something about the closeness of this encounter had every move feeling like it was magnified.

The sharp gust of breath that left the prince's lips surprised me. "You've seen a million naked women, August." I couldn't help but laugh a little. The last thing I had expected to draw a gasp from him was the naked figure of the opposite sex.

"This is different," he admitted, but he didn't match my tone or humor.

"How?"

August was silent and simply watched me in the dim light, his gaze raking over my exposed upper half. The heat in the room was unmistakable, and for a second, I wished he had let me crack the window; it was hard to tell if I couldn't breathe because of the summer warmth or because of the way his eyes settled on me and seemed to look right through me.

"You don't need to be the bachelor prince with me," I told him, feeling exposed in more ways than one.

"That's why it's different," he told me with a sigh and rested his hands on my thighs, almost as if he were scared to give in and touch me elsewhere. "That's all I know how to do, all I know how to be... and I know you deserve better than that."

Again, I was surprised by his blatant confession. This felt to be the most honest he'd ever been with anyone, including himself. I suppose it was to be expected given the events of the day, but even so, it felt like a massive emotional undertaking. At the same time, it felt like he was selling himself short; in the weeks I had known him, he had grown exponentially beyond a bachelor prince. "That's okay," I assured him, taking one of his hands in mine and pressing it to my bare breast. To my surprise, the contact just felt right. "Don't overthink it. Just be whoever you are... and touch me."

His fingers flexed against my chest, and he groaned, a sound so deliciously agonizing that I thought the rest of my clothing may burst into flame. "It's practically all I've thought about, Max," he told me. He sat up so that we were face-to-face and kneaded my chest with his big, rough hands, then dipped his head to suck on one of my nipples.

I whimpered a little, loving the way the heat of his mouth

enveloped me. "Yeah?" I reached between us to undo the ties of his slacks before they tore on their own. I was desperate to set him free.

"I say your name while I'm stroking my cock," August told me when he looked up again, his molten gaze searing into my flesh. A chill coursed through my entire body at his admission. "And I hate myself for it. You deserve better."

"Don't." I pulled him into a kiss to silence him. He was spiraling. I couldn't let him go too far, or we'd be knocked off our path, perhaps forever, and I knew at that moment that I needed this with him. Soon I had his trousers undone, and he fell into my palm, fitting perfectly in my hand. I stroked him as I sucked on his lip, and the way he groaned against my mouth caused heat to bloom in my core. To have any effect on him, let alone have him hot and hard in my palm, had me feeling triumphant and powerful.

"Max." He panted, then squeezed his eyes shut and pressed his forehead into my shoulder.

"August, I'm here."

Before I could do anything else, he'd flipped me beneath him, finally flexing some of the brute strength that came with his powerful, muscular body. My breath left me in a sharp gust, and I marveled at the way he towered over me, his pants halfway down his thighs, and his cock, hard and ready for me, standing at attention. "I need to taste you," he told me as he worked to slide my own pants off of me. I lifted my hips to help him, marveling at the fierce intensity in his expression. "I need you to come on my tongue... need to make you feel good. God, even thinking about it is too much. Do you see how hard I am for you? Do you feel me? It's been like this, Max, for weeks. I can't fight it anymore."

"Don't fight it." I gasped at the boldness of his statement and nodded my breathless consent. It was hard to decipher how much of his need was because of the self-hatred he'd developed in the past day, but I hoped silently that he would still want those things, still want me, when whatever was burning within him settled. When he folded me over and teased my quivering slit with his fingers, then his tongue, it was all I could do not to scream out and agitate our neighbors again. "Oh, August..." He hooked my legs over his shoulders and buried his face between my thighs, eating me like a man starved.

When he pulled away, his face glistened in the moonlight, and he looked down at me like he'd transformed into some unbridled, unrefined animal. "Look at you... so stunning and ready... so wet."

"Just for you," I told him, desperate to encourage the walls between us to fall down. I didn't have it in me to tell him just how reciprocal the feelings were. Instead, I tried to show it with enthusiasm.

"That may be the most beautiful thing I've ever heard," he told me, rubbing the bundle of nerves between my thighs as his gaze remained stuck on mine. "Look at me, Max. Ride my face when you come. Then I'm going to fill you with my cock."

I reached between my thighs to tangle my fingers in his sweat-slicked curls and nodded; the sound of his gravelly voice talking me through our interaction was enough to send me over the edge on its own. I fought to keep my eyes open, to appreciate the enthusiasm in his eyes as he dove between my legs again and fucked me deep with his tongue, only pausing to suck on my clit until a shuddering orgasm tore through my body like a violent storm. I fought to stifle a cry of pleasure, and he reached up to shove his fingers, wet with my own dampness, into my mouth. "Shhh," he told me lovingly as he gripped my thigh with his other hand. "I've got you."

When the prince finally shook his pants the rest of the way off and plunged into me, I arched my back into the floor of the inn room and gasped. I was wet and needy and desperate for him, and still, the sensation of our bodies colliding so intensely rocked me to my core. I crushed my eyes shut and fought against the way I felt so totally on display with him, so open, so vulnerable, and instead of letting me, August took my face in one of his rough hands. My legs were on his shoulders again, and he leaned forward to press a soft kiss to my lips. "Maxine, stay with me, please," he said with such genuine earnestness that I could've cried. He was huge and covered me so fully... between his size and the way he spoke to me, as if it was the first time he'd cared so much about the other person in the interaction, I finally felt like I was being taken care of by someone other than myself.

"I'm here," I said breathlessly.

"Take all of me, Maxine," August said with a groan, my ankles on either side of his handsome face. How long had I denied the beauty of his squared jawline and the way his eyes creased with pleasure? I wanted to lick the cleft of his chin. With each thrust, I felt his muscular shoulders flex beneath my calves and his balls slapping against my ass in perfect rhythm. I wanted to take all of him, I needed more, so I wrapped an arm around his neck and pulled him down to meet me. I kissed him softly at first, meeting the pace and intensity of his thrusting. As he began to hammer into me, I met him there, nipping at his earlobes, running my hands down the thick, defined ridges of his back. When he slowed for a moment, I grabbed his ass to urge him forward. I needed him, needed more, needed every last bit he was willing to give and then some.

"Max... it's too good, I can't..." August's lips were parted in frantic panting, and the boulders of his biceps were tense with his impending orgasm. I chased it with him. I wanted to get there with him, to hear every delicious cry of pleasure, to absorb everything he gave me in those vulnerable, passionate moments.

"I know, ah, God, that's perfect. Don't stop," I nearly begged him, reaching up to run my hands over his hard chest and dig my nails into his pecs. Sweat dripped from his brow onto my bare chest, and I savored it, feeling so heated myself that I was shocked it didn't cause a sizzle. "Yes," I whimpered. "Yes, yes, yes, please, don't stop!"

When the heat of his own climax surged through me, filling me with warmth, I held on to August for dear life. The throbbing of his cock inside of me spurred my own orgasm on, and I pressed my forehead into the prince's neck as I came, overwhelmed by the way it surged through every inch of my body. I felt stripped, laid bare before this man that I had barely known weeks before, that I had despised weeks before, and felt like I was fighting back tears that I couldn't explain. I wanted nothing more than to fall into his arms for the remainder of the night, but when August collapsed next to me, the room went silent. We lay in the quiet of our post-coital panting until our hearts slowed, but when I realized my partner wasn't moving, I ran a hand gently over his chest. "August?"

He shuddered in response.

I was almost scared to ask. "Are you okay?"

"Yeah, fine," he grunted. Then he rolled over so that his back was to me. "You should get some rest."

I lay there for as long as I could stand the painful silence, then got off the floor and got dressed after struggling to find my clothing in the dim light of the moon. My partner, now miles away emotionally, didn't move, even when I pulled my panties from underneath him. I wanted to run, wanted to let August loose and never see his face again, but we both knew that wasn't an option, and that fact made it all the more painful. When I slid out of the room, he said nothing. I made my way to the stalls outside of the inn and sat with Wraith until I was able to steady my nerves.

You're a mercenary, Max, I told myself. *Not a wife, not a lover, not the fantasy of some rich prince. You're a killer. That's it.*

When I returned to the room, August was still on the floor, but he had dressed himself. I couldn't tell if he was awake or not, but I couldn't bring myself to look at him long enough to find out. It almost felt like I'd imagined everything we had just done. I slid into the bed, fully clothed, and pulled the thin, scratchy blanket up around my neck. When desperate sadness overtook me, I bit my lip hard and told myself that it was almost time to get moving again.

WHEN THE SUN began to rise and peek through the curtains of our shared room, I hauled myself out of bed and started packing up to leave. We had a long way to go yet again. I wasn't sure how fate had smashed the two of us together in what was starting to feel like an endless voyage. The sooner I could get us to the end of it, the better. "Tell me about that necklace of yours," I said.

"What does it matter?" August shook his head in frustration, and for the first time since I'd met him, he seemed genuinely unsure of himself. "We need to talk, Max. I... I need to talk to you about last night."

"There's nothing to talk about," I told him, pulling my hood up around my neck as I repacked my bag. "Forget it, August. Message received... last night was a mistake. You had a hard day and picked the wrong way to... be comforted about it. I don't know, it doesn't matter." I had made a mistake letting him in, getting close to him, and I wouldn't be doing that again. There was nothing he could say that would make me feel otherwise. I sat on the edge of the bed to pull my socks and boots on. "But that necklace, I need to know what it is."

August sighed and rubbed his face in frustration. "It's… uh, it was a gift from my parents."

"What's inside of it?" I put my hand out once my shoes were laced up.

August looked confused by my questioning. "I don't know. It doesn't open. They always told me it was to keep me safe and that I should always wear it. You know, it's symbolic."

I bit my tongue to the best of my ability and tried not to sound judgmental, but it was unclear how successful I was. I couldn't wait to be back to not giving a damn about my tone or the implications of my commentary, just like August didn't care about what happened between us. "And you never questioned that?"

"Up until very recently I didn't think I needed to question my parents, so no." August pulled the chain over his neck and dutifully placed the necklace in my palm. I tried to ignore the way his fingers brushed against mine and withdrew my hand quickly.

Before I did anything with it, I gestured to the side of his face. "And the scars on your ears, did they ever tell you what those are from?"

August immediately reached for the tops of his ears, which were currently covered by his hair. The round helixes were crowned by bumpy ridges of scar tissue. "They… I was attacked by a dog as a child… When did you notice them? I thought that my hair…"

"I touched them last night," I commented plainly, keeping my gaze on the jewelry in my hand instead of on his face. My cheeks flushed against my will as I recalled running my hands through his sweat-damp hair, biting his earlobe, and kissing down his throat. Never again.

It didn't feel right to comment on his story, not until I had pieced everything else together. I only hoped that I was wrong, but the pieces of the puzzle were looking bleak. "Everything opens," I told him. "With enough force." When he opened his mouth to argue, as he often did, I put a hand up. "Believe me, you're going to want to see this." I placed the necklace on the floor, then rolled the cylinder under the heel of my boot, where I flattened it with a satisfying crack. I held the broken jewelry up to him, and a glowing bit of green shone through the splintered silver shell. "Look familiar?"

"Is that—"

"Yeah, it's calcinite."

"Why would they want me to wear a necklace full of elf weaponry?" We stood in silence for a moment until August grabbed the necklace, then hissed in pain as the stone touched his bare skin. I shook my head as if to say "don't do that."

I cringed internally at the information I was about to deliver. As angry as I was with him and as annoyed as I was with his entitled life, it pained me to imagine the scene I had to describe to August, and it hurt me even more to think that he'd been carrying that hurt for his entire life. "Probably the same reason they had your ears shaved down when you were little, maybe when you were an infant even. You're not human." Had little August cried? Had he screamed out for help, for comfort? Was it painful to have a part of him stripped away so cruelly? I didn't know. I couldn't show him that I was considering it all either, especially when it seemed to have no effect on his life until now. Hadn't it?

"Max..." August stood nearly speechless. I knew that if I looked at him for too long, I'd be drawn to comfort him, and I couldn't do that anymore. Never again, I told myself.

"I know it's a lot to process," I said coolly. "I'll meet you by the stables when you're ready. I have to load Wraith up for the trip back."

A SILENT RIDE

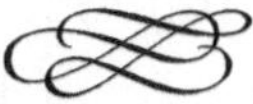

AUGUST

"*M*axine, listen… I—"

"It's Max," she bit out, not bothering to look at me. "Let's get going; the last thing we need is to show up late and draw attention to ourselves." I pocketed the necklace. "You should start to feel better without this on… we'll find somewhere to dispose of it on the way."

"Better?"

"More like yourself," she suggested, though I had no reference point for such a thing; if my mother and father had kept me subdued since childhood, there was no telling who I actually was. Did I have an arsenal of fae magic trapped somewhere in my bones? Or had I been hushed for so long that I was now just like any other human? I had no clue, nor did I know what any of that information would mean for my future. "Whatever that means to you."

The ride back to Barrien was filled with torturous silence. Every time I attempted to speak, unless it was regarding logistics like food or lodging or a spot to relieve myself, Max promptly shut me down and we carried on quietly.

When we approached a small lake in the Grimmaker Woods, Max dismounted only to pull apart my necklace and chuck the small crystal of calcinite into the water. She used the side of her knife to push the metal capsule back into place and then returned the necklace to me because, "it'll look suspicious to your parents if you return without it." When I put it back around my neck, my skin itched.

My captor was already heading back toward her horse when I reached out to grab her arm. "Max, please, just talk to me."

She shook my grip loose and whirled on me in anger. "You're not going to like what I have to say, August!" she said with a hiss.

I let my hand drop to my side and sighed. "I probably deserve it."

Max looked beside herself at my response. "Don't. Even. You don't get to play the victim," she said through gritted teeth. "You think you can just fuck me because you need someone to make you feel better? That's not how it works. You can't just have me when you want and then roll over and shut me out, August! I don't even know why I'm helping you. I can't believe I—"

"You can't believe you… what, Max?"

The way she glared at me then was so reminiscent of the first day she'd met me that I wanted to disappear and never be seen again. We spent months on the road together, shared some of the most traumatic and vulnerable moments I'd encountered in my adult life, and yet, I was nothing more than a bounty to her again: a disgusting, pompous, rich asshole that was worth only the money she could get for me.

"You're the one who's supposed to be answering questions," she bit out. "Not me."

"Questions, indeed," came a voice from somewhere up in the

trees. It was one I had heard before, but the look of recognition on Max's face helped me identify it: the elf from the tavern. When he leapt from his surveillance spot in the trees and landed between us, irritation bubbled within me. Everything was already a challenge, so to have whoever this was now interfering seemed a needless barrier.

"Florian," Max said as she regarded him. She didn't run to him like I feared she would. I didn't know if I could take it if she had. "Following me?"

"Once I realized you were transporting the prince of Barrien, yes," Florian said with a nod, looking between us. When his gaze settled on me, it was icy.

"I'm not turning him over to Emynor."

Florian's tone changed immediately. His brow furrowed, and his grip on his bow and arrow tightened, the wood groaning between his long fingers. "And why not?"

"It's really complicated, Florian." Max shook her head with a sigh as if to say there was more going on than just a war between two kingdoms. There was. Not to mention our own private battle that we still hadn't gotten to the bottom of. Now that Max's ex-lover was in the picture, everything felt more complicated. Selfishly, I hoped she didn't find his presence comforting.

"I've got time, little menace," he purred at her. The nickname made my stomach ache. "I'd love to hear how someone so responsible for malice and murder has convinced you to return him to his kingdom, where he'll continue to reign in terror."

Max chewed her lip as she looked at him. "We don't have time."

"Nonsense. The sun is setting. It's time to set up camp, whether you like it or not. Thanks to you, we can sleep under the stars, but before that, we're going to talk."

AND TALK, we did, much to my dismay. First we built a fire in near silence. I volunteered to catch fish from the very pool that Max had bathed in on our way through Grimmaker before, though Florian pushed back, insisting that he could catch something better and quicker than I could. I insisted, caught the fish, and then Florian cooked it while we all talked. I was shocked that he even gave us the time to explain and equally surprised that Max thought it was worth it, but as I learned more about him, I understood her rationale. He was clearly skilled, passionate, and judging by his attire and equipment, he had resources that we wouldn't have access to until I was on the throne.

"I can't say I'm surprised," Florian told us, scrunching his nose as he took in the information about my parents – whoever they actually were to me – kidnapping me from Emynor and using me to wage war against my own people.

"So you'll help us then," Max suggested as if it were a given.

"That's a lot to ask, Max."

"I know," Max told him, her tone somber. She looked across the fire at both of us. "But it's for a cause you believe in and a fight you've been fighting for a long time. This is the way to finally end it for good and for August to ensure none of these horrors are brought upon Emynor ever again. Isn't that worth it?"

Florian chewed his food in deep thought. I had said very little aside from filling in the blanks about my background and my promise to reunite the elven mother with her young child; it felt like the negotiation here was between the two of them. I could promise anything in my power, but I had very little bargaining power and even less knowledge about how their relationship worked. "What do you need?"

"Crystals," Max told him simply. "We need enough to get back to Barrien and purchase clothing to get into the ball with… five hundred, maybe."

"Easy enough," Florian said with a shrug.

"We'll repay you," I chimed in, desperately attempting to contribute anything to the conversation.

Florian regarded me as if he'd forgotten I was there, then looked back at Max again. "What else?"

"I need you to check on Danny."

The silence that fell over the group was broken only by the crackle of fire and a snort from Wraith, which suggested that she was not pleased with that idea.

"You're joking," Florian said finally, but there was no hint of amusement in his tone. "You don't let anyone 'check on Danny,' little menace." Again, the nickname rubbed me the wrong way, but so did the fact that Max was trusting him with something so important to her. I still had no idea who Danny actually was. Would she ever tell me? Now that we were miles and miles apart, it didn't seem likely. I knew that her outburst had been meant to wound me, but maybe our time together at the inn had been a mistake.

"You'll take Wraith. She can take you to Danny; she'll be too obvious when we re-enter Barrien anyway. No one will bat an eye at Stratus. Danny needs food delivered, some supplies, and he needs to know I'm still alive."

Florian looked over his shoulder at his own horse, a striking, lean thing of charcoal gray. Whereas Max and Wraith contrasted each other, Florian and Stratus were very similar. When the tall elf looked back at us, he nodded. "Fine." Perhaps it was because I'd gotten to know Wraith so well during our time on the road, but something about Stratus struck me as less relatable. Less human, maybe. Then again, it turns out I wasn't human either.

~

WE SLEPT under the stars that night, which felt odd considering the danger we'd been in after dark in those same woods. The fire kept us warm in the cooling night air, and Florian, lithe and impressive as he was, threw up a makeshift hammock between two trees, while we slept on the ground as usual. Wraith and Stratus stood guard nearby.

I couldn't sleep. Despite the exhaustion of travel and the fact that I was still nursing the Umbral bite, my body was alight that evening. I couldn't tell if it was because I was no longer being weighed down by the calcinite in my necklace, the existence of which still made me feel sick if I dwelled on it for too long. It made sense to me that my "parents" in Barrien, whoever they really were, had kept their distance from me during my time growing up; they weren't really my parents, so they didn't actually care about me. I was just a pawn. I didn't really understand their motivation for kidnapping elven children like myself and Heath, but I understood enough to know that we weren't the same type of people. As ignorant as I had been, I wasn't a heartless, murdering monster like they were. The faces of the people who had raised me, sort of, flashed into my mind, and I shook my head in an attempt to rid myself of those memories. The tips of my ears burned, almost as if I was suddenly aware that part of them was missing. I sat up on my blanket and stared into the fire, then looked around at my travel companions. Florian was asleep. Max was, too, but I couldn't tear my gaze from her. I wished that she had given me time to explain myself, that she'd extended me some more grace when it came to what happened between us. Didn't I deserve a little more understanding?

As I watched her form, calm and still in the flickering light of the fire, my mind raced with the previous night's events. Heat rose in my cheeks, and I crushed my eyes shut as I recalled the way she had comforted me, had taken me so lovingly despite my state of heightened emotion. I'd pushed her away because…

"Max, wake up," I said in as loud of a whisper as I could manage.

I half expected her to roll over and flip me off, but in true Max the Menace fashion, she was upright and had a knife pointed at me in seconds. "What do you want, August?" she said with a groan when she realized I wasn't an intruder. The knife came down more slowly than I would have liked, and she rubbed her eyes. "We have a full day of travel ahead tomorrow."

I hated how she could shut me down and shut me out, the way she had done during our entire time traveling together. I knew that she felt like I deserved it for what I had done to her the night before. "We need to talk."

"No," she said with a huff, then flopped back onto her blanket.

I gritted my teeth, irritated that she would talk to Florian all night but wouldn't give me a second. Now that we were partners united by a common goal, she owed it to me to hear me out, even if it meant nothing for our future as romantic partners. "Yes, get your ass up," I snipped at her. I glanced back at Florian, who hadn't stirred and probably looked like some sort of god sprawled out in his hammock, and got to my feet. The last thing I needed was his pretty ass interfering if we woke him up with our conversation. "Follow me."

I took off into the woods, not really caring where I was headed, and not looking behind me. I didn't take into account that Max was much smaller than me and her stride much shorter, so when I heard her struggling to keep up, I slowed a little.

"Where are we going, August? I don't know my way around these woods at night!"

"Away from your boyfriend," I told her over my shoulder.

"He's not my boy—"

I whirled on her, putting us face-to-face again, and scowled. "No? You sure seem a lot more comfortable around him than you are me, despite our most recent encounter."

Max was as confident in her response as ever and folded her arms across her chest, which meant that she was bracing to put me in my place. "I am more comfortable around him," she said plainly. "It's never been confusing to me how he feels. He doesn't push me away after we have sex, and we know what we are to each other. No mysteries."

"So, you have fucked him." I felt sick, but I wasn't sure why. It wasn't like me to be jealous.

"Yeah." Her voice didn't waver one bit. And why should it? I had no claim on her.

"And you regret that you've fucked me," I said, filling in the blanks in my mind.

"I regret that it felt like more than just fucking. Can I go back to bed now?" Before I could respond, before I could process her words, Max had already turned on her heel and headed back to where I assumed our camp was.

I stood there like an idiot and stammered before I finally choked out a louder-than-I-intended "Stop."

She did, but not without question. "Why should I?" she asked as she turned back toward me, having made it quite a few steps away. We were angrily whispering at each other now, as if we might be interrupted at any moment. It felt ridiculous.

Then, I confessed. "Because it felt like that to me, too, and you want to know why I pulled away."

"I don't care anymore. I want to uphold my part of our deal so no more children are ripped from their mothers' arms. That's it."

"That isn't it, and you know it."

"Fuck off, August."

I closed the gap between us in a couple of quick strides and placed my hand on her shoulder to spin her around. When we were face-to-face again, she surprised me by laying a palm across my face in a sharp slap that caused anger and frustration to burst forth from me. "What the hell are you doing?"

"Getting away from you."

"Not until you've heard what I have to say."

"Why should I care what you have to say?"

"You've spent, what, months now ignoring me, shutting me down, pushing me away. It's my turn to have an ounce of control."

She shoved me.

I grabbed her wrist.

"Who's Danny? Another boyfriend? Another Florian?"

"He's my brother, you prick."

"Good, then I don't need to worry about him. Time for you to listen, Max the Menace." When she attempted to shake off my grip, I tightened my hold on her wrist then grabbed her other arm so that I had both of her wrists in one of my hands. I used my body to push her back against a nearby tree and lifted her pinned wrists above her head. She shoved against me. "God, you're stubborn."

"You're an asshole."

"You don't really think that," I told her seriously, forcing myself to meet her gaze. "You want that to be the truth so you can push me away, like you do everyone, even though every ounce of you is screaming to let me in."

Max scoffed, laughed in my face like she did when she was putting men in their place, and I had to fight the immediate embarrassment that washed over me.

I leaned down to nudge her dark locks away from her neck so I could whisper in her ear, could plant a kiss against her neck. "Remember how perfectly we fit together? How I filled you with my come and told you how divine you felt?" She swallowed against my lips. "How it felt *right* for us to be like that with each other?"

"And then you rolled over like you couldn't stand the sight of me."

"I was scared," I confessed, pulling away to meet her gaze again.

Max was furious with me. "Of what, asshole?" she hissed. "You sleep with people all the time!"

"Sure," I shrugged with a sigh. "But I don't do *that*. I don't call out people's names, I don't—" I swallowed hard, my mouth dry with embarrassment. What if I was pushing her so far away that she wouldn't help with our plan in the morning? What if I was ruining everything? "I don't let myself unravel in front of other people, okay?"

"You're mad because you enjoyed yourself. You're mad because it was a good fuck."

"It was more than a fuck," I growled bitterly at her, echoing what she had said only moments before. I didn't move from where I was trapping her against the tree. I resented the fact that I was already straining against my slacks as we stood there, catching our breath in the middle of the woods. "You never want to do that again? Fine, go back to sleep. But you can't pretend it didn't happen. I messed up," I said through gritted teeth again. "Because I didn't know I could be that way with anyone. I got scared. That happens when you're faced with sensations you didn't know you could feel... and I don't know if you've noticed this, but I've been faced with a lot of new experiences lately." I dropped my hands from her sides and took a step back, giving her space to leave. The last thing I wanted was for her to feel forced or trapped, but I'd had to pin her down so that she would at least hear me. She needed to know.

Max said nothing. Her chest heaved with labored breath for a moment before I put my hands up in defeat and took another step back. I rubbed my hands over my face, the reality of the confession I'd just made settling in, and when I was about to turn and walk back to camp, I realized that Max hadn't moved.

"Max?"

She sniffled. "Don't—"

"I'm sorry."

When she spoke, her voice was soft and raw, like all of her walls had crumbled despite her best efforts. "Don't pull that shit again, you big idiot."

I was back to her in seconds, and she fell into my arms in a way that I could've only dreamt of. "I won't, I promise—" I began, but before I could even get out the entirety of my statement, she'd wrapped a hand around the back of my neck and pulled me down to kiss her. In that kiss, I found peace and forgiveness. We undressed just enough to grant access to one another, and within seconds, I had her in my arms against the tree again. When she wrapped her long, muscled legs around my waist, I pressed my forehead to her shoulder and thrusted into her as my belt jingled around my ankles.

Max gripped my hair and pulled me up so that I had to look her in the eyes before she kissed me again, soft and sweet and deep and ravenous. "Hell, Max…" I panted.

"Unravel with me."

"Only you," I told her.

BEATRICE THE APOTHECARY

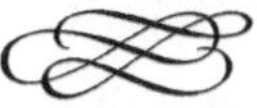

MAX

It was ironic that we ended up back at the Dalcester Street Market together, this time ready to spend money on what might've been considered frivolous when I had to fight August so hard last time not to blow the last of our money. Florian had loaned us a significant amount, and I had taken it without a second thought, leaving it to August to repay that debt when the time came. All I knew at that point was that I would be contributing to the fight by being present. Beyond that, I wasn't sure what would happen if and when August was able to overthrow his parents' rule and right the wrongs that his negligence had permitted to happen. Thankfully, because we were on such a tight schedule, I didn't have time to dwell on what would happen between August and me once all was said and done. Our reunion in the woods had ignited something in me that felt too big to address in the midst of such an undertaking... and yet, when he looked at me across the formalwear stall of the street market, holding an intricate mask of black and gold over his face, my heart skipped a beat.

"What do you think of this one?" he asked in that same care-free, big idiot voice that had accompanied me for many, many miles.

Before I could answer, the merchant owner of the stall chimed in. "Oh, yes, sir, that is sure to garner the attention of every royal at the Barrien masquerade!"

I smirked and returned to my browsing while August shopped, still feeling uneasy at the prospect of mingling with royals when I had spent so much time either avoiding or capturing them. Their behavior, their rituals, and the intricacies of their interactions were all beyond me.

"What are you getting? Let's see it," August piped up again sometime later, after having paid the merchant for his own outfit.

I held up a bundle of clothing, mask and shoes tucked away inside, without much to say. "Guess you'll have to wait and see," I told him, also dreading the idea of dressing up. At least there was a mask involved.

We went to the apothecary next.

Beatrice the Apothecary was a short, chubby, dark-skinned woman with a head of bouncy curls. She wore gold, horn-rimmed glasses that made her dark eyes appear three times their actual size and, at all times, appeared to have glitter on her clothes and skin. I wasn't sure how glitter played into potion making, but the fact that she literally sparkled everywhere brought me immeasurable joy. I'd known this woman for as long as I'd been doing my work and had always admired her craft.

"What's new, Beatrice?" I asked as we entered her domain, a small storefront with vials, bottles, jars, and drawers lining every inch of the walls. The countertops were covered with assorted loose ingredients, from fragrant herbs to dried animal parts.

As if she had been waiting all day for our arrival, Beatrice blew out several candles with one breath, leaving only a single candle that illuminated her from below. "Behold!" she announced theatrically, holding up a vial of swirling gold particles suspended in liquid. "You've heard of Forty-Winks, Fifty-Winks, and even The Final Wink… but I now present to you: Thirty-Winks[1]!"

I must have looked confused because Beatrice then sprang into her explanation about the potion's purpose. "It's the even weaker cousin of all of those other potions. So, it won't kill them or knock them out, but it will disorient them!" Meanwhile, I just hoped that I wouldn't confuse this new brew for its more deadly cousin, which we were also purchasing.

I shook my head a little. "Beatrice…"

Before I could point out the issue with telling them apart, August chimed in. "They're all in the same shaped bottle. Don't you think we might… accidentally kill someone we mean to disorient?"

I jerked a thumb his way. "He's got a point."

Beatrice sighed, then looked at the bottle in her hand in deep thought. "I get what you're saying, but… they're all part of the same line. They have to match!"

I groaned a little, then surrendered. We spent some time explaining our general plan to Beatrice, who had always been a trusted ally, and she supplied us with suggestions for potions that could aid us in our plan. She packed them into a sack, and I got ready to pay before asking, "Anything else you think we need?"

"Well, it's not a potion, but…" The apothecary looked nervous to make her suggestion.

"Go on," I mumbled, waving my hand to spur her on. "Let's hear it."

"You can't exactly march into a masquerade ball at the Castle of Barrien smelling like a mercenary who hasn't showered in weeks."

"She's got a point," August nodded.

"But I am a mercenary who hasn't showered in weeks."

Next to me, August shrugged in agreement. "Also true." I attempted to subtly sniff my clothing and realized that I did not smell like someone who was invited to a masquerade ball.

Beatrice's spectacled gaze pivoted to the prince. "Honestly, you're not smelling so great yourself, royal boy."

August looked beside himself at the suggestion, but before he could say anything, Beatrice was turned toward her wall of vials again. She snapped at the air after squinting at the bottles for a moment. "Morgan, could you light those candles again?"

"Darling, I just lit them," someone responded from behind the counter.

"Yes, but I had to blow them out for the presentation! You know, like we practiced!"

A deep sigh sounded from somewhere behind the counter, and then another person, Beatrice's spouse, Morgan, appeared, dutifully holding a box of matches. "Just a moment…"

"Thank you, my love," Beatrice replied as the light in the room increased tenfold.

I gave Morgan an appreciative nod, and they gave me a small half-smile in return; the two of us were a lot more alike than Beatrice and I, but we appreciated her flair all the same. She pushed her glasses further up her nose, then pointed a chubby finger at a row of vials that shimmered with thick fragrance oils. "For the mercenary…" Beatrice mused aloud, running her finger over vial after vial until she apparently landed on the right one. "Woodsy… earthy…" she shot a glance over her shoulder at me. "Patchouli, moss, and rhubarb." She turned around with the murky vial between her fingers and gestured to my hand. "Hold out your wrist."

"Huh?" I pulled my hand back further reflexively. "No thanks, I don't really try things while shopping. Wrap it up, and I'll put it on when I have to."

August chuckled beside me.

Beatrice rolled her eyes. "I should've known." She held out the vial to Morgan, who dutifully took it to wrap on the counter next to her. "Alright, now for the prince…"

I watched her in silence and let my gaze wander over to Morgan, who was carefully wrapping the small vial in paper and then brown twine. They did so without question, without a fuss, and I couldn't help but think back to my conversation with August at the Invisible Cliffs; he loved the kingdom because it provided everything he needed, and that was how Morgan and Beatrice must have viewed each other, too. They all loved the comfort that they had, the fact that their needs were met without question, and I longed for that.

"Musky, spicy, and warm," Beatrice nodded, running her fingers over the vials again. "I think."

August shrugged. "Should be whichever one reads 'big idiot.'"

"Aha!" Beatrice plucked the right vial from the shelf and turned to face us again. "Vanilla, sandalwood, plum, and—"

"Orchid," Morgan finished, holding their hand out for the bottle of perfume. "I think that's spot on."

We took our purchases with little other conversation and loaded them into Stratus's saddlebags before mounting him together. I still hadn't gotten used to the ease with which I could get onto him and found that I missed Wraith more than I expected. Perhaps it was the fact that everything was so unknown and that I was about to force myself into a situation that would be completely out of my element… and I wouldn't even have my horse with me.

Because there weren't any inns in Barrien that I felt comfortable at, let alone any that would have vacancy with the ball being such a big event, we opted to prepare for the ball in a small clearing of a nearby forest that I had used to observe the castle months before. It felt strange and out of place, dressing in such fancy garments in the middle of the woods, but it certainly wasn't the strangest thing I'd done in the name of justice. The sun was setting, and the arrival of other guests was visible from our viewing point, as it had been when I had used it.

"You can see my bedroom from here," August mused, pulling his shirt over his head while I situated myself behind Stratus's lean body to get changed.

"Mmmhm," I responded, feeling a little strange that I'd been found out even though it wasn't like I'd been ogling him. "Anything of note happening in there now?"

"No, it's empty. But I can't imagine what all you saw while staking out the place," August replied, the sound of paper being torn coming from the other side of the horse. The merchants had all wrapped our items a little too thoroughly.

I smirked to myself, then bundled up my daily clothes and stuffed them into the saddlebags. When I pulled my clothing out of its careful paper packaging, I held it up in front of me to get a better look and couldn't stifle the sigh that left my mouth. I hadn't worn a dress in, well... for as long as I could remember, and this wasn't just a dress, it was a gown. "I have no clue how I'm going to get on and off a horse in this..." I muttered to myself. It was simple enough: a flowing black gown with a neckline that plunged almost to my navel, and a sweeping train of sheer fabric. The front of the gown was embellished with an intricate, golden floral design. When I slipped into it, I was impressed by how easy it was to move in and the way the warm summer evening breeze made its way through the fabric. While I waited for August to finish dressing, I replaced my knives where they normally lived on my daily clothing; I tucked one into a strap on my thigh and hid a few others wherever I could manage without it being too obvious. I felt bare as I stood there, letting my hair loose so it could fall over my shoulders. Before I stepped out to see how far August had gotten, I remembered the perfume and dabbed a little on my wrists and neck. It felt strong, overwhelming, but then again, I wasn't used to smelling like anything but myself. I closed my eyes and took a deep breath, willing my steadfast and self-assured mercenary persona back into place. I tied the mask of matching black and gold around my head. "Ready."

"Come on out then," August told me.

I did as I was told and felt less graceful than ever as I watched each step in the soft forest floor with the heels I'd been sold. I hated them, but my guess was that I looked like exactly the type of person that would be at this ball. When my gaze settled on August, I couldn't help the surprise I felt. I shouldn't have, though, because he looked more at home than ever in his all-black attire, which was accented by a knee-length coat that had similar embellishments to my dress. He gave me a bow and then raised an eyebrow as he looked me over.

"Wow..."

"It feels like a lot... and the perfume, I'm not sure it's me." Hell, I sounded like a royal priss. Why did I care if I identified with a certain perfume oil? After that night, none of it would matter.

"That's the thing about perfume," he told me, closing the gap between us. "It smells one way in the bottle, but once you've got it on your skin and it warms up, it takes on a whole new scent." He raised my wrist to his face, where he inhaled my flesh deeply, then pressed a kiss to my exposed veins. "You know, that's why they tell you to put it where your pulse is... so the pumping of your blood can heat up the oil. I'd say your heart is racing right now." He must have been correct about the mechanics of perfume oil because from where I was standing, I could smell what Beatrice had given the prince, and the scent was unmistakably him; he still smelled like the man I'd rolled around with in the tavern after a torturous day, still smelled like the air of the woods mixed with fresh sweat, but then the scent of vanilla and orchid amplified his natural musk and made my mouth water. When I let my wrist fall from his fingers, my heart thudded hard against my chest, screaming from the onslaught of sensation.

"And yours?" I asked.

He swallowed hard, then gave me a lopsided smile as if I was trying to pull one over on him. "Now, now, don't think you can tear down all of my walls so quickly." We didn't have time for it, but I found that I wanted nothing more… one day, maybe, when the dust settled and the chaos cleared.

"You look nice," I confessed.

August looked at me curiously, suppressing another smile. "Nice? Is that a compliment I hear coming from you, Max the Menace?"

I bit my lip. "Don't make me regret it, but… yes. It suits you. And you really don't need to call me that."

"No?"

"It's not like I picked it myself," I said with a scowl. "I probably would've picked something cooler, like, I don't know… Max the Battle Ax. It's more of a marketing tool at this point than anything."

August looked as if he were considering his options, then nodded. "It *does* remind me of your boyfriend's nickname for you, after all. What shall I call you then?" he asked, tucking a strand of hair behind my ear before he tilted my chin up so we were face-to-face.

I opened my mouth to argue. "He's not—"

He cut me off, as he had a habit of doing. "Nightshade, perhaps."

"Why?"

"It's beautiful and deadly, just like you."

---

1. Thirty-Winks: used to disorient a victim.

THE MASQUERADE BALL

AUGUST

We arrived at the Castle of Barrien in the nick of time and almost to my dismay, as Max had just pulled me into the most passionate kiss of my life when she realized we needed to get going. While most others arrived by carriage, Max and I had only Stratus at our disposal. I hoped that he wouldn't give us away, but thankfully Florian's obsessive maintenance of the horse's mane and expensive taste in saddles made him look high-end enough for us to get by. We rode him to the entrance of the castle, where guests were being led inside, and I helped Max off of his back as gracefully as we could manage, given the fact that we hadn't practiced.

"Not bad," I whispered to her as she touched the ground, her gown falling neatly around her. We followed the procession of guests through the castle to the main ballroom, a path I could've navigated with my eyes closed.

"Is it strange… being here, without anyone knowing?" Max asked under her breath as we walked. I could tell the questions were a way for her to distract herself from the formalities surrounding us. Perhaps she felt right at home, masked and sneaking around, but I didn't.

I nodded.

"Have you missed it?" I sensed a hint of regret in her voice.

"Not the parts you might think."

When it was our turn to enter, I made up a name for us on the spot and provided it to the master of ceremonies.

"Introducing the Lord and Lady Nightshade."

The way that everyone moved together, mingling, drinking, dancing, as if nothing was wrong made me wildly uncomfortable. At the same time, I was glad to be masked and able to observe them without being identified; I would likely never have this chance again regardless of how the evening panned out. I pulled Max onto the dance floor of the ballroom and into my arms without asking if she was ready. I knew she would say no.

"I told you, I can't dance," she said, looking up at me through the slits of her mask. I could sense the desperation in her voice despite her best efforts; Max the Menace was used to being in control, especially with me, so this was new and terrifying for her. I liked being the one to take her to that place.

"I can," I assured her. "You'll have to follow my lead for once." She didn't argue, so I took one of her hands and placed it on my shoulder, then positioned mine on her hip before taking her other hand in mine. Though she wasn't a dancer, her speed and stealth were clear in the way she moved with me, and I felt the agony of the past few months melt away as we moved together. Even though the marble floor of the ballroom felt native and comfortable beneath my shoes, I longed for the softness of the forest floor... but only if I still had this woman with me. I could go anywhere with her, I realized, and I would be able to view it as a grand adventure, no matter the terrors we faced.

As we danced, I leaned down to bury my face in her neck and

breathe her in. The scent transported me away from the dance, from the ballroom of the kingdom of Barrien, and deep into my memories of Max, where there was endless comfort even in her teasing, even in her pushing my boundaries and causing me to face painful truths. It was then that I heard the sound of a voice I had not been prepared to hear again. I should have expected it, but I hadn't been prepared for the way it would shatter the solace of my bubble with Max.

"He's been ill, unfortunately," my mother said from somewhere in the ballroom where she was undoubtedly mingling with her guests. I couldn't bring myself to look her way and instead just listened while we glided past her conversation on the dance floor.

"Oh dear, is it serious?" the guest asked in faux concern. I couldn't place the woman's voice, and it was likely that she had never actually met me. What did she care if I lived or died?

"I'm afraid so..."

Her voice hammered in my head, pinging around in my skull with the agony of realizing that this was the beginning of their faking my death. They hadn't cared that I was kidnapped, which was why they hadn't sounded the alarm. I imagined my mother's made-up face when she received a letter that I'd been turned over to Emynor as a bargaining chip. Perhaps she would turn up her nose and shrug. Such a shame after all we've given him, she'd say, oh well. Just like that, they would squash the warring kingdom's one chance at bargaining for their freedom. Then they'd tell their guests that I had died from the mysterious illness that overtook me around the time of the masquerade. Were they planning to announce my demise that evening? The room spun as we danced, and I felt the strength in my legs falter.

"August?"

"I can't..."

"August, stay with me." Max must have sensed my lead of the

dance falter because she tightened her grip on my hand and shoulder. "What's going on?"

I shook my head and attempted to refocus on what was before me, but all I could hear was the dismissal in my would-be mother's voice. I wanted to run. "Let's go."

"Where?"

"Away, forever."

"We can't, August," Max told me with a firmness that I needed at that moment. She reached a gentle hand up to stroke my cheek, and I closed my eyes to lean in to her touch. "I imagine there's still time before anything happens here, though. Let's step out."

To leave the ballroom seemed like it would get me too close to leaving altogether, but I complied. I would be useless if I didn't have my wits about me. Once we were in the hall adjacent to the ballroom, where only servants were puttering around to prepare for dinner, I leaned against the wall and tried to catch my breath. It was dim, cool, and quiet in comparison to the room we'd just come from.

"Talk to me," Max suggested, standing in front of me as if her small body could guard me from anyone that got too close. She looked uncomfortable in her dress, and I wanted nothing more than to rid her of it.

"They're going to pretend I've died," I explained, staring down at her from the cover of my mask. "It's sick."

Max chewed her lip. "All the more reason to go through with your plan."

I felt spineless when I confessed, "I can't confront them." The boldest move I'd ever made was killing the man who had captured and assaulted Max, but that was not in my nature. I'd lived a sheltered, privileged life up until my time with Max, where I'd been forced to question everything I knew. Right then, however, I felt confident that I wouldn't be able to follow through. Being privileged and sheltered also meant that I had grown up aware of the order of things and being submissive to that order; you don't disobey your royal parents. But then again, if they're not actually your parents and they're responsible for your abuse and genocide of your people, perhaps there is some wiggle room.

"You can," she told me without pause. "You will."

I ran a hand through my hair in frustration. "Do you enjoy pushing me?" It was starting to feel like it. The entirety of our trip together had been one harsh reality after another.

"I only push you when necessary. Listen to me, you big idiot." Her tone was harsh, but a whisper of a smile crossed her shapely lips.

"Nightshade," I said with a growl.

"You have to confront them. It will be painful, but it's necessary. You know that," she told me as she squeezed my hand. "That's why you're going to do it."

I steadied myself with a deep breath that was sucked straight from my lungs when she pulled me into an unexpected kiss. She pulled me down with a hand on the back of my neck, and I gripped her satin-clad hips. When she nibbled my lower lip, my knees nearly gave out. "Before the night is over," I told her, panting between stolen kisses, "you're going to ride me on the throne."

Then, she said something that I'm sure Max the Menace had never said before or since. "Long live the king."

THE FINAL WINK

MAX

We slid back into the ballroom just as the sound of silverware hitting a crystal glass chimed through the air. Years of entering high-stakes situations for a living, and this was the first time I felt truly uneasy. Normally my jobs were much more planned out, to the point where I had a clear advantage. This, on the other hand, felt highly dangerous; we were in a room stuffed with people who could easily overthrow us if we weren't convincing enough. I chewed my lip as we entered the room and mapped out each potential exit as we walked, August's hand in mine, toward the area where the king and queen were about to address their guests.

"Our esteemed guests, how lovely it is to spend this evening with you each year, on the night of the Autumn Equinox!" the queen said, projecting her voice across the room. She bore no resemblance to August that I could see, which made sense, but I wondered how they had passed him off as their son. Her hair was graying but had very clearly been blond at one point, and her eyes were a pale blue. The woman was short and thin, her spindly fingers wrapped around the stem of a glass of sparkling wine.

August's hand was damp within mine as we stood and listened to her speech. We were only a few feet from them, and I felt oddly on display, despite the fact that we blended into the crowd perfectly.

When the king took over, I was taken aback by his appearance, which I'd never witnessed before. August was the spitting image of him, only older, and confusion riddled my brain. It didn't make sense. He raised his own glass. "In addition to thanking you all for your attendance and continued support of our beautiful land, we wanted to take this time to announce that our son, Prince August Theodoric III—"

"Oh, father!" August spoke up from my side, letting his hand slip from mine as he approached his parents and took his place at their side. When he slid his mask off, the couple could not hide their surprise. "Please, allow me. After all, I think the people of Barrien should get used to seeing my face, don't you?"

There were murmurs in the audience.

"I didn't even know he was here…"

"His mother said he was ill. He looks perfectly fine to me."

"Oh my, I sure hope he's not announcing an engagement. I'd like a chance at that."

I rolled my eyes beneath my mask.

"Oh, well, I…" the king stammered. August was turned away from me, but I could guess that he had either mouthed something to the older man or given him a look stern enough to change his tone. "Of course."

"Thank you, Father," the prince bit out before turning back toward his guests. "Yes, yes, thank you all for joining us this evening." August's tone was as even and clear as someone who had been addressing ballrooms full of pompous guests for a lifetime. "As my father mentioned, part of the reason we've gathered you all here is to make an exciting announcement. After decades of exemplary ruling, my father will be abdicating the throne, and I will be taking his place as king of Barrien."

I stifled a laugh at his phrasing. Meanwhile, there were gasps around me.

In a move that left his parents no room to argue, at least not publicly, August concluded his very brief speech with, "As such, my coronation will occur first thing in the morning so that all of you lovely people can be in attendance and witness this moment in Barrien's history!"

I began clapping immediately, then elbowed a man next to me, who joined in. Within seconds, the room was in uproarious applause and conversation, and August was exiting the platform with one last comment: "Please, enjoy the evening!" The way he snapped at a group of nearby guards before exiting the room with my hand in his, causing them to follow him obediently, radiated power. "Escort the king and queen to the throne room immediately," he told them, sending a few off without him.

Seconds later found us locked inside of said throne room with the guards standing by the doors. August had since released me, and I found myself against the wall, unsure of my place in this confrontation. While we were walking, I felt the hilt of a sword that I didn't realize August had purchased rustle against the fabric of his coat. I couldn't argue that coming armed was a smart move, but it caused me to wonder how exactly he planned for this confrontation to pan out. After he'd killed Striker in such a quick manner, I couldn't help but wonder if there was a violent, impulsive killer within him.

He gestured to the guards. "Wait outside. I'll call you when we're finished."

I turned to leave with them, my fingers itching to wrap around a dagger for safety, when August called to me. "Not you, Max. Stay."

The looks on the royals' faces were impossible for me to read. There was a heavy silence between them all before the queen spoke up. "Oh, darling, you're safe!"

August's brow furrowed immediately, and when his mother approached him, he backed away. "Yes, no thanks to you. How is it that no one knew I was missing, Mother?"

"Well, I… we… didn't want to worry the people, my dear. You know it's our job to keep up appearances, no matter what's happening in the castle!"

"Didn't want to worry them or didn't want them to know that you were okay with my murder?"

The king chimed in immediately. "What does it matter? You can't just storm in here and make claims like you did in there! You'll have to address the guests again and right this immediately, August!"

"Like hell I will," he snipped. "I am no longer under your command."

I nodded at him from my spot on the perimeter of the room.

"You are," the king growled. "And you will be for the rest of your life, the length of which remains to be seen."

"Do you really think a death threat will have any effect on me at this point?" August argued. "What did you think would happen when I was kidnapped, Father? Did you think I would be turned over to Emynor and they'd kill me on the spot? No, not so. I saw everything… the destruction you have dealt to that city, the heartbreak… and for what reason? Why are you destroying their homes and ripping their babies from their arms?" August was yelling now, and his pain resonated through the throne room.

"They're savages!" the queen barked, the look on her face one of a victim who was defending killing their attacker. It was all an act.

"Savages? So that's what you think I am, too." August scoffed. His hands trembled at his sides as if he were considering drawing his sword. I hoped, for all our sakes, he would wait and get his questions answered first. If he killed them, or even if he sent them away somehow, that window of opportunity would close.

"What are you talking about?" the king asked.

"I know I'm an elf," said August. This was the first time I had heard him use that label on himself.

"Only part," the queen chimed in again.

"What?"

"You didn't think we'd just pluck some random elven brat from Emynor and make him our son, did you?" The queen's submissive expression was gone, and her face had returned to its resting state of posh annoyance.

"No?" August sneered, turning toward his mother, but keeping tabs on his father. It was easy to see that he had lost all trust in the pair. "Then tell me why!"

"We don't owe you an explanation," his father said with a scoff, holding tight to one last shred of power he thought he had.

Without warning, August drew his sword and pointed it to his father's throat. He was trembling, and the tip of the blade touched the older man's neck, where it drew a prick of fresh blood. "Tell me why," August demanded again.

The queen stepped over and hesitantly put a hand on her son's shoulder, but the way he slid away from her touch sent a pang through my heart. "When your father was a young soldier..." she told him, "he made a mistake while on an assignment in Emynor."

"A mistake?"

I stood in silence but wanted to run to August, to shield him from the disgusting commentary of his parents, who made clear that they didn't have an ounce of real love for this man, whether he was their real son or not.

"So when a young elf woman showed up at the castle doors, claiming that her newborn child was the son of the king, we had to deal with that *mistake*. We took you in and told the people that you were ours, that we'd been private about my pregnancy all along and that we were welcoming the new prince of Barrien to the world. We raised you as our own!"

"Hardly!" August said, turning so that his sword was pointed at the queen now. "I never saw you. How long did it take you to notice that I was missing? Did you even actually give a damn when you realized?" It was clear that he did not want to hear their answer. "And what happened to her? The woman, my real mother."

"She died," the queen replied, eyeing the sword.

"She died, or you killed her?" August lowered his blade a little.

"I would imagine her bones are at the base of the Invisible Cliffs now."

August's body jerked in a way that suggested he was swallowing bile. I had told him the purpose of the Invisible Cliffs when we visited, not knowing that it would ever have such a personal connection for him. Now it had multiple; his mother had been murdered there, and his people had been mining the very gem that kept him powerless and subdued, as it did for the elves of Emynor.

"You killed her and you… subdued me… for what? Couldn't you have just let me live on my own with her?"

The queen laughed. "Of course not. We couldn't have people finding out that your father was an unfaithful man with a bastard child—"

"It wasn't my fault! She… she seduced me with her whorish elven magic." Pathetic.

August ripped the necklace from his throat and tossed it on the floor in front of his mother. "So who cut my ears?"

"Oh darling, we couldn't have anyone – not even the family doctor – know where you'd come from. I did that myself." The blatant lack of remorse in her voice made me uncomfortable. How had this woman even raised a child? Probably with the help of the kingdom staff.

"I was a child," August said in response. I imagined the queen holding his tiny body down as she carved up the tips of his ears. "I was a baby!"

"There are requirements for fitting in with the royal family, August. Would you rather we had just disposed of you, left you to die somewhere?"

The silence in the room was deafening as August considered her question as if it had not been rhetorical. He looked from his mother to his father and then back again. "Yes, perhaps. If I had known this would be my fate… and that I would be responsible for the horrors occurring in Emynor. You ruined me," August choked out, "and then used me to ruin the lives of others."

He swallowed thickly, then pointed the sword at his father again. I drew a dagger from the strap on my thigh, ready to step in and approach whoever August wasn't able to handle on his own. "It's my job to attempt to reverse some of the damage you've wrongfully done. I know that you made me prince as a scapegoat, so that I would sign whatever you put in front of me without question. Thankfully that has awarded me other rights that you won't be able to undo at this point. You will obey, or you will draw your last breath this evening."

The king gawked. "You'd kill your own parents to—"

"Just like you'd kill your own son!" August screamed, his fair face going red. I held my breath and hoped that he would be able to control himself. I was a killer, sure, but August wasn't. He couldn't begin his reign of reparation this way. Silence settled over the room and August snapped his fingers, sending the guards in immediately. "Lock these two up pending trial for treason."

When the throne room had cleared and the air hung heavily with regret, sadness, and triumph, August turned to me with bleary eyes.

"August, I'm so sorry—"

"On the throne," August commanded me immediately. In any other circumstances, I'd be averse to someone ordering me around, especially someone in legal power like August was about to be, but this was different. The look in his eyes said he wouldn't stop me if I were to turn and run, but when I complied, the sword dropped from his grip, and he followed me.

When he crushed me against the throne, his muscular body over mine, all rational thought left me. I found his lips in a frantic rush and bit his lower lip, matching the intensity of his need and the frustration he clearly needed an outlet for. How did it feel to learn that he'd never actually been loved by the people who claimed to be his parents? That he had been used as a means to an end and that they likely felt no remorse for it? I couldn't imagine.

August's rough hands hiked up my dress while I struggled to unbutton his intricate shirt. "I can't..."

Wait," he said gruffly, then stood back to shrug out of his coat. The light in the hall was dim and subtle, but enough for me to see him undress in front of me. I sat, still shoved back in the throne, panting. He gripped one side of his shirt and with a swift yank, sent the buttons flying. The sound of them rolling across the marble floor of the throne room echoed throughout, and I found my breath caught in my throat as he shed the fabric, exposing his muscled chest and abdomen. Finally, I could appreciate it without guilt. He came to me again, this time less restricted, and pulled me to him in a kiss. Our size difference allowed him to pick me up and slide beneath me so that I was straddling his lap, the fabric of my gown tearing slightly with the new positioning. I didn't care. I ran my hands down his chest as our tongues explored each other, then pulled away to slide from his lap onto the floor before him. Again, I was faced with a situation that had me more submissive than I was used to and far more submissive than I would've ever been with the August I'd met months ago. But now…

August watched me through a hooded gaze, his usual talkativeness nowhere to be found, as I unlaced the front of his trousers. He ran a hand over his face in disbelief as I set his cock free and stroked it. "Now… that is quite the sight."

"One you've seen before?" I asked, feeling vulnerable and unleashing my fears into the cold marble room. Though the August before me was different from the one I'd originally kidnapped, they had the same history. I knew his playboy ways and could only imagine how many surfaces within the kingdom he'd fucked people on. I hoped this wasn't also one of them.

"Only in my very recent dreams, Max," he assured me as he reached down to stroke my cheek. The way he sat in the throne, his throne, so comfortably lit a flame within me. That type of power did not normally impress me – quite the opposite usually – but knowing what he had been through to get there and what he intended to do with that power impressed me.

That was all I needed to hear. I ran my tongue up the underside of his length, my eyes locked on his, before taking him into my mouth. Soon I was stroking him, taking him deep into the back of my throat while I massaged his balls, and he was gripping the armrests of his throne with the tension of a building climax. "God, Max…" he panted, but before I could bring him to the edge, he pulled me off of him and upright.

"What is it?"

"I need you out of that gown," he told me, "as stunning as it is on you." He stood, a sight to behold with his pants around his ankles and his cock thick and hard for me. He saw nothing off about the arrangement, though, and helped me out of my dress only to place me in his seat and dive between my thighs.

"What are you— ah, August!"

He was ravenous as he ate me, lapping at the cleft of my sex before he plunged a finger, then two inside of me. He wasted no time in bringing me to the edge with his synchronized finger flexing and sucking my clit until I came, stifling my cries with a hand over my mouth. August, of course, noticed and swiped it away with his free hand. "Again," he demanded, "but this time, let the whole castle hear it."

The prince made me come again and again until I was ragged and boneless, barely able to hold myself up in the massive throne. When he stood and leaned over me, he kissed me hard and deep, and I savored the way I tasted on his lips. I kissed him back. I tangled my fingers in his sweat-slicked curls, I pulled him close and kissed the butchered tops of his ears.

"Are you afraid to let go?" I asked him, fearful myself that all we had experienced was inadvertently driving us apart, despite how much we had grown together. Now that we were back in Barrien, would he withdraw and return to his old ways? I didn't think so, but I couldn't help but be nervous. People were predictable and to change his ways entirely went against that.

"No," August grunted, stroking himself as he stood upright in front of me again. "I've been saving this moment because it takes so little with you. Spread your legs, Nightshade." When I complied, he laid his cock, heavy and throbbing against the lips of my cunt. He notched himself between my thighs, only the head of his cock entering me, and looked me in the eyes. "Touch yourself for me."

I felt I couldn't possibly come again, but I slid my hand down my belly and rubbed my clit for him. The room had been frigid upon our arrival, but now the air between us was hot and slick.

"Yes," he whispered harshly, watching as I worked myself in a show for him. "Beautiful…"

"Unravel with me," I told him and reached out to run my nails along his tensed abdomen. The muscles rippled in response.

"Only you," he said, then gripped the armrest of the throne and groaned, biting his lip as his cock jerked and shot thick ropes of come across my flesh.

We stayed in the silence of the deserted throne room until the masquerade's guests were long gone.

RECLAMATION

AUGUST

The next morning, the guests of the masquerade and the people of Barrien were invited back to the castle for my coronation, which was arranged on the shortest notice the kingdom had ever seen. I ensured that the staff of the castle took to the streets to invite everyone in the city who would hear them; I was determined to have my people know my face and feel my involvement in their world. Merchants from surrounding farms and cities provided us with food, flowers, decor, and clothing for the event, having worked late into the night to make it so once I had made my announcement.

When I dressed, seeing myself in the full-length mirror of my chambers for the first time in months, Max stood behind me. I couldn't place the look on her face. "What is it?"

She shook her head as I fastened my cufflinks. "You want them there?"

I turned to look at her. "No, but they have to be there to hand over the throne," I told her with a sigh.

"Then it'll be brief," she assured me. "And I'll be the one to escort them." Before I could argue, she closed the gap between us and ran a hand through my hair, tucking a few stray curls behind my ear. It was almost as if she wanted the scarred ridges of carti- lage to show, as a reminder of why I had come back, why I was so determined to change the path of Barrien. Despite my time without the necklace from my parents, I didn't feel any supposed magic returning to me. I supposed I didn't view it as a loss because I couldn't remember a time when I'd had those abilities. I put my hand over Max's and kissed her.

When we saw each other again, she was indeed escorting my parents, and by their posture, I could tell she had her favorite dagger at their backs.

I was formally crowned, an event that brought me a flurry of emotions, and I gritted my teeth when I surveyed the crowd and saw my parents again, their distaste apparent in their expressions. Max wasted no time escorting them out of the hall once more. When the hall had cleared and she was nowhere to be found, I slipped away from the celebration to the prison cells of the castle.

"Max?" I called, covering my nose and mouth with a sleeve in an attempt to block the rancid stench of the cells.

"Here."

"Oh, thank goodness!" my mother's voice chimed in as I rounded the corner toward my parents' cell. "August, she's trying to kill us!"

Max stood with her back against the wall across from the cell and shrugged when I laid my eyes on her. "Not really," she told me without meeting my gaze. Instead, she glared at my parents, who stood against the bars of their new quarters, looking very out of place in their coronation clothing. "I'm giving them the option of killing *themselves*."

"How can you let this happen, son?" my father boomed, gesturing to the two potion bottles Max had left just outside of their cell. I knew what it was: The Final Wink. It was a generous, merciful offer, especially since Max could've easily killed them herself. I knew, though, that they wouldn't use it; they didn't believe they'd done anything wrong.

"WHAT RIGHT DOES he have to lead the people of Barrien?" my father argued at their trial, meeting the council with arguments and insults rather than a confession. "Two months ago, he hardly knew what was happening right beneath his nose! He'd rather distract himself by fucking anything with a pulse than dealing with the politics of—"

"Enough!" the head of the council declared, rolling his eyes at the irony of my father's blatant immaturity.

I bit my lip to hold back my own commentary; I had presented the facts to the council already. The facts about Emynor, at least. The story of my kidnapping felt too embarrassing, too personal, to broadcast. The way my parents switched from attempting to sweet-talk themselves back into my good graces to callously insulting me was alarming. I still hadn't come to terms with the fact that I'd been living a lie with them since I was a baby.

"Is it true that you've used harmful, abusive tactics to gain control of the city of Emynor, including kidnapping and the use of the Neon Shackle to debilitate and imprison the elves of that city?"

"Who are you going to believe?" my mother said with a scoff, clutching the skirt of her dress, which had become disheveled during her imprisonment. "The king of Barrien or this nitwit?"

One of the other councilmembers cleared their throat. "Former king," she corrected. "With that said, we are basing our judgement on his story alone. Are there, perhaps, other witnesses who can vouch for this story of what you witnessed in Emynor?"

Max shifted at the door of the court. I could sense the changes in her posture, in her breathing, even if I wasn't near her; I couldn't tell if it was a whisper-of-elven-magic thing or just a Max thing. But before she could comment, the wooden door swung open. Florian, of all people, glided into the hall without so much as a sound from his boots hitting the marble of the floor. "I can provide you with a firsthand account of the horrors in Emynor, as well as any number of witnesses. Perhaps you'd like to see, face-to-face, a young elven child who was ripped from his mother's arms by your guards? He's barely old enough to speak properly." Somehow he kept his tone cool and formal, while the content of his words was scathing.

Max looked from me to Florian, then back to the council. "I'm willing to escort a member of the council to Emynor to see for themselves."

My father grumbled.

The head of the council declined the offer. "I don't think that will be necessary," he told the group with a wave of his hand. Then, he turned to my parents. "It's clear there has been an abuse of power here and that atrocities have been committed in the name of Barrien. Now these horrors must be remedied by the new king. But before we determine your sentence, I must ask... why?" The man looked truly sad.

I held my breath, but when nothing useful came from the lips of my parents, I confessed. "Revenge."

The head of the council looked at me curiously. "What for? Have there been similar slights against Barrien, committed by the elves of Emynor?"

I shook my head. "The destruction of Emynor has simply been a decades-long tantrum from my parents because of me: proof that my father had an affair with an Emynorian woman long ago. The elves have done nothing to deserve such horrific treatment."

The council looked mortified, as did Florian, who had not been around to hear my parents' confession on the night of the masquerade ball.

"All of this because you couldn't keep your prick in your pants!" my mother shouted, smacking my father on the back of his head.

"Listen, woman—"

"Silence!" the head of the council boomed once again.

When my parents were later escorted from the hall with a new sentence of life in prison, they did not meet my gaze. Max, meanwhile, left her post at the door to give my hand a gentle squeeze. I offered her a half-smile before turning back to the council. "If I may, there are other matters I would like to present to the council." I spoke in a way that reminded me of my father, when I'd overheard him in his own meetings; perhaps I had been listening at least a little bit.

The woman who had asked for witnesses earlier gave me a sympathetic look. "Now?"

I nodded. "Yes, it must be now. Every moment of inaction that goes by will lead to more death and destruction in Emynor." When the council did not protest, I continued, keeping Max's hand in mine as I spoke. "I propose that we employ Florian as a royal advisor, particularly in our dealings with Emynor. If it is amenable to everyone, his first order of business should involve delivering a message of immediate ceasefire to those soldiers of Barrien currently in Emynor. They should retreat immediately, except for those who will remain to assist in rebuilding the city and providing resources to the elves of Emynor."

I looked at Florian, and although he appeared shocked, he gave me a nod of confirmation. Despite being less than in love with his personality and relationship with Max, I had to admit he brought invaluable insight into the dealings with Emynor and would ultimately be responsible for restoring our relationship with them, as well as returning many elven children to their homes, including little Heath. Not only that, but he was my first introduction to real elf history and culture, and despite his pompous attitude, was a welcoming ambassador into that part of my life.

"But he's not one of us," another councilmember commented, looking around nervously as if he knew he was in the wrong.

"Neither am I," I continued before the council could interfere. "Additionally, I must insist that the Invisible Cliffs be closed and the Neon Shackle no longer be mined, sold, or used by anyone in Barrien. The gem must be forbidden." I gave the council a look that dared any of them to wonder why I disliked the stone, but no one argued.

When our dealings with the council concluded, it was late in the evening. I paid Florian back the loan he had given us, but not before we all had a meal in comfortable silence, aside from Florian's report of Danny's safety. The elf eventually left Barrien, being called to the road, but promised that we could call on him if the time came that he was needed again.

HOME

AUGUST

$\mathcal{D}$ays later, I woke to the first tendrils of morning light trickling onto my face in a room I knew very well. Light streamed in softly through an open window, and with it came gentle warmth. When I followed the small beams of light, they settled on the bare shoulder of the woman lying next to me in bed. Her raven hair was sprawled across her pillow like a lion's mane, her chest rising and falling slowly with sleep. I propped myself up on my elbow and watched her for a while, amused by the small smile that crept onto her fair face as she dreamt. When her eyes flickered open, their dark brown illuminated to the color of wet clay, she rubbed the sleep from them. "What are you staring at, you big idiot?" When she pulled me onto her in a playful embrace, I melted into her.

"You," I told her, burying my face in her hair. "A most welcome sight."

I had been fully prepared to spend another day just as we had been: lying in bed, then eating breakfast together before dealing with continued work on the political front, then exploring the grounds together. To my dismay, however, that was the day Max decided it was time for her to go back to her brother. When she loaded up her belongings on Wraith, I found my heart aching more than I'd expected. Barrien law didn't require kings to be married to ascend to the throne, but many nights when I lay awake listening to Max dream, I found myself wishing that I had that as an excuse to keep her in Barrien. I knew in my heart that we hadn't known each other nearly long enough for such a commitment, nor would Max tie herself to me for the sake of my coronation, but...

"Leave that here," I insisted, putting a hand over Max's as she packed up yet another bag of her clothing.

"I don't know how long I'll be gone," she told me, not meeting my gaze as she fastened another strap on Wraith. The horse had become oddly tolerant – not affectionate, tolerant – of me since her trip with Florian, and I couldn't help but wonder if we had bonded over our mutual annoyance with him.

"Decide," I told her with certainty, willing her to meet my gaze. "Decide to come back."

"I have Danny, August... you know that."

"Bring him with you." It was a huge ask, one that I wouldn't have dared to make if I hadn't been desperate, because I didn't want Max to think I took the situation lightly. I knew that bringing Danny, whom she had kept safe and hidden away for so long, across the continent back to me was probably something she would never consider, but I had to ask. "I'll send you with guards, supplies, whatever you need to feel like the trip would be safe enough for him. He'll be safe here, happy. There are teachers, other children... He can play and thrive and... I'm good with kids. I promise."

The way she smiled at me tore into my heart, and I realized then that it would be painful to wake up without her, to go on without her. "Or I'll come with you," I offered.

"August, this is your home."

I shook my head.

"What?"

"No," I told her, "you're my home. Wherever you are, that's where I need to be. What will it take?" With how our time together had played out – full of obstacles, but also full of pleasant surprises – I was heartbroken when she actually left and didn't make a promise of when she would return. So much had changed about our situation, about me, that it felt almost impossible to exist without her by my side.

Weeks went by, and her scent eventually faded from the sheets of my bed, our bed. One morning I found myself staring out the window of my bedroom, which had remained the same despite the option of moving into my parents' old chambers, and pinpointed the spot in the distance where we had changed for the masquerade ball. The details of that night had long since become a painful blur, aside from the moments I'd spent with Max. Just as I recalled the way she'd looked in her gown that evening, the broad head of a particular black horse peaked over the top of the hill, followed by two passengers: a stunning woman with raven hair and a little boy who looked a whole lot like her. They had come home.

Max once told me that a fortune-teller said that she had an "innate ability to seek out what others are searching for." She always thought that was a reference to her bounty-hunter skills. I've since learned that it means she leads people to the truth, to what they need in life. In my case, she was exactly what I needed.

GLOSSARY OF CREATURES AND POTIONS

*P*OTIONS (ALL CAN BE PURCHASED FROM BEATRICE THE APOTHECARY):

THIRTY-WINKS: used to disorient a victim.

FORTY-WINKS: sleeping potion with a purple haze/smoke. Smells like lavender.

FIFTY-WINKS: stronger sleeping potion, sometimes dangerous. May have caused the death of a few people by accident.

THE FINAL WINK: lethal, produces black smoke.

SAVERS SALVE: general first aid, used for cuts, scrapes, and other minor injuries. Can disinfect serious wounds like an Umbral bite, but cannot heal them.

STORM-IN-A-BOTTLE: creates a storm, complete with thunder, lightning, and rain, to use as a distraction. Its magic comes from lightning striking all of the ingredients as they're mixed.

ALCOHOL:

GLOOM GLUG: cheap dark beer, has an earthy aftertaste.

CRUM CHUG: cheap pale beer, undertones of urine.

TUBER TODDY: strong root liquor, murky, tastes awful but will get you drunk quickly. Great for distracting you from the pains of existence.

CREATURES:

UMBRAL: a giant wolf with two sets of eyes, huge claws and teeth, and toxic saliva. Their saliva is deadly to humans and many other races; elves can recover from an Umbral bite, but the pain of the wound itself is agonizing. Only spotted in the Grimmaker Woods, possibly extinct.

TOOTH FAERIE: cat-sized spider-like creatures which feast on teeth and are typically drawn into a home by those left under children's pillows. Once they identify a target, however, they won't rest until they have extracted all of their teeth. They make a tinkling sound when they move as a result of all of the teeth inside of them clinking together.

LAKE MERMAID: lake creature that appears to be half-human female. Uses its looks and ability to communicate telepathically to lure people into the water, then consumes them with its massive fangs.

MINIATURE DRAGON: a dragon, but miniature. Comes in a variety of colors. Very fashionable!

OTHER:

CALCINITE (also known as the NEON SHACKLE): a neon green gem mined from the Invisible Cliffs. It is harmless to most beings, but depletes the magical abilities of elves and for that reason was weaponized by the kingdom of Barrien during their war with Emynor. The gem is no longer mined, sold, or utilized.

ABOUT THE AUTHOR

Francesca Crispo is a fantasy romance author living near Seattle, WA. She received her B.A. in English Literature from Arizona State University in 2016 and her M.Ed. from Arizona State University in 2018. When she isn't writing or running a business full-time, she enjoys spending time with her family and dogs!

facebook.com/francesca.crispo.author
instagram.com/francesca.crispo.author
tiktok.com/@francesca.crispo.author

ALSO BY FRANCESCA CRISPO

Rabbit Heart: Book 1 of the Terrafolk Trilogy

Seaborne: Book 2 of the Terrafolk Trilogy